MAN KILLER

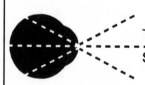

This Large Print Book carries the
Seal of Approval of N.A.V.H.

MAN KILLER

THOM NICHOLSON

WHEELER PUBLISHING
An imprint of Thomson Gale, a part of The Thomson Corporation

Detroit • New York • San Francisco • New Haven, Conn. • Waterville, Maine • London

LIBRARY OF CONGRESS CATALOGING-IN-PUBLICATION DATA

Nicholson, Thomas.
   Man killer / by Thom Nicholson.
     p. cm. — (Wheeler Publishing large print western)
     ISBN-13: 978-1-59722-510-6 (softcover : alk. paper)
     ISBN-10: 1-59722-510-X (softcover : alk. paper)
     1. Large type books. I. Title.
   PS3614.I3535M36 2007
   813'.6—dc22   2007002373

Published in 2007 by arrangement with NAL Signet,
a member of Penguin Group (USA) Inc.

Printed in the United States of America on permanent paper
10 9 8 7 6 5 4 3 2 1

To my wife, Sandra, the better half of
this writing team,
and
to my dear mother, "Boozie," who since
my birth has burned up the prayer-
ways trying to intercede with the
Almighty on my behalf.

CHAPTER 1
IN THE BEGINNING

Death rode across the rolling hills of East Texas. It came as a quintet of riders, their evil stench of debased cruelty as foul as wind blown up from the depths of Hell.

The five riders topped the small rise and reined in their sweating horses. The exhausted animals snorted and blew air through their noses, desperately trying to draw needed oxygen into their tired lungs. The men had ridden the animals hard, almost to death. In fact, as they stood there, the horse carrying the biggest man, a gambler by his dress, simply collapsed with a shudder and exhaled frothy blood from his nostrils for its last breath. For these desperate men, the death of a valuable horse meant very little; they cared nothing for the dying effort of the loyal animal. It was of little consequence to them as long as they could find other mounts to steal. And found them they had.

The leader, a lanky, whippet-thin man with coal black eyes and hair, smirked as he pointed at the small ranch below. "There she be, boys, jus' like I said. And lookie there, they've put half a dozen good horses in the corral fer us, jus' like we'd ordered 'em from a mail-order book."

The gambler wrenched his saddle and gear from his dead horse. "Damn, I'm glad this nag waited until now to drop on me. I shore don't want to carry this saddle any distance on a day as hot as this. One of you boys wanna tote it down to the ranch there on the back of yur animal fer me?"

No man bothered to answer the request and if the truth be known, the gambler had expected none. The men he rode with cared for no one but themselves. With a shrug and several mumbled obscenities under his breath, the big man slung his saddle, sleeping roll, saddlebags, and tack over his shoulder and started walking toward the ranch home below.

As he reached the fence of the main corral, he propped his saddle onto the top rail and looked around. "Damn," he mumbled to himself, "the people who own this place must be right proud of it. I ain't seen one cared of nicer in a long time."

The ranch house was freshly whitewashed,

with blue shutters at every window. Flowers grew in a narrow strip in front of the covered front porch and the sidewalk was bordered with whitewashed rocks. The barn and outbuildings were all in good repair and the fence of the corral was equally well maintained. Several small trees had been transplanted around the perimeter of the yard, promising shade from the hot Texas sun in a few years.

The gambler, who currently called himself Ace Richland, watched as the other four riders rode their horses up to the front porch of the house and climbed off, warily sweeping the area with their cruel eyes. A Mexican ranch hand walked out of the barn, a pitchfork in his hand, and stood by the open doors, assessing the strangers with apprehension. He was clearly uneasy with the appearance of the unexpected visitors.

The leader of the gang whispered something to his Mexican companion and watched with cold indifference as the outlaw walked over to the man at the barn. The two men talked together for a few moments, then the outlaw whipped out his gun and shot the unarmed ranch hand without warning.

As the sound of the shot reverberated around the yard, the front door swung open and a young woman ran out, sliding to a sudden halt as she saw the filthy men facing her in front of the porch. She glanced toward the barn and softly moaned, then turned to dash back inside, mumbling a prayer that she could get to the shotgun before the men got inside. It was not to be.

The leader leaped over the two steps to the front porch and caught the woman by her long, brown hair, jerking her back into his arms. Her neck bowed back until she was facing into the broiling sun, directly overhead. Kicking and screaming, the woman did not meekly surrender even though her pain was excruciating. She clawed at her attacker, trying to get her mouth to his hand or her fingers to his eyes.

The man uttered a guttural laugh and dodged her efforts to bite him. Finally, growing weary of the struggle, he whipped out his pistol and cracked it against her head, knocking her senseless. He held the limp woman in his arms and looked around. "Dammit, Sanchez, how come you shot that Mex? You wanna git the rest of the hands all over us?"

"There are no more, Señor Alva. The rest are gone until tomorrow or the next day, delivering cattle to a buyer in Dallas."

"Good news fer us, then." He looked at

the woman in his arms. "This here gal's a beaut. Sanchez, saddle up a horse fer you and me while I take some o' the starch outta her. You other boys do the same and kill yur old mounts. I don't want nobody using 'em after they've rested up. We'll lay over here a couple hours and then head on. It's only about fifty miles to the border. With fresh horses, we'll make it by mornin'. No posse'll catch us then."

Sanchez nodded and grabbed the reins of two horses, heading toward the barn. One of the two blond men, twins named Swain, spoke up hesitantly. "Boss, can me and Andy have a go at that there gal after you git done? She's a mighty fine looker, fer a fact."

"Ya sure can, Bob. You two done right good back at that bank in Tyler. Kept that guard from drillin' me in the back. Ace, you kin have her after the Swains git done. Sanchez'll go last."

"I ain't so keen on sharin' my gals with others, Al. I'll wait till we hit Kansas. There'll be plenty of gals up there to dilly-dally with."

"Suit yourself, Ace. If you ain't gonna fun yourself, then ride up to the top of the hill back yonder and keep a look out. I don't want no posse sneakin' up on us."

"I'll do it, Al. But, I wanna check around the house first, see if there's anything I want."

"Well, make it quick. I want you on that hill when I come outta the bedroom." He threw the unconscious woman over his shoulder and walked into the front room of the ranch house. The woman had been baking, and the warm smell of fresh bread permeated the room. The inside of the house was as well maintained and cared for as the exterior. The floors were swept and washed, the kitchen pots and pans were stored neatly on their hangers by the stove, the dishes in a walnut china cabinet polished to a high sheen. Clean gingham curtains framed the few windows. Clearly the woman he carried had worked hard to make the simple house a home for her family.

Alva dumped the woman on the bed in the main bedroom and quickly tied her wrists and ankles to the four posters. Taking his knife, Alva skillfully cut away her clothing, then stepped back, admiring his catch. "She's a real looker, fer a fact," he muttered to his reflection in the mirror over the vanity chest.

In the corner, a baby, barely a yearling, raised itself up from its crib and started crying, upset by the stranger suddenly in his vicinity. Alva glanced, irritated, at the interruption. "Bob, come git this brat and shut him up. I don't want to hear his caterwauling."

Bob Swain hurriedly entered the room, his eyes growing wide at the scene before him. He grabbed the crying baby from the crib and clamped a meaty hand over its tiny mouth, causing the scared child to scream even harder.

"Andy, bring me a glass of water," Al shouted over the muffled screams of the baby. "Bob, shut him up, I say."

Andy Swain entered with a glass of water, his jaw slackening at the sight lying exposed on the bed. He grinned lewdly, exposing the gap between his front teeth, marking him as a Swain to anyone who had ever met any of his family.

Alva took the water and sipped a small amount. "All right, you seen what's comin' up fer ya. Now git on outta here. I'll let you know when it's yur turn. Meanwhile, git them horses ready to go, in case we hafta go quick."

The two brothers left the room, lustfully licking their lips in anticipation of their turn at the young woman. "What'll I do with this here brat, Andy?" Bob complained. "He's screaming like a lost cat."

"Whop him up against the fireplace. That oughta shut him up," Andy offered. He watched with indifference as Bob held the screaming child by its feet and slammed it against the rock face of the fireplace. Instantly the crying stopped and Bob dropped the defenseless dead baby on the hearth, next to the small stack of cut wood.

"Come on," Andy urged. "Let's git them horses saddled. I wanna be ready when Al gits done and it's our turn."

"I'll flip ya fer first dibs," Bob offered.

"Deal. I'll take heads. You got a coin?"

Alva sipped about half the glass of water, then threw the rest against the face of the bound woman, bringing her back to consciousness. She gasped and yanked at her bonds, but she was tightly secured. She twisted her head to look toward the cradle, but could see nothing. As Alva began to unbuckle his pants she moaned, then screamed. The entire time he pleasured himself with her, she alternated between screaming, cursing, praying, and pleading with him, all to no avail. She was still sobbing when he readjusted his clothing and strolled out into the main room where Bob and Andy were eating fresh bread and churned butter.

"She's all yurs, boys. Who's first?"

14

"I am, by damn," Andy crowed. He stood and smirked at Bob, still chewing on some bread. "I'll try and save a little fer ya, brother Bob. But not much." He strutted into the bedroom, shutting the door behind him.

Bob snorted and then looked over at Alva as the screaming and crying increased a notch. "She's got a pair of lungs on her, don't she?"

"So what? She's good fun, anyways. Where'd you git that butter?"

"We hit the smokehouse. Sanchez is making up a load to put on the extra horse. We'll eat good till we git to Kansas."

"Ace find anything worth takin'?"

"He got some money from the desk yonder. And he picked up a real nice hat. I think that's about it unless you want the shotgun. It's a dandy."

"Naw, I ain't got no room to carry a shotgun. I'll have some of that there bread and butter. Then I'm gonna sit outside in that rocker on the porch until we're done here. You be sure and tell Sanchez when it's his turn."

"I will, Al, jus' as soon as I'm done. Don't you worry 'bout it."

"Oh, I don't, fer a fact." Al slathered up a hunk of fresh bread with butter and stepped out on the porch. He settled in the chair and ate slowly, savoring the bread's soft texture and the smooth, salty flavor of the butter. " 'Sides bein' good in the sack, that gal can cook," he grunted to himself. On the porch, he barely heard the woman's screams and eventually dozed off, not hearing Bob call for Sanchez, who waited patiently in the shade of the barn for his turn.

As for the unfortunate victim, she did not stop screaming, crying, cursing, nor begging for mercy until Sanchez slit her throat after he had finished with her. By then, Alva was refreshed and ready to continue their flight from the law. He motioned the men to gather around him at the front steps. His first question was to Ace. "Ace, how much money did you find in the house?"

"Twenty dollars, Al."

"Give me half, right now."

Grumbling, Ace passed a ten-dollar greenback over to Alva.

"Sanchez, the pack animal ready to go?"

"Sí, Señor Al. We will have plenty good eatin' for a week."

"Andy, you and Bob kill them used-up horses?"

"Shore enough, Alva. There ain't no animals left fer anybody to chase us with."

"Well then, I guess we may as well be on

16

our way. Didn't I tell you I had a plan fer gittin' away from any posse that got after us?" Alva glanced over at the body lying still by the door of the barn. He led his horse over to the mortally wounded man and quickly riffled his pockets, but found nothing of value. He looked down at the dark eyes, growing duller by the minute, but glaring defiantly up at him. "You're a tough ole bird, José, but I guess you'll be dead soon enough. No need to waste another bullet on ya."

Alva mounted his new horse, marveling at the quality of the animal, and led his men out of the ranch yard, his mind already on problems to face before they were in Indian Territory and away from the posse chasing them from Tyler. Since they had stolen only six hundred and some dollars from the community bank in Athens, the small East Texas town to the south of the ranch, he wondered why the posse even bothered to chase them. He did not know it, but the posse had lost their trail some thirty miles back and had already abandoned the pursuit.

The elderly Mexican cowhand stirred and painfully pushed himself up until he was on his hands and knees. He had promised to watch over the patron's family, and knew he had failed. He willed himself to stay alive until the others returned, to tell them what he had seen, in the hope it would help them find and punish the foul cochinos who had done this awful thing.

Slowly, painfully, he made his way to the porch and crawled inside the house. His face was convulsed with tears when he crawled back outside and onto the rocker on the front porch. He could not stay inside with the horrors he saw there. Placing his hand firmly over the bloody wound in his lower chest, he waited for the other ranch hands to return, praying to the Blessed Virgin that he not die until they did.

He watched with dimming vision as scavenger birds started to circle the ranch, the smell of death having already permeated the hot Texas afternoon.

CHAPTER 2
RANGER BUSINESS

"Dust on a Texas afternoon in July is drier than lizard spit." With that apt statement, Steve Block hacked a gob of something off to the side of the trail.

The man riding beside him grinned and licked sun-dried lips. "By gum, Steve, I do believe that's the most you've said since we split off from the rest of the posse."

"No need to git sassy on me, Marty Keller. I jus' been a'-workin' up to it, is all." Steve glanced at his riding companion. The tall man was slouched in his saddle, his lean body rocking slightly with the gait of his dark gelding with a white blaze down its nose. Even though the man seemed at ease as he rode, Steve saw that his eyes were never still, always looking ahead, to the side, occasionally to the rear, then down to the tracks of the three riders they were following. This was Steve's first posse with Marty Keller, but he could see the man's reputation as a skilled tracker was well earned.

"I gotta admit yur one hell of a tracker, Marty. How you found the trail when them bastards went into the river is beyond me."

"I was lucky. I saw the scrape of a horse-shoe on a mossy rock. Then I just looked for a place I would leave the river if I was running away from someone."

"I'm still impressed. Now, if it turns out yur right about these three headed fer Camp Verde, I'll plumb take my hat off fer ya."

"I'll bet that's exactly what they're doing. These skunks have been on the run for over three weeks now. They've gotta be short of food and provisions. Camp Verde is the only place they can stock up before they cross the Pecos River and drop down into Mexico. If my calculations are right, we can't be more'n a day from there right now, and these tracks keep heading straight for it."

Steve streamed another offering of spit and tobacco juice to the side of the trail, then wiped his lips with the sleeve of his dusty, sweat-streaked shirt. "I wish ole Slim hadn't come down sick on us. I think we'll need his six-guns afore we finish up this particular chore the captain done give us."

"He was definitely too sick to stay with us, Steve. No question about that. I'm just grateful we found that nester family out here in the middle of nowhere. The lady can give him the care he needs while we chase down these comancheros. I reckon he'll make his way to Austin as soon as he's well enough to travel again. I don't see any other way we could have done it, do you?"

"Nah, I reckon not. I still think we're gonna miss ole Slim's skill with the pistol afore this thing's over."

"Next time I'll tell Captain Self that we want only men who never get sick on our patrols. How's that?" Marty flashed a dry grin at his companion.

"The cap'n don't never listen to us, you oughta know that. He thinks one Ranger is worth six regular men."

"Isn't that about right?" Marty teased his morose partner.

"Well, I ain't so sure 'bout that." Steve took off his dusty hat and wiped the sweat from a forehead that was marked by the crease of the brim. He looked at Marty and licked the dust off his lips. "How 'bout you? How come the cap'n lets you sign on fer a posse and then go back to yur ranch? How come you ain't in the Rangers full time?"

"A friend of mine from the Dallas Company served with me in General Forrest's cavalry. He told Captain Self about my skill as a scout and tracker one time when the

Rangers were after some bank robbers and needed help. After we got the crooks, I turned down the Captain's offer to join the Rangers. I wanted to work on my new ranch. Me and Meg — that's my wife — were just getting started. I work with the Rangers now and then for cash money, but my heart's in my ranch."

"Cattle?"

"Some, but mostly horses. I love raising a well-bred horse for use by someone who appreciates good horseflesh."

"You raise 'em before the war?"

Marty shook his head. "No, actually my pa raised cotton over in Mississippi. I was in college, at the Virginia Military Institute. You ever hear of it?"

"I sort of did, I think."

"Major Thomas Jackson was head of cadets. Ole Stonewall didn't have his nickname yet when I first knew him. We called him Ole Fussy Feathers. He certainly made believers out of us before he was killed in '63."

"You fight with Stonewall Jackson, did ya?"

"No, I was with General Forrest the entire time. My pa insisted I come home as soon as VMI dismissed classes early to let everyone join the Army of Northern Virginia. I was the only cadet in my class that didn't fight with Stonewall, I guess." Marty looked at Steve. "How about you? You see the elephant?"

"Yeah, at first I was with Kirby's brigade. We got trapped in Vicksburg. After we surrendered in July of '63 and got paroled by that scoundrel, Ulysses S. Grant, I came back to Dallas and joined the Second Ranger Brigade. We stayed in Texas the rest of the war. I was in a little scuffle with the Yanks during the Red River fight, but that was it fer me."

Steve stopped his pony and stretched his back. Marty let his horse take a quick rest as well. He swallowed a sip of warm water from his canteen, then recorked it and hung it from his saddle horn. He let his eyes wander the countryside, looking for any sign that would indicate an ambush ahead. Steve stood in his stirrups and did the same, stretching his legs while in the saddle.

After a few quiet moments they started again, keeping their eyes on the tracks that led across the dusty land toward the southwest and Camp Verde. As if they had not stopped, Steve began talking again to Marty.

"So you rode with Forrest?"

"Yes, I was his captain of scouts. We had a few scrapes that made me think I was destined for a very short life."

"So how'd you end up in Texas? Not interested in cotton-growin' after the war?"

"Not so much not interested as unable. My pa died while I was away and our place was behind Union lines from '64 on. When I came home, the Union tax assessors had already seized the land for unpaid taxes and parceled it up and sold it off. When I tried to get it back, the court threw out my case. A fine homecoming, huh?"

"Damned carpetbaggers," Steve agreed. "They're worser than any scum-suckin' pig I ever saw." Steve spit to emphasize his disdain for the hated moneygrubbers from the North. "What happened then?"

"Well, I got lucky, I guess is the best way to put it."

"Do tell. Even after losin' all yur land to them Yankee sumbitches?"

"As I walked out of the courthouse in Jackson, the state capital, a young woman walked up and hugged me. She was wearing a homespun dress that was worse off than any of our female slaves ever wore before the war. Her shoes were Union Army clodhoppers, and her bonnet was hardly fit to cover a scarecrow. She was bone-thin and sun-browned and still the loveliest thing I had seen in four years.

"She looked at me happy like and said, 'Marty Keller, is it really you?'

"I mumbled something, not sure who had ahold of me. I gotta admit that whoever she was, it sure felt fine to have her huggin' me like that.

"The lady stepped back and grinned at me. I tell you, Steve. The gal was so good-lookin' it took my breath away. 'Don't you know me?' she asked.

" 'No, ma'am, I don't think I do,' I said.

"She flashed me the most wonderful smile I ever saw and said, 'Oh, Marty, you ninny. It's me, Margaret Sue Lyman. I've lived down the lane from you all my life.'

"When I got my voice back, I said, 'Meg Lyman. I didn't recognize you. You've grown up since I saw you last. You're beautiful. Oh, I'm sorry, I didn't mean to be so fresh.'

"She smiled real sweet again and said, 'Don't be. I'm happy you like the changes. I'm afraid I'm not as glamorous with these clodhoppers and this old dress as I once might have been. It's good to see you, Marty. I'm glad you survived the war. I went to your poppa's funeral. It was real nice. Everyone there said good things about him.' She smiled at me again and tugged on my arm. 'When did you get back? Come on, let's go to the hotel and have a cup of what passes for coffee these days. You have any money?'

"Not quite sure what she was after, I answered, 'I've got some greenbacks, I took from some Yankee prisoners a while back. Some.' I wasn't too keen on tellin' her just how much I had. The bankroll in my sock was all between starvation and me. I swept my eyes over her again. 'Where's your pa?' I asked.

"She said, 'He marched off in the last countywide draft levee taken the first of '65. Any man forty-five or younger had to go. Pa just made it. I got one letter from him saying he was in some artillery unit and headed to Texas to fight a Yankee general named Banks. That was in early March. I haven't heard a word from him since. All I can do is pray for him and wait, I guess.'

" 'I'm sorry, Meg,' I said. 'Maybe he'll show up yet. Meanwhile, let's eat. I could use some food myself.'

"She smiled at me with her blue eyes shining. 'Wonderful. I just spent my last dime paying off the lawyer that's tryin' to save my property from being seized for nonpayment of taxes. All I got to show for it is one more week, and then I'm off the place for good.'

" 'You too?' I said. 'I know the feeling.'

"Meg squeezed my arm. 'Oh, Marty, they get your place?'

" 'More'n a month ago. It's already been sold to some speculator. According to the county registrar in there, I have to get permission to even go back to the house and pick up stuff that's mine.' I jerked my thumb toward the courthouse. It really burns me that they sold it so fast once pa died. It was like they were vultures on a fence, ready to pounce just as soon as he passed away.

"Then Margaret's face grew thoughtful and she said, 'I was by your old place day before yesterday. Nobody's there, as far as I can tell. Come on, let's get something to eat and I'll tell you what I think.' She gave me a rueful grin and confessed. 'I haven't had a lick of food for two days now. I've been pickin' wild blackberries and sellin' them to the colored soldiers on occupation duty here in Jackson. The berries around Yazoo County are just about all gone now, and I'm busted. Do you mind?'

" 'No, that's fine by me,' I said. 'I'm sort of hungry myself.' "

Marty grinned at Steve. "I can't say I was too hungry, but I sure didn't want this fine-lookin' gal giving up on me and going

27

somewhere else to cage a meal."

Marty paused, checking the tracks they were following, to insure they were still on the right trail. "Meg knocked off a large stack of flapjacks faster than you could count to ten backwards. I ate my stack down and enjoyed watching her eat. Over coffee she told me what was on her mind.

"She finished her coffee and smiled at me. It damned near lit up the room. 'Marty,' she said, 'I hope you'll forgive me for acting like a starved puppy. I sure was hungry.' I had to admit that she looked a mite better now, a bit of color was back in her cheeks.

"I smiled at her and said, 'I've been hungry myself a time or two these last few years.'

"Her gaze touched my heart with its tenderness. 'Was it bad for you?' she asked.

" 'Not as bad as some, I guess. Bad enough.' I worried the cup rim with my finger. 'Now it looks like I've lost my place, dammit.'

" 'I've got a proposition for you, if you are interested.'

" 'I'm listening.'

" 'I saw you and your pa about the first of the year. I was working in our north field one morning when you two rode by in that nice wagon your pa had. Is it still at your place?'

" 'It was the last time I was there.' I had just come home for a short furlough. Good thing too, since pa died a month later.

"Meg nodded. 'I'm glad you got to see him one last time. Marty, can I count on you to keep a secret?'

" 'Sure.'

" 'I've got two real good horses. Pa kept them in a hidden meadow next to the slough to the south of our place. The Confederate government acquisitioners never found them. What I don't have is a wagon.'

" 'You don't say.' I was torn between admiration for her audaciousness and my memory of good men left behind because they didn't have a good horse to ride against the bluecoats.

" 'I've got things I want to keep. You've got some too, I know. Let's take my horses and your wagon, load it up with what's rightfully ours, and light out of here. We have no future in Yazoo City or Mississippi, so let's go somewhere else and get a new start. We can start tonight, if you like. Partners.'

"I looked hard at that little slip of a gal, not yet twenty, yet smarter than I was about what had to be done. I stuck out my paw. 'Deal.'

"Meg gave me the sweetest grin a man could get. 'Come on, then. Let's head out to my house and get my horses. As soon as it's dark, we'll slip over to your place and pick up your things. If the wagon is still there, of course.'

" 'I don't know why it wouldn't be. Pa didn't say anything about getting rid of it.'

"We rode together on my worn-out roan to her place, already talking about where we wanted to go. When we got there, she showed me her horses. They were purebred stock and high-quality animals. I spent the rest of the day getting them used to a saddle and harness again. After all the months they had been hidden away, they had forgotten what they were born for."

Steve pulled up his horse. "I gotta take a leak, Marty. Hold my hoss fer me, will ya?"

As soon as they were underway again, Steve pushed to hear more of the story. "So what happened next?"

"Where was I?"

"You and Margaret was a'goin' to sneak back to yur old home and get yur things afore the land grabbers got 'em."

Marty smiled at the memory. "That's exactly what we did. We grabbed stuff from my place, including the good wagon my pa had, the Sharps rifle I had brought home to him in '64 during a visit, the shotgun I hunted with as a boy, my ma's dresser and good china and silver that Pa hadn't sold yet, along with some clothes that still fit me."

"Yur Margaret get her things too?"

"Yep. We filled the wagon with things of hers. We had more than enough to start over, when we finally settled outside of Greenville. We sold one of her good horses for enough to pick up a small ranch for back taxes. So, in a way, I'm as bad as the sumbitches who robbed me of pa's place."

"Not likely, to my way of thinkin'. At least you work yur land, like any honest man oughta. Them land-grabbers jus' hold on to the land without no regard fer what's right."

"Well, we surely do work hard on our place. We're finally seeing some light. We've got twenty good horses for breeding stock and some cattle that I'm trying to cross-breed to a Mexican Brahman bull I bought. I think it's gonna turn out to be an excellent beef cow before I'm done."

"And yur Margaret? When did ya marry her?"

Marty laughed. "We hadn't made it to Shreveport, Louisiana, when I told her we had better get married or I wasn't gonna be responsible for my actions around the campfire. She looked me square in the eye and said, 'Silly man, I've loved you since I first saw you when I was barely twelve. Of course I want to marry up with you. That's been my plan from the second I ran into you in front of the courthouse in Jackson.'

"So we hunted up a preacher, got hitched, and things have gotten better and better with every passing day. Now, we've got a little tyke, name of Matt. He's a real delight. Always happy and smiling. He'll chase grasshoppers till the sun goes down, laughing like a clown and checking to see if Meg is watching him. He's a pure joy." Marty shook his head. "I'm one lucky guy, and I really mean that."

"I'd have to agree, iffen you was to ask me, pard. Now, do ya think we could stop and grab a bite to eat? My stomach's been rubbin' agin my backbone fer the last hour. These jaspers we a'trailin' are headed fer Camp Verde as sure as grass is green. We'll catch up with 'em there. Ain't no outlaw alive can pass up spendin' some time and money at a saloon when he's jus' off the trail with cash in his pocket."

Chapter 3
Ranger's Justice

"Well, there's Camp Verde, Marty. The place shore don't look like much, do it?"

"You're right about that."

The town built around the army outpost was grubby and sparse. Adobe huts stood beside green wooden structures with front façades attempting to imply more than their true worth. A dozen buildings flanked the rutted main street, while several side streets had numerous soddies, tents, or adobe structures for living quarters. Only the post seemed to be in a state of normal repair.

Marty spit dust from his mouth and wiped the back of his hand across his dry lips. "I'm surprised how careless these boys were, Steve. Riding straight as a hound's tooth for this place ever since they split off from the rest of the gang."

"They had money in their pockets, pard. I done told ya how hard it is fer outlaws to pass up a chance to whoop it up when they been out robbin' and killin'."

"Well, it's gonna cost 'em. Come on, let's ease on down and check things out. I'd like to put an end to this thing and get on home to Meg and little Matt."

"Fine by me. There's the town livery. What say we start there?"

"Sounds good," Marty grunted. "All I want is to get off this hay-burner for a spell and stretch the kinks outta my back."

The two men dismounted their horses at the entrance to the livery and walked the tired, dusty animals inside the dim interior. The old barn had ten stalls in two rows on either side. The musty smell of hay, manure, and dust tickled their noses. A balding man with a pronounced limp hobbled over to them from a cluttered office in the corner of the barn. He flashed a friendly grin and stuck out a grubby paw. "Howdy boys. Welcome to Camp Verde. Lookin' to board yur ponies fer a spell?"

Marty took the offered hand. It was as hard as iron. The man had the hands of a smithy, and the grip to match. "Good afternoon. You the man in charge here?"

"Yep. Theo Tackleberry, owner, swamper, and farrier, all in one package. What can I do fer ya?"

"I'm Steve Block and this here is Marty

Keller, Mr. Tackleberry. We're Texas Rangers. You don't have a problem with that, I hope?"

"Not in the least, Ranger Block. However, ya still gotta pay to board yur animals with me. Sorry."

Steve nodded and looked over the man's head at the stalls. Five had horses in them. "We're after some bank robbers from up Dallas way. Three men. They drop off their horses here, say sometime yesterday?"

"Yep, them three at the end. I shoulda knowed they was bad. They had too much spendin' cash on 'em. Paid fer three days. Said they was gonna drink the saloon dry, poke all the whores silly, and then buy some supplies fer their pards who were out on a cattle drive. Wanted to buy a team and wagon from me. Was workin' on the bill of sale when you two rode up. Shore wish you'd a waited another day till I got paid fer it."

Marty smiled. "Tough break, Mr. Tackleberry. They won't need any wagon now. Have any idea where they might be?"

"They were in the cantina down at the far end of the street about an hour ago. I stopped by to have a short beer. They was drinkin' and playing cards till the gals come down fer the evenin'."

Marty looked at Steve. "We may as well head on over, I guess."

"Wait a minute, Marty. Them boys is parked fer a spell. I'm dirty and hungry. What say we clean up and git us some hot grub afore we brace 'em?" He looked at the livery owner. "Any place to git a bath and shave and some hot grub, Mr. Tackleberry? I missed my usual Saturday night bath."

"Shore enough, Ranger. The hotel has a tin tub on the second floor. Ya rent a room fer the night and they'll give ya hot water and store-bought soap fer two bits. The hotel café has the best food in town."

"You have a sheriff and a jail here?" Marty queried. "If we stay the night, we'll have to put 'em somewhere."

"No sheriff. The Yankees being so close helps keep the peace, as a rule. Are ya plannin' to take 'em alive?" Tackleberry asked. "Be easier to plug 'em, wouldn't it?"

"Alive, if we can. That's the way Rangers work. Still, if they try anything, all bets are off." Steve gave his best ranger scowl to the livery owner.

Tackleberry nodded. He understood Ranger terms. "When we need a holdin' jail, we use the Thompsons' root cellar. It's rock lined and has a door a mule couldn't kick his way out of. Ya could cool 'em off in thar fer the night. The town magistrate usually locks drunks and such up thar."

Marty nodded at Steve. "Let's have a look at the cellar before we decide, Steve. If we can't secure them properly, we may as well head on back to Austin with them tonight."

"All right, Marty. But I shore do wanna clean up and git some hot food afore we brace these jaspers. Grit has done worked its way clean down to the door of my long handles."

"I'm outta clean shirts," Marty said as he scratched the week's long stubble on his chin. "Mr. Tackleberry, if I was to want a new one from the store, how much would it be?"

A merchant's gleam lit up the livery owner's eyes. "My missus makes shirts fer the Yankee soldiers stationed around here. I reckon she's got a couple that would fit you boys that was ordered and not picked up. Ya got any aversion to wearin' Yankee blue shirts?"

Marty grinned. "Wore plenty of 'em during the late unpleasantness. We sorta depended on the Yanks to keep us supplied."

"Good. I'd let you two, cause yur Rangers and all, have a couple fer two dollars hard silver or three in greenbacks."

"And for one more greenback, Mr. Tackleberry, would you sit on the porch and watch for our desperados? If they head toward your livery, you must get us immediately."

"I reckon so. It's sort of my civic duty to assist Rangers anyways. You boys plan on checkin' in with the Yankee Army fellas over to the fort?"

"I don't think so," Marty answered. "We Rangers sorta handle our own problems."

The root cellar proved to be as strong as any jail, buried deep in the earth behind the Thompson house, only half a block from the livery. Marty and Steve paid for the room while Tackleberry headed home to get the new shirts. Marty lost the flip and waited until Steve had soaked, soaped, and scrubbed the week's accumulation of trail dust off of his body.

Meanwhile, Marty shaved, luxuriating in the hot water and scented soap provided by the hotel. He sighed in contentment as he slipped into the tub and motioned for the boy holding a bucket of steaming water to pour it over him. He finished his bath and waited for Steve to complete his shave. The new shirts fit and were well made. They were of pale blue cotton, lightweight and comfortable.

"Damned iffen we don't look like Yankee

dandys, Marty."

"Feels good, doesn't it? Come on, let's get you stoked up with food. I don't want to brace those boys after dark."

"What's the difference? We oughta let 'em git all filled up with whiskey. They'll be easier to take."

"Whiskey makes some men braver than good sense dictates, Steve. You've seen that, I know."

"It also makes 'em slower and dumber, as a rule. Come on, let's git some grub. I'm 'bout half-starved."

Not interested in a serious argument with Steve, Marty accompanied him to the dining room. They each devoured a large pan-fried steak and piles of potatoes, finishing with dried-apple pie and two mugs of hot coffee. Marty stopped the waiter, a young man not yet out of his teens.

"Where'd you get the good coffee, son?"

"We worked a deal with the commissary sergeant over to the fort. The Yankees has got more good food than ya can shake a stick at."

"Certainly goes down smooth, doesn't it, Steve?"

"Can't really say when I last had real coffee, pard. Mighty nice." Steve leaned back in his chair and worried at a piece of meat with an ivory toothpick he carried in his hatband.

After a few minutes, he got up and stretched, then jammed on his sweat-stained hat. "Ready to do the job?"

"Let's get 'er done," Marty agreed.

Steve slipped his .44 Colt from his holster and opened the cylinder. "You'd better put another pill on yur popper, Marty. These fellas are bad cases and might want to shoot it out." He slid the deadly pistol back into its holster and then checked the .36 Navy revolver riding on his left hip. Marty was armed in the same fashion, except he carried a new Remington revolver chambered for the .44 brass center-fire cartridge, rather than a Colt .44 cap and ball. Marty then checked the load of the Navy .36 he also carried as backup. They slipped the pistol butts forward into the waist holsters on their left hips. Marty tied his holster to his right thigh with a leather strip, then nodded to his companion. "Ready, Steve."

The two men stepped out on the veranda of the two-story hotel. Tackleberry was seated in a rocker in the shade of the top balcony, slowly rocking back and forth.

"Hello, Mr. Tackleberry. Our boys still at the cantina?" Marty looked across the dirt street as he adjusted his hat.

"Yep. Say, them shirts look right becoming on the two of ya. Mighty good. Ya want me to accompany ya to the cantina and point out yur fellas fer ya?"

"I'd appreciate that, Mr. Tackleberry," Steve answered. "You can point them out and then back off. Me and Marty will take care of the rest."

"Fine by me. Like I say, I think I oughta help, but I ain't no gunhand. I'd jus' be in yur way iffen lead was to start a'flyin'."

"Let's hope it don't come to that, Mr. Tackleberry." Marty and Steve slowly walked up the rutted dirt street toward the cantina at the far end of the little town. It had the rounded adobe façade consistent with many Mexican bars, and the words, CANTINA BLANCO, written in faded white-wash over the swinging batwing doors.

The three men casually entered the dim interior and walked to the bar. The place held a dozen men, some leaning against the triple wooden planks that formed the bar and some playing cards at two of the tables.

"Three beers," Marty ordered, his back to the men at the tables. Tackleberry stood between the two Rangers and slowly looked around the room before turning to the bar. He sipped from the foam-topped glass and softly spoke to the rangers. "Two of 'em are

41

at the table in the corner, playin' cards with the two soldiers. The half-breed in the bowler hat and the big blond fella with the knife scar on his left cheek. I don't see the Mex, but then I don't see Rosita, so he may be upstairs pokin' her. Her crib is the end door on the right."

Marty looked up. The hallway overlooked the cantina below, and five doors led to rooms, all of which were closed at the moment. Tackleberry finished his beer and swiped the back of his hand against his lips.

"Well boys, I'll mosey along. Good luck to ya both."

As the livery owner limped to the door, Marty whispered to Steve, "Want to wait a bit and see if the Mex comes down?"

Steve sipped his beer and nodded. "Yeah, we'll give him a few minutes." He turned and leaned his elbows against the bar, casually surveying the people in the room. Tackleberry stopped at the far end of the bar, where he could duck down behind the huge beer barrel that served as the legs for that end of the bar. He did not want to miss any of the coming action. It would be the talk of the town for weeks.

Jim Hawk had been an outlaw since he was fifteen. He had killed and raped his way from one end of Texas to the other. His heart was as cold as solid ice on the river at Christmas, but he had the senses of a wolf. He had seen the three men come into the bar, one of them the cripple from the stable. He watched from under the brim of his dingy bowler as the cripple limped away from the other two men, then stopped at the far end of the bar by the barrel and waited, as if expecting something to happen shortly. His eyes narrowed as the one man turned and looked the crowd over, his elbows hooked on the bar top.

Jim watched as Steve's eyes swept the room, not looking directly at the two men, but still taking in everything he could in the encompassing glance. Nervously, the stranger's right thumb flicked the leather safety strap free of the hammer of his pistol. He had done the move without conscious thought, but its meaning was clear to the wary half-breed outlaw. Jim's face hardened.

"Damn it to Hell, that's a lawman." He muttered to himself.

"Bob, thar's two lawmen at the bar. Bob, dammit, you hear me?" Jim whispered to his outlaw friend, who was so drunk he could barely hold his head up. Jim Hawk's urgent tone of voice cut through the hazy fog of his companion's intoxication.

Stone sober, Bob Baker was as mean and dangerous as any rattler shedding its skin. Drunk, his fierce, wild nature grew even worse. Roaring like a cornered bear, the drunken outlaw leaped to his feet and fired at the first target his whiskey-sodden eyes could make out. A dry-goods drummer from Dallas took the bullet in his back as he leaned against the bar and pondered where he could possibly sell the wagonload of glass jars used in canning vegetables that was headed his way. There weren't a hundred white women who canned vegetables between here and Ft. Bliss, which was over three hundred miles to the west.

Screaming in shock and pain, the drummer fell heavily to the floor, raking several glasses and a nearly full whiskey bottle off the bar as he did.

Marty spun around, drawing his pistol as he did, startled by the sudden chaos in the bar. Things seemed to be exploding in all directions around him. Steve had slapped leather at the first shot and was in the process of putting two bullets through the torn left shirt pocket of the drunken Baker, not one inch apart. Dust jumped from the shirt as the two slugs ripped into the man. The blow of the hot lead slammed Baker against the wall, where he clawed at the pain burning through his chest. He slid slowly to the floor, a bloody streak on the wall defining his dying progress.

The half-breed, Jim Hawk, pulled the card table over on its side, hiding behind its wooden top as he pulled his pistol. Moving as if running through Mississippi mud, Marty jerked his hogleg out while rolling the nearest table around until he was shielded behind its round surface. He saw Steve crouching low, bobbing his head up and down as he tried to see over the tops of several tables still standing, his smoking gun pointed in the direction of the table behind which Jim Hawk hid. Neither ranger had a clear shot at the man, but Jim Hawk couldn't shoot them, either, without exposing himself to their fire.

Meanwhile, in the midst of the gunfight, the other patrons in the bar scrambled to get undercover or out the door before they suffered the same fate as the dry-goods drummer. Chaos reigned for a moment, followed by silence, with only Marty's breath whistling in and out of his mouth registering to his senses.

"Rangers, Bub. You shuck the gun and come out with yur hands up. Do it now!" Steve shouted the standard command with forceful authority, although he looked like a frantic chicken, bobbing up and down as he tried to get a shot at the half-breed outlaw without exposing himself to return fire.

Jim Hawk's only reply was to blindly fire two shots in Steve's general direction, causing the ranger to duck back on his haunches. Marty quickly put two return shots into the tabletop near the barrel of Joe's smoking six-gun, without result. He pulled his head back as Joe answered his fire, two .44 caliber lead balls slamming into the wooden table, but not penetrating the tabletop's thick wood.

Marty peered around the rounded edge of his table, easing his pistol toward the outlaw's position. He spotted the outlaw's boot, exposed by the round tabletop. It was Marty's only chance.

Carefully, he aimed his pistol and gently squeezed the trigger. The heavy gun bucked in his hand, gray smoke obscuring his vision for an instant. His aim had been true. He blew Jim Hawk's left big toe clear off, as well as smashing two other toes. Screaming in agony, the half-breed outlaw leaped up, hopping on one foot while trying to get at the injured one with his hands, any thought of the Rangers erased by pain.

Steve took the opportunity to put a .44 lead pill right over Jim's right ear, putting him down and out of the fight. Steve stood up, a grim expression on his face. "You boys woulda been better off givin' up, it 'pears to me."

During the excitement, while tables crashed to the floor and bullets filled the air, the Mexican member of the outlaws, who had been rudely interrupted during a spirited ride on the Mexican whore, Rosita, reached for his pistol. The ensuing gunshots caused him to leap to his feet and struggle into his pants and boots. Carefully, he crept out of the door toward the balcony railing where he eased up behind a pillar until he could see the floor below. The stealthy approach had taken enough time for Steve to shoot Jim Hawk in the temple. The Mexican saw the lanky ranger stand up and mutter something to the fallen 'breed. The Mexican thinned his lips in a ghastly grin as he aimed his Navy Colt at Steve's back.

As he pulled the trigger, Marty instinctively glanced up and saw the barrel of the gun behind the pillar. He shouted, "Steve, look out!"

The ranger half turned to gape at Marty, causing the shot aimed at his spine to enter his left shoulder, shredding flesh, then striking and breaking the collarbone before passing out to slam into the sawdust-covered floor.

Groaning in pain, Steve slumped to the floor. "Marty, Marty, I'm hit."

CHAPTER 4
THE LONG
ROAD HOME

Steve slowly slumped to the floor, trying to stay upright, but failing. Marty saw the shape of the Mexican shooter hidden behind the balcony railing. The outlaw shifted his position so he could take aim at Marty, exposing more of himself.

Marty fanned three quick shots upward, hoping to get a hit before the man fired down at him. Two whistled past the man's head, not even close, but the third ricocheted off the top railing of the banister and flattened out like an oversized nickel. This hunk of misshapen lead, although drastically reduced in energy, was still moving fast enough to cut its way through the man's lower jaw and slice into the outlaw's brain. It lodged against the skull, too spent to bust through the tough bone.

This was enough. The outlaw's head slammed back, then forward, before he pitched over the railing, turning a complete rotation before crashing down on a card table below, smashing the table to pieces. There was absolute silence for a second, then pandemonium broke out, as the on-lookers rushed back to look at the dead and dying, or to gather around Marty kneeling beside Steve, working feverishly to staunch the flow of blood pouring out of the tall ranger's wound.

Tackleberry limped to Marty's side, wild exultation in his voice. "Gawd damned, but was that some shootout! I ain't never seen nothin' like it in my life. What a ruckus. He gonna make it?" Tackle-berry solicitously asked as Marty jammed Steve's kerchief into the bloody hole in his back.

"If he gets some proper medical attention. You have a town doc?"

"Nope. We use the fort's sawbones when we got somethin' bad."

"Well, this is bad. Get someone to fetch him, pronto."

Tackleberry looked around, then called to one of the onlookers, "Theo, git over to the post and ask Doc Summers to git over here real quick like. Tell him we had a shootout and got some men bad hurt. Git a move on now."

One of the younger men dashed out of

the bar, running as fast as he could up the street.

"Ole Doc Summers is a right fair sawbones, Ranger. He'll take good care of yur pard."

Marty held Steve's head in his lap, pushing hard against the fierce wound in his back. "You hear that, Steve? Help's on the way. Just hang on for a few minutes. You're gonna be fine. Hang on." Steve looked up at Marty, pain ravaging his homely face. "Marty," he gasped, "check out the comancheros. Make sure we got 'em."

"Mr. Tackleberry, would you have a look at the men we shot? Are any still alive? Please confiscate their weapons."

"Shore thing, Ranger. Be right proud to." Tackleberry limped away, while Marty continued trying to staunch the blood seeping out of Steve's wound. The post doctor arrived just as Tackleberry returned. Marty thankfully turned over the care of his companion to the crusty old physician and stood, shaking the cramps out of his legs.

Tackleberry chuckled as he reported to Marty. "That blond fella breathed his last whilst I was checkin' him, and the other two was as dead as last week's beer soon as they hit the floor." Tackleberry pointed his chin toward the still form of the dry-goods drummer. "The drummer is croaked as well. Shot square through the brisket. Didn't even know what hit him."

Marty nodded his appreciation. "Thanks. Bad luck for the unfortunate fellow. He didn't deserve it. Would you see to his necessities, please? I'll leave you funds to bury him."

"Shore will."

"Thanks. Now, I need some paper and pencils. Bartender, you got any?"

At the bartender's nod, Marty continued. "How many of you men can write?" Several held up their hands. "Good. You men who can write, sit down and write out what you saw, in your own words. Austin will want to know what just happened here."

Marty supervised the taking of several written accounts of the events, then followed the doctor and two soldiers as they carried Steve to the post hospital, using an extra door from the saloon as a stretcher.

While the doctor attended Steve, Marty reported to the post commander, a Major Peyton, explaining what he and Steve were doing and why. The major, a gruff regular and a veteran of the war, angrily tapped the ashes from his pipe into a small ceramic dish.

"I don't see why you Rangers can't let us

help you in these kind of situations. That's what we're here for."

"We are sort of used to doing it ourselves, Major. We've been doing it since Texas was a republic, you know."

"I know, I know. You're also too proud to let Yankees help you, just because we are Yankees, if the truth be known. Well, you got an innocent man kilt who might still be alive if you had let us help. Well, so be it. You can rest assured I will send a full report to army HQ in Austin, explaining the incident. I'll let General Sheridan make a decision as to what to do, if anything." Major Peyton held out his hand. "I heard about the shootout from the soldiers who witnessed the entire thing. Sounds like you and your partner did a right smart job on the outlaws."

Marty took the offered hand and grinned at the major. "We almost got in too deep, I'm afraid. Will you allow me to leave Steve here until he can travel back to company Headquarters in Dallas?"

"I suppose. We wouldn't want the Rangers to think the U.S. Army wasn't cooperating with them in bringing the law to Texas. Why don't you get some sleep and check in tomorrow morning. The doc is a right handy man to have around. If your pard can be fixed up, ole Doc Summers is the man to do it."

"Thanks, Major. I thank you and will see you tomorrow." Marty slowly walked back to the town's hotel, winding down from the hypercharged excitement of the past few hours. He ate and went to bed, sleeping better than he thought possible. He awoke to a new sun, the cloudless sky already a harbinger of the hot hours to follow. He ate a hearty breakfast of flapjacks and ham, then walked down to the livery, where he found Tackleberry at work on his books. The livery owner pushed his Franklin-style glasses up on top of his balding head and nodded at a chair in the corner.

"Grab yourself a chair, Ranger. How's yur partner?"

"I'm headed over there in a few minutes, Mr. Tackleberry. First, I wondered what happened to the three outlaws?"

"I put 'em in the saloon beer cellar. It's cool in there. Thought they'd keep fer a while, until we can plant 'em."

"You have an undertaker hereabouts?"

"Nope. I sorta handle them chores when it becomes necessary."

Marty laughed. "Mr. Tackleberry, why doesn't that surprise me?"

"A man's gotta do what's necessary to

scratch out a livin' these days."

"Did you go through the dead men's pockets? Any of them got a name I can turn in?"

"Yep. The half-breed is Jim Hawk, iffen a bill of sale he was carryin' is kerrect. The other two didn't have no names nowhere. As to the rest, I was a'hopin' you wouldn't bother to ask." The livery owner opened a side drawer in his worn and scarred rolltop desk. He pulled out a few papers and ten twenty-dollar gold pieces, as well as several greenbacks. "They had two hundred thirty-two dollars on 'em. The papers don't tell much. Old letters, a map to some farmland in east Texas, the bill of sale fer a .36 Navy revolver from a gun shop over to El Paso del Norte, and a shoppin' list fer enough grub to feed thirty men fer a month."

Tackleberry grinned at Marty. "Old man Haycock over to the general store is gonna be plumb hurt you didn't wait till they made their purchases."

Marty grinned and shrugged his shoulders. "Luck of the draw. You're gonna come out better than you thought. I'll be buying your wagon. I'll need it to get Steve back to Dallas. I'll take the outlaws' horses as the team. You can have the tack as payment for planting them in boot hill. Fair enough?"

"The tack ain't worth much, Ranger. It's been used hard and not took good care of. I'll do it fer one of them twenty-dollar gold pieces and the tack. That's fair enough. Also, forty fer the wagon. That's what they was gonna pay. When will ya want it?"

"Not for a couple of days. As soon as I'm certain Steve can handle the trip. If the bed of the wagon is filled with hay, it ought to be fairly comfortable for him, don't you think?"

"Shore nuff. By the bye, them boys you kilt were armed right nicely. The guns are over there," he pointed at a table against the far wall. "The Navy Colt revolver the man upstairs was a'carryin' — the one you plugged under the chin — is a mighty nice one. You want it?"

"I'd better take them all, Mr. Tackleberry. The Rangers always have a need for good weapons. Roll 'em up in a blanket and hang on to them until I'm ready to go. You can go ahead and put the dead in the ground whenever you are ready."

"Might as well, I reckon. They're only gonna keep gettin' riper as the day wears on. Y'all wanna be at the final plantin'?"

"No thanks. I'll pass this time."

"Everybody in town is a'talkin' about the shootout. I'll bet we have a bigger crowd than when old man Evans was put under six weeks ago."

"Always nice to make the local folks happy," Marty laughed along with the livery owner. "Meanwhile, I'd better mosey on over to the fort and check out Steve. If he's not dead, he's probably griping about the food or about being laid up."

Marty took his leave and headed for the post. As he walked up the main street, several townspeople waved and wished him a good morning. It felt good to do something that was right and just and be appreciated for it. He was in a good frame of mind when he presented himself to the post doctor at the dispensary.

"Welcome, Ranger." The old doctor wiped his hands on a soiled towel as he stepped out of the back room.

"Howdy, Doc. How's Steve getting along?"

"Surprisingly enough, he's doin' quite well for someone who lost as much blood as he did. Just shows the power of a good bleedin'. His collarbone is broken and I cleaned out and sewed up the hole in his pectoralis major muscle — the one under the collarbone," the doctor tapped the heavy muscle of his chest. "If he doesn't get sepsis in it, he should heal up jus' fine. He'll not be able to use the arm fer about five or six weeks, I reckon."

"When can we travel? I'll be taking him back to Dallas, to Ranger Headquarters there." Marty pushed the nagging worry from his mind. He had been gone longer than he expected already.

"Give me a few more days. I'll let you know by Friday. I imagine if he's not infected by then, you can head on out. He'll have to ride in a wagon; he can't sit a horse fer some time yet."

"I suspected as much. I've already purchased one. I'll load the back with hay. It ought to make a fairly comfortable bed."

"Sounds good. Well, go on in and see him. He's been askin' for ya all morning. I just finished wrapping his wound. He'll be asleep afore long, so make it short."

"Thanks, Doc. I'll check on him and then clear out."

Marty stepped into the ward. Steve lay on a cot, and a heavily bandaged soldier lay on one across the room from him. "Howdy, Steve. How you feelin'?"

Steve smiled, but his ruddy face was wan and pinched. "Poorly, Marty. We git 'em all?"

"Yep, every one. They'll be planting them this afternoon."

"Good. Serves the sumbitches right. Damn, boy, but this here arm shorely does hurt."

"The doc says you're gonna be fine, Steve. He says you'll be ready to travel around the weekend. I've got a wagon and I'll fill it with hay. You ought to ride in style all the way to Dallas, just like a king on a golden coach."

Steve nodded, but his expression showed no confidence in Marty's promise. "You git statements from the eyewitnesses?"

"I have six. Right here in my pocket."

"Anything on the dead men the Rangers can use?"

"Only the name of one of them. I took the weapons to give to Captain Best. Also the ponies. We'll use them for a team to pull the wagon. That way we won't have to put our horses in trace."

"Good ideer. The rangers can use good horseflesh anyways. Marty, check in with the camp commander. He may have a courier going to Austin. They can wire Captain Best that we're on our way back, that we've taken care of the three he sent us after."

"I will, Steve. Now, you take it easy and get some rest. We don't want to have to lay about here all summer. I gotta get back to Meg and my boy, and you gotta get back to

Mrs. Block. I'll check in on you tomorrow."

Steve nodded, his face drawn and weary. "You said it. I'll look fer ya tomorrow."

Marty slipped away, then headed over to Major Peyton's office. He sent a brief message to Captain Best, care of First District Ranger HQ in Dallas, telling him of the situation and his plan to transport Steve back by wagon just as soon as the doctor released the wounded man. The major promised to send it out in the next dispatch run.

The next few days passed slowly, but by Saturday morning, just as the sun rose above the eastern plains, Marty sat on the wagon seat and checked Steve, laid out on a blanket in the hay-filled wagon, "You ready, Steve?"

"Take me home, boy. I'm as ready as I'll ever be."

CHAPTER 5
BACK TO DALLAS

"Dammit, Marty, my shoulder jus' ain't helpin' me none. It don't matter if I sit up here with ya on the seat, or lay back there on the hay. It's shore a'painin' me."

"Give it some time, Steve. It's only been three days since you got shot. I keep telling you that it looks like it's healing fine. I calculate we're not far from water. As soon as we hit it, I'll stop and set up camp. A good night's sleep may make all the difference."

Tall cottonwoods and a thick layer of velvet-green grass bordered the small stream where Marty pitched their camp. Marty got Steve comfortable, his bedroll laid over a scattering of fresh hay. Marty took care of the horses, hobbling them inside a picket rope stretched in a triangle around three large trees, then walked over to the stream and stripped off his shirt and undershirt. The cool water was a soothing balm to his tired, sweaty body. After washing, he took the bucket hanging from the wagon and filled it with clear water.

He carefully washed the area around Steve's wound, then gave him the rag and bucket. "Wash off some, Steve. It'll make you feel a lot more human."

"I gotta admit, Marty, you're the washin'est rascal I ever did meet. You take a bath every day, do ya?"

"Not that often, unfortunately, but as often as practical. I got tired of being dirty while I was in the army. Now it's like a habit. I think it makes me feel better. I know Meg likes me cleaner rather than not. She's always as clean and fresh-smellin' as a Texas rose. Makes her a real pleasure to be around at the end of the day."

"Well, I reckon if you can stand all that water on ya, I'll git by. Give me a hand with my boots. The cold water'll feel right good on my tired ole dogs, I'll bet ya."

"You want some help with your pants?"

"Hells bells, sonny. I ain't no button child. I can handle my own duds, thank you very much."

"Whatever. Just wash some of that stink offa you. We're both a mite gamey."

"I declare, things have come to a sorry state of affairs when a body's gotta wash up and it ain't even Saturday."

Marty flashed a grin at Steve and walked back to the creek. He stripped off his clothing and eased himself into the cool water. Sitting down, he was submerged nearly to his shoulders. He scrubbed off with a sliver of lye soap he carried in his bedroll, shaved, and washed his hair. Then he sat on a rock and used up the rest of his soap cleaning his clothing. After squeezing out as much of the water as he could, he laid the wet clothes on a rock and walked back to camp with only his blanket loosely wrapped around him.

Marty squeezed his bare feet into his boots and then gathered enough wood to make the campfire. He fried up the last of the salted pork and corn dodgers for their supper. After they both ate their fill, Marty took the horses back to the creek to water them, and then put on his clothes. By the time the sun had dipped behind some thunderheads to the west, he was comfortably dry and clean again.

He returned the horses to their makeshift corral, and then settled back against his saddle, his bedroll spread out under him. "A nice evenin', don't you agree?"

"Tolerable, I reckon," Steve answered as he struggled to roll a smoke with his makings. "Damned shoulder, it just ain't workin' right yet."

"Want some help?"

"Nah, I'll git it sooner or later. I'll need to do it myself after I git home. Mary won't help me, that's fer sure. She's agin all tobaccy, fer a fact."

"Same as Meg. She's after me not to smoke or drink. I can't get away with it around the house. She does let me puff a pipe now and then, thank goodness." Marty chuckled at the image in his mind of Meg, standing in that way of hers, with a hand against a cocked hip, determination all over her pixie face. He could hear her voice, just as if she were there with him: *Now Marty, let's not fuss. Just do it my way.*

"I reckon I oughta meet that little gal of yurs, Marty. She sounds like a real dandy."

"You bet your britches, Steve. She's the one person who got me right with the world again, after the war. I was plenty burned up by the fact that we gave so much for nothing. I really had a case of the chapped ass. Meg straightened me right up. She said to put it behind me, get on with my life with what I had. And I had a lot. A whole me, not half shot to pieces like so many men I knew. My health, enough money to get me away from Mississippi, and best of all, her.

She's a hundred percent wonder, Steve, that's as sure as the day is long."

"So's my Mary. But then I reckon we're supposed to feel thataway."

The two men sat in silence at the campfire, both engrossed with their personal reflections. Finally Steve broke the long stillness. "Whatta you gonna do next with yur ranch?"

Marty grinned and threw a small branch into the flames, absorbed by the shower of red sparks that exploded upward. "A lot. Meg and I are just about to turn the corner. Every spare cent we've made or saved has gone into good horseflesh. Next year I should be able to sell fifty head of horses, at premium prices. My six best mares are at the main house right now, ready to breed. If this stallion I'm riding is any good at all, I should have some prime yearlings to move. It's been a hard pull, but I do think we're at the crossroads, the good Lord willing and the creek don't rise."

Marty looked over at Steve. The wounded ranger was gingerly trying to find the most comfortable position to sleep. Marty supposed Steve asked the open-ended question to distract himself from his pain. Marty continued his rambling discourse.

"There's a good chance a couple of sections just to the north of our land are gonna become available next year. The current owner has already approached me to see if I was interested in purchasing them from him. That would double our grass and give me a second source of water. With that, I could add a second herd, and possibly some cattle. I read in the Dallas newspaper that an English cow, called the Angus, is a good candidate to replace the Longhorn. Lives just fine off grass and has more meat on its bones."

Steve spoke up, a sleepy drawl to his voice. "No way, pard. The Longhorn is the only cow what can make it in Texas. Mark my words on that. Ya put any credence in that kind of foolishness, yur gonna loose yur shirt."

"Well, it was just something I read. I suppose a body'd best look real carefully at any hasty decisions when it comes to replacing the Longhorn. The old mossybacks have been around a long time. It's just that they're skin, bones, and horns. Not enough meat."

"Maybe so, Marty, but you mark my words. A Longhorn'll stomp any English cow flatter than a run-over rattlesnake iffen you was to put one on the range." Steve pulled his blanket up to his chin with his good arm. "Well, pardner, I'm gettin' mighty weary. See ya in the morn."

Marty sat for a few more minutes, thinking about the ranch and the plans he and Meg had made. He tossed another branch on the fire and lay back, his hands cupping his head, looking up at the dark sky. A zillion stars twinkled in the velvet blackness. He hoped Meg was sitting on their front porch looking up at the same sky.

" 'Night, sweet darling, Meg. 'Night, little Matt. I'll be seeing you soon. I pray that Steve can go a full day tomorrow. That'll make me just that much closer to you both."

It was not to be. Steve started off strong, but by noon, his shoulder was seeping blood and every jar of the wagon brought a gasp of pain from him. He tried to cover it up, but Marty saw his distress. Finally, in a small grove of trees next to a small stream, Marty pulled the wagon off the rutted trail.

"Reckon I'll ride out and look for some venison, Steve. We're just about out of meat."

Steve gave Marty a rueful look. "Sorry, pard. I want to keep goin', but my arm is hurtin' somethin' painful."

"Let me have a look." Marty helped Steve to a seat next to a downed tree, where Steve could rest his back. The wound was red and fearful looking, pink fluid oozing from the puckered hole. Marty opened the stitches that held the wound together. He snagged a tiny thread sticking out of the hole and pulled out a shred of fabric from Steve's shirt that had been punched into the muscle tissue by the outlaw's bullet.

"This could be it. One thing we learned during the war, was to get everything out of the bullet hole, so the muscle can knit back together."

"You gonna try and sew me shut agin?"

"Nope. The ole doc who rode with us in the Texas Legion, said the best way to let a bullet wound heal was from the inside out. Just keep the hole clean, and make sure the patient has plenty of red meat to eat." Marty carefully bandaged the wound, using a clean strip of linen he tore from a sheet given him by the Camp Verde doctor. He made a small campfire and put a fresh canteen of water next to Steve, along with the ranger's weapons.

"Steve, I'm gonna try and scare up a deer. We could use some fresh meat. I think you'll be all right, but if someone comes along or you see any Injuns, pop off a round and I'll hurry back."

Steve settled back gingerly, easing his arm in the sling Marty tied around his neck to a comfortable position. "I'll git along, pard. Some fresh venison would hit the spot. Good huntin'."

Marty rode away from the camp site, a bit hesitant about leaving Steve, who seemed to be almost completely helpless; but he also knew how important a source of fresh meat could be to the wounded ranger's recovery.

Marty slowly rode along the green collar of the stream, an emerald necklace in a landscape of brown grass and earth. He knew that any animals in the cover of trees would be stirring after waiting out the noontime heat. It would only be a matter of time before he saw something. It was only a few minutes later that he flushed a small herd of Texas Whitetail deer. He stopped his pony and dismounted. The animals would not run far if they sensed there was no pursuit. He took his .44 Winchester "Yellow Boy" carbine, from the saddle scabbard and quietly jacked a round into the chamber. He dropped the hammer to half cock, then carefully followed the tracks left by the bolting deer. Marty spotted the herd munching some grass in a small clearing next to the stream.

As he watched, three more deer walked out of the trees to the sweet grass. One was a spike buck, not yet two years old. Marty took aim and dropped the animal in its tracks. The rest of the herd immediately bolted back into the trees and out of sight.

Marty walked back to his pony and led him to the kill site. He looped his lasso around the dead animal's rear legs, threw the other end over a tree limb, and hoisted the carcass off the ground. Skillfully, he gutted and skinned the deer, wrapping the liver and heart in a swath of the skin. As he worked, he sensed a sudden stillness to the air. He dropped his knife on the skin and took up his rifle, which was propped against the tree. As he jacked another cartridge into the chamber, a movement across the creek on a small knoll caught his eye.

Four mounted Indians rode over the top, spotted him, and reined in their paint ponies, looking at Marty and around the area, as startled as he was by the unexpected encounter. The swell in the earth had apparently masked the sound of his rifle, else they would have been more careful as they crested the hill.

Marty immediately held out his hand, palm up and extended. The four Indians were Comanche, not painted for war, but not above taking a white man's scalp under any circumstances. For a moment, the four Indians sat still and motionless, staring at

Marty with cold, calculating eyes.

Marty made an eating motion with his hand, cupping it toward his open mouth. Slowly, he lowered the rifle, took his knife and cut a rear haunch off the carcass. Carefully, he tied it and the skin holding the selected innards to his pony, then nonchalantly climbed on his horse. He rode away, leaving the rest of the deer for the Comanche warriors. He rode back to his camp with one eye looking over his shoulder, alert for any pursuit, but the Indians must have decided to take Marty's offering and spare him for another time, because he returned alone.

Steve shook his head as Marty related the story. "Yur one lucky son of a gun, pard. Them Injuns musta been right hungry, else they'd have come at ya from all four sides and took yur scalp as well as the deer."

"I think they knew what kind of rifle I was carrying. I'd have knocked at least two of them outa their saddles before they reached the creek. Sometimes discretion is as smart as anything else."

"Well, I'm plumb glad you got back with some of that there deer. It shore smells good, a'cookin' over the fire."

Marty nodded. He was roasting the liver and heart, the best parts for a man fighting sepsis and blood loss. "It'll be done in a minute. After we eat, I'll try and grab a little sleep if you think you can stay awake a spell. Then I'll take over for the rest of the night."

"Them boys ain't gonna bother us tonight. They don't want to try and find the happy huntin' ground in the dark, you know that."

"Yeah, but they're not above sneaking in to help themselves to our horses, night or not."

"And iffen they do, what am a I supposed to do about it? I can barely hold my head up."

"Just call out. I'm going to bring the horses in close and tie them down. They'll have a chance to eat their fill tomorrow, after the sun's up."

"All right, pard. You're the one callin' the cards. I gotta admit you've took right proper care of me so far. Ain't no need to change now. It 'pears to me that the meat is done. Let's eat."

Marty let Steve rest the entire next day. He prowled the perimeter of their campsite, but saw nothing of the Indians. At the first blush of dawn the following morning, he was on the move, Steve bedded in the load of hay, complaining that he was feeling so much better that he should be allowed to ride on the seat next to Marty.

After supper, the two men discussed their options. Marty was anxious to continue. He felt the need to get home even stronger now.

"Well, Steve, how you feelin'? Up to riding on a while?"

"Not too bad. Stopping over fer a day helped, I feel plumb refreshed. You wantin' to ride on in to Dallas, aren't ya?"

"We're only about six hours away. It would be near midnight, but you could sleep in your own bed tonight, if we did. I'll leave it up to you."

"You've been a good pard, Marty. Took your time when I was a'hurtin' and didn't complain none about havin' to handle all the chores yurself. I'll give it a go iffen you want to drive on. I know yur in a hurry to git back to yur place."

"I can't explain it. It just seems like something's urging me to get back home. It sure makes me uncomfortable."

"Then let's git a'goin'. We're wastin' time."

As they rode into Dallas, a heavy storm shook the sky with thunder and lightning, while fat drops of rain drenched the two men. Marty unloaded Steve at his home, helped his anxious wife get the wounded man into bed, and took his leave. He stomped the mud off his boots at the doorway to Captain Self's office. A young man he did not recognize greeted him.

"Yes, sir?"

"Hello, I'm Ranger Keller. Where's the captain?"

"He's away on a posse, Ranger Keller. I just got here this afternoon myself. I don't know much more than that. There's hardly anyone around here but me."

Marty put the witness depositions on the desk and quickly briefed the young ranger on what had occurred. "I'm going on home. Tell the captain I'll come back in if he has any further questions that Ranger Block can't answer."

Marty rode away from the Dallas Ranger Headquarters, tucking his chin down in the opening of the rubber-coated poncho he used as rain gear. The thunder and lightning increased in intensity, the white flashes illuminating the wet ground and making spooks out of the trees and bushes next to the road. Marty shook his head as his imagination created all sorts of weird things out of the shadows, and dancing illumination from the lightning flashed. The ghosts of his past, the men he had killed in the war, outlaws and Indians from his Ranger days, all appeared along the road every time the lightning cut through the wet, black night.

Marty swallowed his uneasy thoughts. He had to get home. The urgency to return to his family roared through his brain like a runaway locomotive.

"Meg, darling, I'm coming. I'm almost home. Just hang on until the sun rises. I'll be there then."

The sun had barely cleared the mist to the east when Marty rode onto his land. As he topped the small hill that overlooked his ranch, he paused to breathe deeply. His land, his air. He spotted two of his wranglers coming out of the bunkhouse. He waved his arm and shouted, "Hello."

Surprisingly, the two men immediately jumped on their horses and spurred them hard toward him, instead of waiting for him to ride down.

"Hector, Anselmo, I'm back," Marty greeted them. "Glad to see you."

Anselmo swung off his pony and rushed to Marty's side. He clutched Marty's leg, anguish covering his face. Tears spilled from bloodshot eyes as he sobbed up to Marty, who sat stunned on his horse.

"Jefe, forgive us. We have failed you. Madre de Dios, we have failed you."

"What, what is wrong? My God, man, what's wrong?"

Chapter 6
Heartbreak
in Texas

In Marty's anguished mind, the next few hours passed in a dizzying blur. The grief-laden confession came first. His men were late returning from the sale because of a delay in receiving the payment money. Then a hard rainstorm rumbled through and they wasted a day waiting it out. They returned to the ranch to find José desperately trying to stay alive long enough to tell the gruesome tale of carnage.

Anselmo, his face convulsed with grief, described the intruders. "Five men, Jefe. A tall one — thin, dark-haired, and mean. He was the leader of the gang. Another one was a Mexican, named Sanchez. Two blond-haired men, maybe brothers. Big but not very smart. An older man, wearing sleeve garters with scalps dangling from them. They took our best mares, Jefe. Then they killed your child and his mamma. The angels have taken the señora and her niño.

Your Margaret and little Matthew are gone, Jefe. They were dead when we arrived, José not long after."

Marty would have fallen from his saddle had not the two vaqueros grabbed him and helped him down. Marty leaned against his horse, clutching his saddle horn to stay erect, trying to comprehend the magnitude of the horror he was confronting. "What, what are you saying? My Meg, dead? Little Matt?"

"Sí, Jefe," Anselmo answered, tears streaming steadily down his weathered cheeks. "They sleep over there, under the big oak. They are with the Holy Mother of God now. We are so sorry, Jefe. So very sorry."

With the help of the two wranglers, Marty stumbled to the twin graves under the shade of a towering oak tree at the south corner of the yard. He stood for a moment, staring at the fresh dirt mounded under the two wooden crosses, carefully made by his men. One simply had MATTHEW carved on the crossbar and the other MARGARET. From each cross, one of his men had hung a crucifix, the tiny, silver crosses twinkling in the sunlight.

Marty stood silently, then dropped as if he had been struck by lightning. He fell across the twin mounds, his face in the fresh dirt, his hands clawing deep into the loose soil. Marty did not know how long he lay on the graves. In his grief he wondered, *Where are the tears? Why aren't I crying?* Miserably, his two men stood in the shade of the tree, holding the horses and waiting for their friend to work through his grief.

It was late afternoon before Marty stirred. Slowly, he got to his knees. He smoothed the dirt that he had disturbed. He prayed, asking a God he suddenly needed to take his wife and son into His eternal embrace. Marty softly pleaded for his wife and son. It was hard to say the words. He wondered if he could ever believe in the goodness of the Almighty again. His heart was broken, yet his rage was already consuming his soul with fire. If he lived to be a hundred, he would not rest until the filth that had committed this evil were dead, as dead as his family and his dreams for the future.

"Anselmo," Marty whispered as he turned away from the graves, "tell me again what happened."

Walking slowly back to the house, Marty listened as his foreman repeated what he knew, including the final words of old José, just before he died. "Where is José?" Marty queried.

"Phillipe took him to his sister in Waco. He was buried in the family plot there two days ago."

"Where are Roy and Sean?"

"As soon as we found out what had happened, they rode to Dallas to tell the Rangers. Captain Self brought a posse back to track the evil ones and Roy and Sean rode with them. I stayed to tell you the sad news when you returned."

Marty listened as the old Mexican cowboy finished the story of the gruesome discovery, and then had him repeat it again, from the beginning. The information seared into his brain as it tore the fabric of his heart. He would need every bit of knowledge to fulfill his vow of vengeance.

As darkness fell, Marty picked at the beans and bacon served by the younger Hector. He sat on the porch in the evening darkness, still wondering if he ever was going to cry, the ache in his guts and the sense of loss so overpowering it was almost unbearable. It was after midnight before he walked into the house and went to his bedroom. He could not sleep on the bed that he had shared with Meg. Instead, he took his bedroll and walked to the big oak. He lay down beside the silent graves and waited for the coming dawn.

Anselmo was waiting for him when he returned to the house the next morning. "Jefe, here is the money for the cattle. Two hundred twenty dollars."

Marty tried to concentrate on what the old cowboy was telling him, but the mind-numbing pain prevented any rational discussion. He dropped the money on the rolltop desk in the living room and stalked out.

Anselmo hurried after him. "Jefe, the killers took the good mares. They killed all the horses they didn't steal. Hector and I drug them to the ravine beyond the south hill and buried them."

"Good."

"Jefe, what do you want me to do?"

"You and Hector ride out and see if they took the rest of the horses. I'll need to know how many are left."

"Captain Self and the posse each took one horse, so they could ride hard after the killers. There are no more horses left on the ranch."

"How many cows are left?"

"About fifty. The breeding females and the two bulls."

"Bring 'em in close to the ranch."

"Sí, Jefe. We will leave immediately. Will you be all right?"

"Sure, compadre. I want to stay close to

home today. I don't feel like doing much."

"I understand, Jefe. We will be back by dark."

"Don't worry about it. I'm gonna putter around here. If you have to stay out tonight, I'll be all right." The two vaqueros rode off, casting anxious glances back at him as they left. Marty sat down in the rocker that he liked to use after a hard day's work. He and Meg would sit on the porch and watch the sun go down, he rocking and smoking his pipe, and Meg darning or sewing on something. That would never happen again. The bitter thought choked him in its grim finality.

The day passed slowly, seeming to take twice as long as any other day. Marty wanted to cry, to feel the release of an outpouring of bitter grief. He dwelled on thoughts of Meg and little Matt, their times together, the things they had done. Nothing worked. His heart had turned to ice and his mind blazed afire with only one thought: retribution.

Marty remained in the rocker. He watched the sun set and the sun rise, still in the chair, wondering if he would ever sleep again. He didn't care.

Anselmo and Hector had just ridden in to report that the cattle were gathered on the meadow behind the barn, when Captain Self rode into the yard at the head of twenty, trail-dusty, grim Rangers.

Marty endured the seemingly endless parade of dirty, sad-faced men who shook his hand and offered their condolences in halting, subdued voices. Finally he shook the last hand and sought out the Ranger captain. "Captain Self. Did you find them?"

"No, son. Nary a sight. We trailed 'em clear across the border into Injun Territory, up to the Washita River. Just as we got there, a real gully-whomper rainstorm hit. After it quit rainin', we lost the trail. We looked fer over a day, but it warn't no use. They got clean away."

"Well, let's go back. We'll spread out. They can't have gone up in smoke. They left a sign somewhere."

"The rain took the sign, Marty. We looked. All signs had been washed away."

"Well, they'll show up in some town. All we have to do is poke around until we cross their trail again."

Self shook his head and put a strong hand on Marty's arm. "It's no good, Marty. We're Rangers, tasked by the state of Texas to uphold the law. In Texas. You know that, Marty. We have neither the authority nor the mandate to go outta Texas to chase outlaws, even though every man in my command was willing and ready to do just that. We're deeply sorry for your loss. It's a rotten thing to have to endure. We just don't have enough men or time to track these scum-suckin' hellhounds down. No matter how hard we want to. I'm takin' the men back to headquarters in Dallas. I'm sorry, but that's the way it is."

Marty jerked his arm away from Self's grasp. "It's not right, Captain. I went out for you. I got the men I went after. While I did my job for Texas, someone killed my family. You have to help me catch them. You have to."

"I'd like to, son. Nothin' would give me more pleasure. I can't. If your heart wasn't hurtin' so, you'd know I'm right."

Marty gritted his teeth. "You're not right. You're not. If the Rangers won't help me, I'll do it alone. To hell with the lot of you. To hell with Texas. I'll chase them down by myself, even if it takes the rest of my life. I swear it."

Self did not back down at Marty's outburst. "Don't, son. It'll be a dirty trail and there won't be any satisfaction at the end. You'll just become harder and more bitter the longer you look. Stay here, where your folks are, and make a new life for yourself."

"Not as long as there's breath in my body. I'll find those bastards, if I have to follow them clear to Hell. And when I do, I'll kill them. Just like they killed my family."

Self shook his head, a sad look in his eyes. "And then you'll be just like them. Is that what your wife would have wanted for you?"

Marty shook his head and turned away. His face was set, his eyes burning with determination. He spoke very little to the tired Rangers as they watered their horses, grabbed a quick meal of jerky, dropped off the extra animals they had borrowed from him, and trotted away, headed back to Dallas.

As soon as they had gone, Marty took stock of his situation. He had a dozen horses and fifty cattle he could sell. That would bring nearly a thousand dollars. His ranch might bring a couple thousand more. He owed the bank and his ranch hands about five hundred of that. He would have enough to stay on the trail for a year, maybe more, if he was careful with his money.

He started to carry out his plan the very next day. He sent his men off with the cattle and horses, back to Dallas with instructions to sell them at any price. He rode along for part of the way, stopping at the land office in Greenville, where he sold his ranch to the local speculator for a third of its true worth.

"I'm mighty sorry to see you go, Marty," the man said. "Your place was a real nice example of what a small ranch should look like. I don't reckon I'll have any trouble sellin' it. The folks around here all liked you and your nice missus. We're sure gonna miss you."

Marty looked at the paper. He dreaded what he was about to do, yet it was the only way. "Just remember your promise, Mr. Northfield. Whoever buys my place has to maintain Margaret's and Matt's graves out by the big oak."

"I give you my word I'll make that part of any deal. We all know about your loss and have the deepest sympathy for you. Everybody wants to do everything he can to help you."

Marty signed the papers and rode back to the ranch. His men returned at the end of the week, the animals all sold. Anselmo gave Marty the money received for the animals, and Marty told them he had sold the ranch.

"Jefe, what of us?" the old vaquero asked. "What will we do when you are gone?"

"I talked to Mr. Northfield. He's agreed to keep all of you on the payroll for a month, while he tries to sell the ranch to someone. If he does, the new owner will likely offer all of you jobs. I'm giving each of you two months' pay, to carry you over. You all were good men. Any man would be fortunate to have you as his employees. That's the best I can do for you."

"Can we go with you, boss?" Sean hitched his gun belt as he spoke, unconsciously mimicking a gunfighter about to go into action.

"No, it won't work. I don't know how or when I'll find the men responsible for killing Meg and Matt. You can't stop living your lives just because of my problems. You're good men. Stay here and see if you can work for the new owner with the same dedication and loyalty you gave to me."

"You know how sorry we all are, don't you, boss?"

"I do, and I appreciate it. It wasn't your fault. It was mine. I never should have left them for so long. I'll live with that the rest of my days."

By Monday, he had disposed of everything he could not carry with him and was ready for the trail. He took the boy's clothing to his nearest neighbor, who had two small children. They would use Matt's clothes with gratitude. Margaret's, he sent into Greenville to give to women of the church.

Marty got some small satisfaction in the gift. Meg had always enjoyed going to the tiny church, the odd times they had been in town on a Sunday.

On his last day at the ranch, Marty sat by the graves, saying his final good-byes to Meg and little Matt. It was a quiet time, where once again he recalled their life together, what they had accomplished, and what dreams they once had. Marty felt like he was close to his family then. At the end of the day, his eyes remained dry. He shook his head in disgust. He could not believe he had not broken down in tears once, even though his heart ached for his family. Early the next morning, riding his favorite stallion and leading a pack mule loaded with provisions, Marty Keller rode away from his home, his dreams, his future.

He did not look back.

CHAPTER 7
A GRIM
SEARCH BEGINS

The trail left by the murderers had ended at the Washita River in Indian Territory, so that's where Marty headed. He rode steadily, sparing neither himself nor his horse. The vermin he chased already had a week's head start. He did not want to fall any farther behind them.

In three days he was at the river, the place where his so-called friends, the Rangers, had abandoned the chase for the filth that killed Meg and Matt. He rode up and down the water's edge, looking for sign of fording, old campfires, anything that might be a lead. There was nothing. Marty built a small fire next to the river and considered his next move. He talked to the weakening flames as he drank the last of his coffee. "They have money in their pockets. They're reasonably certain nobody will trail them beyond the Texas-Oklahoma Territory border. Where would they go?"

Marty called out, his voice strident and profane. "Where did you bastards go?" The only reply was the soft voice of the shallow river gurgling over rocks as it flowed serenely along to its meeting with the Sabine River to the south, inside Texas. The next morning, Marty rode north, looking for any major pathway across the grassy landscape. Indian Territory was thinly populated and roads were few and far between.

Late the following afternoon, he spotted a low building, setting at the lee of a long sloping hill, a rutted, dirt road to its front. As he drew nearer, he saw it was a combination trading post and saloon. The sides were adobe and the roof was sod. A shaky corral held three tired nags. Marty swung down from his pony and led him to the water trough, allowing the tired animal to drink his fill. Marty turned his horse loose inside the enclosure and walked to the door of the low building. The Dutch door was open at the top, allowing the stale air inside the building to escape.

Marty had to duck as he stepped inside, stopping at the doorway to allow his eyes to adjust to the dim interior. The one-room building was shelved with goods on its south wall, while the northern half held a rough, wooden plank bar and four round tables surrounded by chairs. Two customers sat quietly at one of the tables, nursing glasses of beer while a man stood behind the bar, slowly wiping whiskey glasses with a dingy gray rag. He had an apron wrapped around his waist, and the sleeves of his shirt rolled up to the elbows. He was middle-aged, with a high forehead and thinning, sandy hair combed in an effort to hide the obvious.

Marty moved to the bar, his eyes taking in everything about the room. He looked the bartender over and pulled a silver dollar from his pants pocket. "A small beer, please."

"Sure enough, friend," the bar tender answered, expertly filling a glass to a foam-topped draw from the beer barrel set on a rack behind the bar. He took a flat stick and scraped the towering foam off the glass, then slid the drink across the bar top to Marty.

"Here ya go, friend. Will ya be needin' any supplies? This here is the only chance to get some fer sixty miles, if yur headin' north."

"Possibly. You have any canned peaches or such?"

"Yep. Got a couple. A dollar for the pair."

"Little steep, isn't it?"

"Not fer the Territory, friend. We're a long way between trade wagons."

90

"I reckon that's true. Well, here's your dollar. I'll have 'em." Marty dropped another dollar on the bar, where the bartender scooped it up just as quickly as the last.

Marty sipped his beer. It was lukewarm, but did a good job of cutting the trail dust from his throat. He waited until the barkeeper returned from the store side of the room with his peaches, then leaned closer to the man. Instinctively, the barkeeper leaned closer to Marty.

"I'm looking for five men. Maybe rode past here about two weeks ago. You seen them? One's a Mex, two were blond and probably brothers."

"Listen, mister. We don't talk about our customers in this here establishment. I mind my own business and I reckon you oughta mind yurs."

Marty reached across the bar and grabbed a handful of the man's shirt. He twisted his hand and pulled until the barkeeper was on tiptoes, trying to keep from being pulled over the bar. His voice was choking as he fought to get air past the obstruction around his neck. "Easy, mister, I — I can't breathe."

"You'll have it worse than that if you don't talk to me, and right now."

"Back off, back off. Lemme get a breath." The man's face was reddening, and his eyes bugged as he fought for breath.

Marty heard the soft scraping of a chair as it was pushed away from the table. He spun around, his right hand pulling his pistol as he turned. He glared at the two men sitting at the table. "You fellas want to die, stand up. Otherwise stay set and stay shut until the bartender and I finish our discussion."

The two men looked at Marty and the pistol in his hand and relaxed. They had no desire to start trading bullets just yet. Marty returned his gaze back to the barkeeper. "Now, will you think back? Did five men stop off here, about two weeks ago?"

"Mister, I don't think —" The bartender stopped as Marty twisted the cloth of his collar.

"Don't think. Just answer. Five men. Two weeks ago."

The answer was little more than a gasp. "Why do ya need to know, anyways?"

Marty's pulse jumped. They had been here. "Two weeks ago, five men rode into my ranch. They killed my wife and baby son, and one of my hands. They rode this way on five of my prize horses. They all got a killing coming and I plan to oblige them. Now, did they stop here?"

The bartender looked into Marty's eyes. He saw madness lurking there, so he talked fast and true. "Yeah, they was here. About ten — twelve days ago. Right, Smokey? Ole Smokey there, he played cards with a couple of 'em. Five men, right, Smokey?"

The older of the two customers nodded. "That's right, Sid."

Marty nodded. "One of them a Mex, two blonds?"

"That's them. What really caught me eye was their horses. As fine a bunch of horse-flesh as I ever did see."

"What else?"

"They stayed about eight hours. Bought some supplies. Rode on. Oh, yeah. The thin one — he seemed to be the leader — asked the best way to git to Wichita."

"Wichita. Good. Thank you." Marty released the man's shirt, allowing him to settle back off his tiptoes.

"I'm sorry 'bout yur loss, mister," the bartender said, rubbing his throat. "I didn't know them fellas had done such hurt to ya."

"Thank you," was Marty's response. He turned to the older cowboy. "You played cards with them?"

"Yep."

"What do you know?"

"Not much. The tall thin one is the boss. Calls hisself Al. The gambler is named Ace somethin'. He seemed different."

"How so?"

"The thin guy, he was plain mean. Worst than that, even. Ace seemed better, somehow. Like he was in with a bunch of folks he didn't wanna be with."

"Go on."

"The two blonds. Al called them, what was it?" The cowboy scratched the two-day stubble of beard on his chin. "A and B. A and B. Bob, that's it. Bob and something that starts with A. I thought it were funny. Twins, I think, named A and B. I never hear what the Mexican was called."

"Sanchez," Marty answered for him.

"Oh, yeah," the cowboy suddenly interjected. "I remember somethin' about the thin fella. Talked like he was from Alabama or maybe Tennessee. He had only three fingers on his left hand. The last two was gone at the first knuckle." The cowboy nodded. "He said something about the war, so he most likely lost 'em then. I saw him rubbin' 'em with his glove off. He saw me lookin' and glared at me like he wanted to cut my heart out. Put his glove back on, real quick like."

"You sure?"

"Yep. I had a friend that lost some fingers. The ones left were always crampin' on him. Maybe a fella uses the fingers that are left somehow different when the others are gone. He fer certain had lost two fingers, and wore a fancy kidskin glove to hide the fact."

"They say anything about Wichita?"

"I think somethin' was said 'bout that."

"That all?"

"Yeah, 'cept the thin one, Al, fancied hisself a sharp card player. He ain't — not by a long shot."

"How about the other — Ace, was it?"

"He could play. He was a sharpie fer a fact."

"Thanks. I appreciate the information."

"I'm happy to give it to ya. I hope you catch 'em."

"Oh, I will. If I have to trail them to Hell and back, I will."

"Mister, I believe ya."

Marty turned back to the bar and grabbed his peaches. "Give me a bottle."

The bartender passed a full bottle of some rotgut over to Marty. Marty grabbed the bottle by its long neck and dropped a five-dollar gold piece on the bar. "Drinks on me, gentlemen."

Marty stalked from the bar, the bottle in his hand. He took a deep breath as soon as he was in the fresh air. He had come close to losing control inside. He would have to be more careful. In a crowd, there might be someone who would decide to take him on when he challenged them like he had the men inside.

He rode a distance down the road, until he spotted a small creek. Finding a suitable campsite, he made himself and his animals comfortable and cooked some supper, rewarding himself with one of the cans of peaches for dessert. He lay back, his head resting on his saddle, gazing upward at the dark sky as the stars began their nightly appearance. He never ceased to wonder at the magnitude of them.

He opened the bottle of whiskey and took a sip. "Meg, darling," he muttered, "I have a need for this. Hope you'll understand."

Silence, interrupted by the pop and sizzle of burning wood were his only companions. Marty slowly sipped the whiskey, thinking of his family and times they had shared. He was not used to the potent alcohol, and soon became far drunker than he had ever intended. It relaxed the demons in his brain and soon he was talking to Meg and Matt as if they were at the campsite with him. He even had an argument with Meg over drinking so much.

Deep inside his brain, even in his drunken ramblings, Marty kept asking himself, *Why can't I cry? Why can't I cry?* He went on ranting and raving in a drunken frenzy until the fire was but glowing embers. He suddenly tipped the last of the bottle and passed out cold, to sleep better than he had since the moment he arrived at his ranch, so many hard days ago.

Marty awoke with the sun halfway up the sky, his head pounding and his dry mouth tasting like a trail herd had marched through it during the night. Cursing himself and the rotgut he had drunk, Marty quickly made ready and hit the trail, riding hard, not sparing himself or his animals. The thumping in his head matched the hoofbeats of his horses as he rode through the day and deep into the night. He made a cold camp, mostly as punishment to himself, and was up at daybreak the next morning, ready to ride on.

"Let's get a leg up, pony. We need to get to Wichita. Some men there have some dying to do."

CHAPTER 8
A TIME TO RUN

Alva Hulett stirred in the whore's bed. Stretching his long arms above his head, he rolled his shoulders and sat up, his back against the headboard. He barely noticed that he was alone. The woman he had purchased had slipped out of bed early and was downstairs, near the rest of her friends. She wanted nothing else to do with the red-necked, sexually cruel cowboy. He was bad medicine, a driving machine that needed to know he was inflicting pain to really enjoy a sexual liaison. Just the touch of him made her skin crawl.

Alva hooked his hands behind his neck, supporting his head, while he let memory talk to him. Alva had grown up in Tennessee, his ignorant family ruled by a grandmother who believed in spells and spirits, and voices from beyond. Naturally, Alva believed as well.

He had gone to war when only sixteen,

ending up with Bloody Bill Anderson and William Quantrill. He had thoroughly enjoyed the hard riding and easy killing the two guerrilla leaders had offered him, not to mention the booty gained from looting and robbing.

Feeling the urge of nature straining his bladder, he swung his long legs off the bed and pulled on his pants. The stiff, trail-stained garment showed the effects of hard riding from the ranch in Texas to the cat-house in Wichita. He pulled his boots on, never having worn a pair of socks in his life, before stepping over to the dresser where he dumped some tepid water from a porcelain pitcher into the bowl beside it. He splashed water over his face, and casually wiped his front teeth with a horny forefinger. He rubbed back the dark, dirty hair from his eyes and grimaced at his reflection in the spotted mirror hanging above the dresser.

Belching loudly, he stepped from the room and headed out back to the convenience. As soon as he was right with the world, he started looking for his men. He found them in the sleazy hotel room still sleeping, the twins on one bed and Richland on the other. Sanchez was sleeping at the livery, up in the hayloft, which was good enough for a Mex. Besides, by sleeping there, he could keep an eye on their horses. Alva had never had such a fine animal under him before. He wanted to keep it as long as possible. Al knew that Richland had probably spent most of the night gambling, but he did not care what the man did on his own time. He just had to ride and kill when Alva told him to, without compunction.

"Wake up, you worthless slugs. Time to make some plans. Wake up, dammit." Alva kicked the bed holding the twins, knowing he could. He did not try it with Richland, uncertain if the gambler he had recruited for his skill with a pistol was fearful enough of him not to react. He had just about enough of Richland, anyway. After the next job, he would cut him loose — maybe the twins as well — then strike out for Colorado and the gold fields. Hulett knew he would keep Sanchez with him. The ex-peon was fanatically loyal, and had already saved Hulett's life more than once in the past.

He watched as the men struggled out of their beds. The twins were good to have around when times were flush. They did exactly what he wanted, no questions asked. But they ate and drank beyond their worth if times were a little tight. Alva made an easy decision. He would go on to Colorado with just Sanchez. He could always get new men if he needed a bigger gang in the gold fields.

"What's up, Boss?" Bob Swain asked, rubbing the sleep out of his eyes.

"I've got a feeling we need to move on right away." Al motioned to the twins. "You two, take this twenty dollars and buy some grub. Meat, beans, flour, and coffee. Also git some tobaccy and two bottles of whiskey. Only two, ya got that?"

"Yep," Bob said, scratching the blond stubble of his beard. "We'll do it. Where we headed?"

"Tell some folks that we're off to San Antone with the Lazy 6 crew. One of them told me they was leaving today at sunrise, headed back that way."

Richland looked out the window. "Then we've already missed 'em. They're long gone."

CHAPTER 9
BANK JOB

"Hell's bells, I know that," Hulett said. "I jus' want people to think we're headed fer San Antone, not where we're really goin'."

"Where're we a'goin', Boss?" Andy Swain asked as he viciously rubbed the sleep from his eyes. Bob sat dejectedly on the side of the bed, so hungover that he could barely focus.

"I'll tell ya once we're on the trail," Hulett answered impatiently. "All you boys gotta do fer now is let everyone you see know that we're headin' fer San Antone. Someone's after us, and I aim to put him way offa our tracks."

"What makes you think that?" Richland asked.

"It's jus' somethin' I feel in my gut. I ain't never been wrong. You wanna stay here, go ahead. But me and the rest are headin' out jus' as soon as we can get supplied and saddled up."

Richland stood and pulled on his pants. "I oughta stay, but my instinct says to follow your instincts, Hulett. You're part wolf, to my reckoning."

"Yur damned right I am, Richland. And don't none of you boys ever fergit that. Now, iffen yur done gabbin', Ace, git on out and tell Sanchez to check and saddle up the horses. I wanna be on the trail by noon, at the latest. Then go to a saloon let everyone know where we're a'headed."

The three men roused themselves to do Hulett's bidding. He nodded, satisfied, then returned to his room. He packed the few belongings he possessed in his saddlebags and left the fleabag brothel. He turned in to the next doorway south, which was the Hi-Lo Saloon. He glanced around the nearly empty saloon, insuring there was little danger to him there and then walked to the bar. This was where he had overheard the cowboys from the Lazy 6 Ranch talking about leaving for the return trip to San Antonio after driving two thousand cattle to the railhead in Wichita.

He ordered a small whiskey. "Pour me one, Tiny."

The bartender was a giant of a man, over three hundred pounds, and taller than the lanky Hulett by several inches. His mighty hand surrounded the whiskey bottle and expertly filled a small shot glass to the brim. He slid the glass to Alva without spilling a drop and raked the man's four bits into the wide palm of his other hand. As he dropped the coins into the cashbox, his deep voice rumbled like mountain thunder.

"Looks like a hot one today."

"Fine by me, I like it hot. Hate cold weather. Makes my rumatiz act up. Say, Tiny, how would I best git on down to San Antone from here? I got some business to transact down that way."

"It ain't so hard, I reckon. Too bad ya didn't ask yesterday. The Lazy 6 crew just brought up a herd from down there last week. They left this morning, headed back. You coulda rode along with 'em. Made it nice while ya cross the Injun Territories. They was about thirty strong."

"Left this mornin', huh?"

"Yeah, 'bout sunup, I reckon."

"Hell," Hulett smiled, at least with his mouth, if not his eyes. "I suppose I can catch 'em if I hurry along."

"Maybe so. I know I wouldn't want to cross the Territory alone. The Comanche are on the prod lately."

"Me neither. I'm gonna ride as hard as I can and catch up with the Lazy 6 boys.

Thanks fer the info. I'll see ya the next time I visit Wichita."

"My pleasure."

Tiny watched the lanky man exit the saloon. He thought back, but could not remember ever talking with him before. The man acted as though they had talked at some time in the past. Well, he met many men at his bar, how could he remember them all?

"Must be gittin' old," the bartender muttered to himself.

Alva stepped out onto the sidewalk whistling softly. He was certain that anybody looking for him would make their way to the Hi-Lo eventually, and talk to the huge bartender. He would remember that Alva had spoken about heading for San Antonio, and direct any pursuers the wrong way.

He slowly wandered to the livery, where he found Sanchez getting one of the horses reshod.

"She threw a shoe, Señor Alva. The smithy will be done very shortly."

"No hurry. The others arrived yet?"

"Señor Richland was here, to check on his horse. Then he went to the cantina down the street to buy two bottles of whiskey. He said he would be right back. The brothers, I have not seen them this morning."

"It's all right. I sent 'em to the store to pick up vittles fer the trail. We're goin' to be on the ride fer about a week or so."

"Where then, Señor Alva?"

"We're gonna hit a bank I've had my eye on fer a spell. Then you and I are splittin' up from the rest of these bummers, and headin' fer the gold fields of Colorado. Don't let on none about it, though. The twins are so dumb they'll think I want 'em along."

"Of course, Señor Alva."

"I'll let the rest know where we're a'headin' as soon as we git outta town. You ask the smithy if he thinks the shoe will last to San Antone. I want everybody to think that's where we're a'headin', even if we ain't."

"As you wish, señor."

The two sat smoking and softly talking about their plans until the Swain twins arrived with four sacks filled with foodstuff. Richland was right behind them with a burlap bag holding two quart bottles of whiskey.

"You boys say anything about goin' to San Antone like I said?"

"You betcha, Boss," Bob replied. "We talked it up real good at the store."

"How 'bout you, Ace?"

"Sure, just like you said."

"Good. Let's get loaded up."

The packhorse was quickly loaded with the food, and the men saddled their mounts. Every man was responsible for his own loading, since Hulett would not allow the men to drop the chore on Sanchez as they would have liked, and would have done had he not protected the Mexican outlaw. Alva led his four unholy companions out of Wichita before the sun was halfway up the sky, riding southwest, toward Texas.

CHAPTER 10
HIDING THE TRAIL

For a couple of miles, Hulett followed the tracks left by the Lazy 6 crew as they rode toward the southwest. As they crossed a stream that cut across the road, Hulett pulled off and followed the meandering course for three hundred yards, then pointed his horse into a small clearing nestled among a grove of river cottonwoods.

"Well, gents, here's where we head to the sweetest little bank in Missouri, jus' waitin' fer us to pick the peaches outta its vault."

"Missouri?" Richland queried. "We're headed fer Missouri?"

"That's right, Ace. Ya got a problem with that?"

"No, course not. I was just wonderin'."

"A little town called Carthage. We had a dandy little fight with the Yanks there back in '63. I ain't never forgot how bad them local folks looked down on us when we came through town. I seen the bank then —

it looked right prosperous. I told Bloody Bill that it looked ripe fer pluckin'. Unfortunately, the Yanks run us so far outta town, we never had a chance to git it. Now I aim to set things straight."

"How far we got to go, Boss?" Andy Swain asked.

"Oh, I reckon about five days. We'll ease up to the town real careful like, look things over and hit it Saturday, late afternoon."

"How much you think we'll git?" Bob Swain chimed in.

"Who knows fer certain," Hulett answered. "Enough, I reckon."

Hulett climbed on his horse and rode on, the others straggling after him until they were closed up tight. He rode due east the rest of the day, stopping just as the sun touched the horizon. He swung down and stretched a kink out of his back, then, looked over to Sanchez, who was already stripping the saddle from Hulett's tired horse.

"Amigo, as soon as yur done, whip us up some grub. Bob, you and Andy gather up some wood fer a fire. I'm plumb hungry. Ace, picket the horses so they're safe."

"And what are you gonna do, Al?" Richland asked, his voice bold and demanding.

"I'm gonna figger on how we can take that

bank without gittin' our butts shot off. Ya got any problems with that?"

"No, I guess not. I just think we all oughta help around the campsite."

"I reckon I'll do my share, Ace. You jus' worry about doin' yurs."

As Al and Sanchez walked the circumference of their little camp later that night, just before Al planned to go to sleep, he grumbled to his loyal Mexican sidekick. "That damned cardsharp. Why the hell I ever took him on, I don't know. I do know that this is the last job fer this bunch. We're fer sure gonna dump 'em as soon as we hit the bank and make our gitaway."

"Sí, Señor Al. I think you are right. Señor Ace, he is getting mucho bolder every day. Soon he will not obey your orders, I think."

"He does that and he'll see my six-gun up his nose. You watch him, though. If I have to call him out, you know how to back my play."

Sanchez's lips spread in an evil grin that would have shamed a gargoyle. "Sí, Señor Al. I know what to do."

Hulett nodded, satisfied he had his back covered if he had to face down Ace Richland. He finished his reconnaissance and settled down by the fire. Before he fell off to sleep, he sensed a tremor in his primal, feral psyche. Someone was trailing him, but the feeling was fainter than before. He had diminished the unseen threat. Hulett settled in, content that he had put some time and distance between himself and the unknown pursuer. He wondered, ever so briefly, if it could have been the owner of the Texas ranch where he and the others had stopped that afternoon. He shifted into a more comfortable position and drifted off to sleep, not really concerned.

The five outlaws rode on, crossing eastern Kansas without encountering another person along the way. Hulett stayed away from the well-traveled roads, sticking to back trails or simply going cross-country. Alva did not want anyone noting the five men riding so purposefully toward the Missouri border.

They reached the southwest Missouri border town on Friday, just after noon. Hulett had the men split up and cruise the streets, looking the place over. He gave the Swains some more of his reserve cash to buy supplies for their escape after they hit the bank. As the sun was setting, Hulett led them back to the clearing where he had previously waited for the fight against the Yankees five years earlier, about an hour's ride south of the town. They made camp next to Spring Creek, which was running deep and cool.

Hulett looked around the small opening in the grove of oak trees where he had camped that summer night years earlier. It had not changed much. The scorched earth from earlier campfires marked where the three hundred men in Bloody Bill Anderson's Irregulars had cooked their meal that peaceful evening. He walked over to the very spot where he had placed his ragged bedroll that night. He dropped his saddle and unrolled his new bedroll.

"If I'd had somethin' this comfortable back then, I'd have been able to sleep a lot better."

The Swain twins snickered. They had never served in the army, being blessed with utterly flat feet, which had kept the duo from being drafted during the many levies imposed on their home state of Iowa during the war.

"I reckon you'll sleep all right tonight, won't ya?" Bob asked.

"I reckon so. First, let's go over the plan fer tomorrow. You all saw the bank? Here's the plan. We'll ride in two groups. Me and Ace, followed by the Swains ten minutes later. We'll meet in front of Casey's store, next to the bank. Me and the Swains'll go inside the bank. Ace, you'll hold the horses and watch the street. Sanchez, you'll ride in alone and hide in the alley across the street. You'll cover our backs as we come out. After we ride out on the south road, you follow. We'll meet back here if we git out clean, or back at the state line on the south road if they follow us outta town. Everybody clear?"

The others nodded their understanding. After all, this was not their first bank job. Hulett was satisfied. The town was just as he remembered it. It should be a snap to knock off the bank. He dozed off, replaying in his mind the satisfaction he would feel once the snooty town's money was in his pocket and not their precious bank.

The men set out the next day under a steady drizzle. The damp weather was a good cover for the gang. With their ponchos on, they were just another group of soggy citizens riding in for some Saturday shopping. The four men stood for a moment under the overhanging roof of Casey's General Store. Hulett saw Sanchez standing by the edge of the alley, the tip of his rifle barely visible under the hem of his poncho. He nodded at the swarthy outlaw and turned to Ace Richland.

"Here we go. Ace, don't let nobody come in behind us whilst we're in the bank. Andy, you go right, and Bob, you go left once we get in the door. Put everyone on the floor and try not to shoot your gun afore we get any money. Somebody gives ya trouble, swat 'em on the head if ya can. Here we go."

The three men walked into the bank and swung their ponchos up to free their gun hands, filled with menacing six-guns.

"Everyone on the floor!" Hulett shouted, waving his gun in the direction of the two tellers and three customers at the cash cages. A portly man rushed out of an office, right into Bob Swain's pistol. Bob let the man's fat stomach press up against the end of his gun barrel before he fired. The sound was so muffled it scarcely registered to Hulett, standing with his back against the twin front doors. The dying manager hit the floor with a *thump,* and never moved again. Hulett pulled the shades down on the glass fronts of the doors, denying passersby a view inside the bank.

Andy Swain leaped over the barrier and hurried to the open safe built into the rear wall. Bob walked through a waist-high swinging door and started gathering up the money in the tellers' cages, shoving it into a canvas sack. Andy stuck his head out of the vault.

"Need some help here."

Bob hurried to help Andy, dropping a fistful of greenbacks on the floor as he did. Hulett kept the cowed customers and employees covered, and held his tongue. He almost shouted Bob's name to pick up the dropped money. Andy must have found something good to call for help like he did.

As soon as the twins exited the vault, Hulett ordered the terrified captives, "All right now, git up and git in the vault. Hurry up, git in thar." They crowded into the walk-in vault. Hulett slammed the door and spun the locking handle.

Each Swain had two bags filled to the brim in his hands. They ran past Hulett and out the door. Hulett took a quick look around. A coal-oil lamp was standing on the work table in the center of the customer area. He knocked it over, stepping back as the oil spread out, dark and shining, as menacing as the red pool of blood seeping out from under the body of the bank manager, lying where he'd fallen. Hulett fished a cigar from his shirt and struck a match. Holding the burning matchstick, he grinned as he lit his smoke, then casually flipped the burning sliver into the spreading pool of oil. The oil flared up in a greasy blossom of dark smoke and a red glare.

Hulett stepped to the door and looked

out. His men were already on their horses, awaiting him nervously. He shut the door to the bank and lithely leaped into his saddle. He calmly led his men out of town in an easy camber. Just as they came to the end of the street, he heard the first shouts of alarm.

"Fire! Fire! The bank's on fire!" Hulett laughed out loud as he whipped the ends of his reins against the flanks of his pony, leaning into the rain as he galloped away from the town, without a second thought for the unfortunate souls trapped inside the burning bank building.

Hulett waited until Sanchez arrived at their campsite before climbing off his horse. "Any posse after us?"

"No, Señor Al. The whole town is at the bank, fighting the fire. I saw no one chase after you while I was there."

"Good. Boys, let's see how much we got. Ace, you cipher as good as anyone I ever knowed. Count up what we got."

Richland took the four sacks of money and emptied them on a bedroll flipped open by Andy Swain. He quickly fell to counting the wads of greenbacks and loose coins.

"We got thirty-seven hundred and six dollars, Al."

"Good. Pile it in six equal stacks."

"That would be six hundred and seventeen dollars a pile, with four dollars left over." Ace had quickly done the necessary math in his head.

Alva nodded. "Each man take a stack. I'll take two." He looked hard at Ace. "Any problems with that?"

"Nope," Ace grunted, slipping his money into his pockets. "I'm happy."

Hulett's grin was evil personified. "Good. Now, here's the plan. We're gonna split up and ride out in all directions. Every man git some grub from the pack animal. We'll meet in a week at the place where we left the road to San Antone. There was a good spot to camp there, remember? Wait four days past tomorry. Anybody not there by then gits left. Swains, I know you two won't split, so you both head northwest fer a few hours, then cut around and come our way. Ace, you go south. Sanchez, you and me will go north once we hit the Kansas border then cut back west in a couple of days."

Hulett looked at his men, a sneer on his lips. "Let's see if you fellas can get anywhere without me to do yur thinkin' fer ya. Now git a'goin'."

He gave a slight nod, and Sanchez responded with a quick nod of his own, always eager to follow Hulett's lead. The other men climbed on their mounts and rode away, leaving without a backward glance.

Hulett waited until the men were out of sight, then grinned at Sanchez. "Ole buddy, we're headed fer Kansas City. We'll relax there fer a spell, then git on out to Colorado and the gold fields. Yur with me, ain't ya?"

"Of course, Señor Al."

"Come on then, let's put some miles twixt us and them scum buckets."

Ace Richland breathed a sigh of relief as he rode away. He was headed for Ft. Smith, not the San Antonio road. He vowed to never again allow himself to get tangled up with so foul a group of men. His relief was palpable as he hurriedly put miles between himself and Hulett. "I pray to God I never cross paths with that bastard again."

The Almighty granted his wish.

CHAPTER 11
A BITTER LESSON

Marty's emotions grew ever more intense as he approached Wichita. It was the mixture of apprehension and excitement one feels before an impending battle. He was steeling himself for the killing that was to come, not unlike what he had experienced during the war.

It was nearly midnight when he rode into town. Marty was exhausted; he knew he would be putting himself at a disadvantage if he started anything in his current state. He turned his horse into the only stable open so late and bought himself a bed in the hayloft for an additional two bits. He went to sleep vowing to his beloved Margaret and little Matt that on the morrow he would avenge them.

Marty slept well past daybreak, and rose rested and alert after the hard sleep. Remembering Steve Block's admonition that a gunfight was best made with clean clothes and a full stomach, Marty had a bath and shave at a nearby barber and a hearty breakfast of steak and eggs at a café across the street. After a cup of coffee, he walked outside and scanned the street.

He stopped a young man hurrying past. "Pardon me, but can you direct me to the town sheriff's office?"

"Sure." The man pointed down the street. "Go to the corner and turn left. It's half a block down, on the left. You'll see the sign."

"Many thanks." Marty walked quickly down the street and turned into the sheriff's office. A middle-aged man was sweeping the floor as Marty stepped into the office. He looked up and nodded.

"Mornin'."

"Good morning. You Sheriff Sedgwick?"

"Naw, I'm Deputy Thomas. The sheriff is up to Topeka, testifyin' at a grand jury called by the state attorney. Can I help ya?"

Marty pulled the warrants signed by Captain Self, asking for the arrest of five men, descriptions as furnished, for robbery and murder. Marty passed the warrants to the deputy. "I'm looking for these men. I think they came here after they robbed a bank in Texas and killed a woman and child as they escaped."

The deputy looked at the warrants. "There

ain't much in the way of description here, Mr. . . . ?"

"Sorry. I'm Martin Keller, a sworn Texas Ranger." Marty figured a little exaggeration would be of help with the deputy. He only needed a few minutes with the men he was after, and his mission would be complete.

"Well, Ranger Keller, you know you don't have any arrest authority here in Kansas?"

"I understand. I'll find the men and call for you and the sheriff to make the arrest."

"You want me to go around the town with ya while you look fer these jaspers?"

"No thanks. I know you're busy. I'll notify you if I find them."

"Fair enough. Just don't fergit."

Marty nodded, and headed for the nearest saloon. He walked in, looked around, then headed for the bar. The bartender moved toward him.

"What'll ya have, cowboy?"

"I'll take a beer." After it was delivered, he took a quick sip and asked his questions.

"A tall, lanky fella with some fingers gone, and twins with blond hair and gapped front teeth? Nope, I can't say I saw 'em. There's twenty-three saloons in Wichita though. Maybe they did their drinkin' in one of the others."

"Maybe." Marty looked hard at the bartender. The round-faced man with a dark mutton-chop moustache covering the bottom half of his face stared back, honest puzzlement on his face.

"Honest, Mister, I ain't seen 'em."

"Good enough. They're wanted for murder, don't forget. It would be worth fifty dollars to me for the man who lets me know where they are. And I'll give him the one hundred dollar reward from the state of Texas."

"I reckon I'd be willing to point them yahoos out iffen I was to see them." He wiped the bar top with a soiled rag. "Of course, I might get so busy that I plumb missed 'em walkin' in. You know how it is, when a man is busy, I mean."

Marty shrugged. "I think I get your meaning. What if I were to give you twenty right now? Would that help you keep your eyes open?"

"Yep, that just might do it."

Marty quickly ran through five more twenty-dollar greenbacks without success. As the last bartender took his money and folded it and put it into a shirt pocket, he made an observation.

"You know, Mr. Keller, there's over twenty saloons in town. You may have to visit them all afore you hit pay dirt. However, there're only four liveries in town. Why not try them first? Them outlaws hadta use one of 'em. Wouldn't you agree?"

Marty smacked his palm against his forehead. "Of course. How stupid of me. Thanks. You'll keep your eyes open anyway, I trust?"

"Fer twenty dollars? You bet a cat's meow I will."

Marty headed for the nearest livery, silently cussing himself for not thinking of the plan himself. At the second livery, run by a man called Jules Neville, he hit pay dirt.

The short, stocky man was also a blacksmith, and was pumping the bellows to his forge when Marty arrived with his questions. Neville kept on pumping as they talked.

"You bet I remember those horses. I never saw any five together like that which were finer. Much too good for the riffraff riding 'em. The only who cared a'tall about 'em was the Mex fella. He slept up in the hayloft and kept a close eye on 'em. He brushed and currycombed every one of 'em. Heck, he even watched me shoe a couple of 'em. What was his name? San, yeah, Sanchez. The fella who seemed to be in charge was called Al, I think. The two blond guys was sort of the sweepers fer the others, if you get my meanin'. The dark-haired one, Al, would tell 'em to do things, and they'd jump to it. I don't recollect what their names were."

Neville took a cherry-red horseshoe out of the burning coals with a pair of metal tongs and set it on the anvil that stood next to the glowing charcoal forge. He took a six-pound hammer in a brawny hand and tapped it on the anvil. The sweet ring of steel on steel rent the air of the room.

Ping! Ping! Bang! Two taps on the anvil, then a hard blow against the glowing iron of the shoe. Fascinated, Marty watched as the skilled artisan shaped the shoe against the round point of the huge anvil. Neville started talking loosely in tempo with the ringing blows of his hammer.

"Where was I? Oh, yeah. Them fellas up here 'bout noon on Monday, and they rode off. I asked the gambler if they would be interested in sellin' any of their horses, thinkin' they might have lost all their travelin' money at the tables over to the Rusty Nail Saloon. That's where they sorta hung out, I think. I saw 'em there a couple of times when I stopped by to wet my whistle after lunch." He carefully finished the shaping of the shoe, then shoved it deep in the glowing pile of coals and started pumping away with the bellows handle, forcing air to whistle through the pile, increasing the heat of the burning charcoal.

Replacing the newly reheated shoe on the anvil, he took a heavy awl and drove it through the iron metal, making the nail holes, four to a side. Holding the finished shoe up for a final inspection, he nodded, satisfied and tossed it into a bucket of dirty water, where it steamed and boiled until the finished shoe was cooled and hardened, ready to be placed on a horse's hoof.

Neville looked at Marty, waiting patiently, and continued, as if he had never paused in his narrative. "I noticed the gambler and the tall fella, Al, spent a lot of time at the gamin' tables. The gamblers over to the Rusty Nail are pretty good, so I hoped I might git me one of those horses. They gotta be worth two, three hunnerd dollars apiece, at least. No luck for me. Those two musta held their own at the games. Anyways, the gambler said no deal." Neville scratched a muscular forearm. "I don't think I ever heard the gambler's name." Neville shoved another straight bar of rolled iron into the forge. "It seems to me the Mex asked me if the shoes I put on his horse would last to San Antonio. I told him they'd get 'em there and back. You might find out more down to the Rusty Nail."

Marty nodded, "I wouldn't have taken four hundred each for them six weeks ago. Now, I'd give them to you for what you've told me, if I could. I want to thank you, Mr. Neville. You've been a big help." Marty reached for his money. "May I pay you for your trouble?"

"Land's no. I'm sorry to hear of your loss to them bastards. I jus' hope you find 'em real soon."

Marty's hand softly brushed against his holstered pistol. "I plan to, sir. You can bet on it."

Marty spun and walked out of the livery, heading for the saloon called the Rusty Nail. Jules watched him go, slowly pumping the bellows handle. "And I wouldn't wanna be those fellas when you do find 'em. You got the look of death in your eyes, and that's a fact."

At the Rusty Nail, Marty pushed through the batwing doors into the dim interior. The floor was covered in sawdust. The smell of spilled beer, sweat, and other unknown malodorous scents assaulted his senses as he looked around the large single room. It was a typical saloon, a bar along one side, several gaming tables and gambling paraphernalia filling the rest of the room. There were half a dozen customers idly killing time and spending their money on drink or gambling. A worn-looking floozy circulated among the customers, hoping to finagle a drink of watered booze or a quick trip upstairs to her boudoir.

Marty stepped up to the bar. The bartender, stoop-shouldered and prematurely gray, gave Marty a gap-toothed grin and asked, "What's yur pleasure, mister?"

Marty had the drill perfected by now. "A beer and some answers."

As he held the glass of beer, he began, "I'm looking for five men. Bank robbers and killers wanted in Texas. There's a reward for any help I get capturing them. One's a gambler, wears sleeve garters that have scalps hanging from them. Calls himself Ace. I understand he was gambling in here just recently." Marty dropped a couple of silver dollars on the countertop. The bartender scooped them up and nodded his head.

"Yep, I reckon he was. Ain't seen him in three or four days." He looked past Marty toward one of the tables where a solitary man was carefully shuffling a worn deck of cards. "Solly, weren't you playing against the dude with the fancy sleeve garters a few times last week?"

Marty turned to look at the lone individual sitting at the card table. He was well past middle age, his hair nearly snow white, the veins in his hands clearly visible as he caressed the cards he was shuffling. A large nose showed the effects of too much whiskey consumed over many years. The eyes were sunken in the worn, thin face — a face that had not seen much sunshine on it lately.

"That I did, my friend. That I did."

Marty moved to the table and sat down across from the old gambler. He put a five-dollar greenback on the table. "I am looking for the man. Can you help me? I'll make it worth your time."

The gambler looked at Marty, an amused smile flittering across his face. "Let's play twenty-one while we talk." He shoved five chips toward Marty. Marty nodded, willing to play the man's little game. He pushed one chip in front of the others. "Fine by me."

The gambler quickly dealt the cards. Marty had a natural twenty-one, beating the dealer's seventeen. The gambler pushed two chips to Marty and dealt again. "You asking about Ace Richland, I take it?"

"Yes. He played here, with you?"

The gambler took the hand, twenty to

eighteen. "Yep, for four days, ole Ace played me. He was a good player — almost as good as me." The gambler dealt another hand, winning again. The conversation went on, Marty and the man trading wins, questions asked and answered, information passing from one to the other.

"Did this Ace try and cheat while he played you?"

"Nope. Ole Ace is definitely a card shark, but he played me straight up, perfessional to perfessional, so to speak. We had some good games. He even came by to say so long afore he left."

Marty pushed another chip out and awaited the next deal. "And did the other man, the one named Al, ever play with you?"

"Oh yes. He thought he could play me head-on, but he quickly learned he wasn't up to it. After that, he only played the other cowboys, not any of the house gamblers."

Marty pushed another chip out to his front. "You have any idea where they were headed next?"

The gambler won the chip and shuffled the cards, his withered hands fairly flying as he dealt the next round. "Ace came by and said he was headin' fer San Antone. He picked up two bottles of whiskey from the bar and left. I don't know what he did then, but I suspect he left with the others. To San Antone, I guess."

Marty looked down. He had nineteen. The gambler turned over his cards. He had two jacks. "Twenty. I reckon you lose."

Marty looked down. His five dollars' worth of chips were gone. He looked up at the old gambler and nodded. "Sure enough. Thanks. I reckon I got what I was after."

The gambler nodded and went back to slowly shuffling the deck of cards, his watery eyes recalling something deep in his memory, Marty already forgotten.

Marty walked to the store just across the street from the saloon. There, he heard about Hulett's statement that they would join the Lazy 6 crew for the return trip to San Antonio. He stocked up and was riding south from Wichita before the sun crossed the top of the sky. He was satisfied. He had closed the gap to only four days.

"Meg, darling. I'm getting closer. Soon, honey. Very soon." He rode hard, his mind focused on his mission: death.

Chapter 12
A Dead End

Marty pushed his horse hard, so hard that he began to wonder if maybe the loyal stallion would break down before they reached San Antonio. "Just get me there, big boy. I'll let you rest good and proper once we're there, I promise."

As if drawing strength from Marty's vow, they did reach the town, the horse near exhaustion. Marty headed directly for the best livery stable in town. He swung down from his saddle and gave the stable hand a pair of silver dollars. "Brush him down and give him all the oats he wants. He earned them." Marty patted the tired horse's velvety nose. "Thanks, old boy. You got me here, and we're not more than a day behind our targets. Thanks."

Marty headed for the sheriff's office, colocated with the city jail, a block off the main street. He had met the sheriff, a salty old lawman named Rogers, while on duty with the Rangers. He walked into the office and asked the deputy for the sheriff.

"He's over to the Chinaman's Café, havin' lunch."

"Many thanks." Marty headed for the café, just down the street from the jail. He walked in and spotted the sheriff, seated alone at a table against the far corner from the door. Marty glanced around the dining room, but saw nobody who fit the description of the men he sought among the many diners having lunch. He approached the sheriff, who was busy sawing on a piece of fried steak with his knife and fork.

"Sheriff Rogers."

The man looked up, a flash of wariness quickly replaced by recognition. "Why Ranger Keller, how do? Sit on down. You here on Ranger business?"

"Personal this time, Sheriff." Marty pulled up a chair and quickly covered his reason for being in the city of the Alamo. Rogers sat quietly and listened, his face reflecting the revulsion and sadness of Marty's grim story.

When Marty finished, Rogers grasped Marty's arm. "I'm mighty sorry for you, son. Those bastards don't deserve the hangman's noose. It's too kind a death. They oughta be staked out on ant hills and smeared with honey." He wiped his mouth with the back of his hand. "You think they rode in with the Lazy 6 crew? They were here yesterday. Left for the ranch about midday I guess. Come on, they all stopped for a drink at the W B Travis Saloon. I hoisted a beer with 'em, myself."

Rogers dropped fifty cents on the table. "Let's go. Cecil is the bartender over there. He knows every one of the Lazy 6 hands personal. If any strangers was with 'em, he'd have knowed it."

Marty followed Rogers to the Travis Saloon. The interior was paneled in polished wood, the floor clean and freshly mopped. It was the nicest drinking house in town. A portly man with dark, slicked-back hair and a huge walrus moustache stood behind the polished bar, serving a round of drinks to men clustered close, laughing and talking as they washed the dust out of their throats. Rogers nodded his head toward the group of men.

"Them's the King Ranch boys. Just got in this morning from a drive to Dodge City. The railroad's extended its tracks all the way to there now. Howdy, boys. Welcome home. Have a good drive?"

"Howdy, Sheriff. Yeah, not too bad. Delivered thirty-six hunnerd outta nearly thirty-eight started," one of the trail-weary men replied. "Didn't run into no Injuns or rustlers. Had a little trouble crossin' the Red River. Some lightnin' spooked half the herd while half was still on the other side. They ran into the badland washes and scattered some. We had a hell of a time findin' and gatherin' 'em all up. That's where we had most of our trail losses."

"Doesn't sound like it was too bad fer ya, all in all. Dusty, this here is Ranger Keller. He's a'lookin fer some murderin' bank robbers that mighta snuck into town with the Lazy 6 boys yesterday. Marty, describe yur men to Dusty and his boys, in case them vermin has split away from the Lazy 6 bunch and showed up out at the King."

Marty shook the foreman's hand and quickly described Hulett and his gang. When he was done, Rogers asked the bartender, who was leaning on the polished top, listening to Marty's description, "Cecil, you see anyone lookin' like that yesterday when the Lazy 6 boys was a'wettin' their whistles?"

"Shore didn't, Sheriff."

"See any strangers a'tall?"

"Nope. Just the regulars, plus the three Gunther brothers, who hired on jus' fer the drive. You know 'em. From over to Fredericksburg?"

Sheriff Rogers nodded his head. "Yeah, I think I know who ya mean." He turned to Marty. Come on, Keller. I'll go with ya out to the Lazy 6 ranch. We'll find out if anyone rode back from Kansas with 'em."

"Thank you, Sheriff. I appreciate your help."

"It's my pleasure, son. I sure would like to be there when you find those skunks. I doubt many of 'em would make it to the hangman's party. Am I right?" Sheriff Rogers looked at Marty, a knowing expression on his face.

"I've given it a lot of thought, these past few days," Marty admitted. "If they were to surrender immediately, I suppose I'd bring 'em in. If they cause me the slightest bit of grief, I'm gonna kill 'em deader than a stepped on cockroach."

"I guess a fella couldn't ask fer more than that. Come on, let's get our horses. We got a five-hour ride to the Lazy 6. I reckon we'll have to spend the night. Lemme go by the office and tell my deputy I'm gonna be out of town overnight."

The ride to the Lazy 6 ranch was mostly quiet. It was too hot and dry for conversation. Both Marty and the sheriff rode with their private thoughts to pass the time away.

They rode into the central compound of the ranch just as the hands were arriving for the evening meal. One of the men recognized the sheriff and waved as Marty and Rogers stepped off their horses and stretched the kinks out of their backs.

"Howdy, Sheriff Rogers. What brings you out this way?"

"Howdy, Lou. Is Jace home?" He turned to Marty. "Jace Spangler is the owner of the Lazy 6."

"He's inside. Follow me. I'll announce ya."

"Thanks, Lou. Marty, you'll like ole Jace. He's a pure bred ringtailed Texas wonder. Been here since afore the war with Mexico."

They entered the main house, a large adobe with whitewash on the outside and polished wood paneling inside. The thick walls had the interior at a very comfortable temperature. Colorful woven rugs hung from the walls, along with several oil paintings. A white-haired man walked out of a side room into the main hallway.

"Why hello there, Bill. What brings you out to the Lazy 6? Some of my boys cause a commotion in town yesterday?"

"Nope, Jace. I wish all the ranch hands were as well behaved as your men are. Jace, this here is Ranger Marty Keller. He's a'lookin' for some murderin' bank robbers. He tracked 'em to Wichita, and was told they was a'comin' back to San Antonio with your men from the cattle drive. Marty, meet Jace Spangler of the Lazy 6."

Marty held out his hand, which the older man enveloped in a crushing grip. "My pleasure, Mr. Spangler."

"Howdy, Ranger. Welcome to my place. So you was told some murderin' skunks were hidin' out among my men?"

"That's what I was told by several folks in Wichita, yes, sir."

Spangler turned to the man accompanying Rogers and Marty. "Lou, as soon as the men finish supper, gather 'em around the front porch. We'll get to the bottom of this right quick."

"You bet, Boss." Slim turned and left the room.

Spangler smiled at his guests. "Can I invite you boys to sup with me? I think we're havin' fried ranch turkey."

At Marty's puzzled look, Rogers laughed. "He means fried chicken, Marty. His cook's been with him fer near thirty years. She's a wonder in the kitchen." He turned back to Spangler. "Thanks, Jace. We'd be plumb happy to join ya."

Spangler nodded, a satisfied grin in his

weathered face. "Maria," he shouted back toward the rear of the house. "Two guests fer dinner. Chop, chop." He motioned to the two lawmen. "A sip of dust cutter while we wait fer her to git everything all set up?"

"That'd suit me jus' fine. How 'bout you, Marty?"

"Thank you. I could use a drink about now. I'm as dry as an old bone."

Spangler took them into his library, where he poured generous amounts of amber whiskey into three glasses. "This here is prime sippin' whiskey. I have it shipped to me all the way from Tennessee."

Marty and Rogers both raised their glasses and nodded their approval. "Mighty fine liquor, Jace," Sheriff Rogers proclaimed. "I'll have to stop out this way more often."

"Wait'll you try Maria's fried chicken," Spangler boasted. "You'll want to take up residence."

The dinner was all that Spangler boasted it would be. They had just finished their coffee when Lou knocked on the doorjamb and entered the dining room. "Boss, the men are all out front."

"Thanks, Lou." Spangler pushed back from the table. "Come on, you two. Let's find out what's what."

Marty soon realized that he had come all

this way for nothing, although one man did step forward after hearing Marty's description of the men he was seeking.

The slender cowboy rubbed a hand through his brown hair and dug a toe into the dirt like a young kid who was explaining a wrongdoing. "I think I had a drink with the dark-haired fella you described. I told him we was fixin' to ride back to San Antone the next mornin' around sunrise. He just wished me a safe trip and took off. I'm sorry, that's all I know."

Marty's disappointment was evident and bitter. He thanked the assembled men and followed Spangler and Sheriff Rogers back inside the main house. The old rancher ushered the two visitors into his library.

"Well, Ranger, it 'pears the skunks used my boys to throw ya off their trail. It's gettin' late. I hope you both will accept my hospitality fer the night. You don't wanna ride back to San Antone in the dark, do ya?"

Sheriff Rogers accepted for both of them. "Thanks, Jace. We'd be pleased to accept yur offer."

"Brandy or whiskey?"

"Whiskey, Jace. Thanks. How 'bout you, Marty?"

"Whiskey for me as well, thanks."

As the three men sipped their drinks, Rogers read the anguish written on Marty's face. "Sheriff Rogers, what should I do?" Marty asked.

"You tracked men before, son. You got to go back to where you know they were last and start agin from there."

"That means going back to Wichita."

"Huntin' men was never easy. These men are worse than animals. They're sly, wary, easily spooked. Like a wolf, they'll be hard to track, harder to corner. You jus' gotta be tougher, smarter, and more determined."

Marty slammed a fist into his other palm. "Then that's what I'll do, by all that's holy. I'm gonna find these vermin and rid the earth of them, so help me."

Sheriff Rogers and Jace Spangler both toasted the vow by raising their glasses. "Hear! Hear!" Then Spangler spoke up. "You have a mission worthy of any man, Ranger Keller. It is my fervent hope you catch those bastards and issue them the justice they deserve."

"They'll get just what they deserve, don't ever doubt it." Marty accepted a refill of his empty glass. He needed the time with the two men, their friendly conversation and company, a balm to his tired and lonesome soul.

Marty left the ranch early the next morning. He rode steadily, but not like his desperate dash to San Antonio. He stopped at the first small town he passed and replenished his supplies. As he hefted the gunny sack filled with food, he spotted a row of pint bottles of whiskey. "Give me a couple of those," he requested of the teenaged clerk.

Marty rode on, determined to spend every daylight hour on the trail, back to the place Hulett and his gang had last been seen. After a hasty meal over a low fire, Marty lay back against his saddle, one of the whiskey bottles in his hand. He watched the sparks whishing upward in the smoke from the fire and thought of his wife and son. Before he realized it, the bottle was half gone. Marty slept good that night, better than he had in a long, long time.

The next night he finished the bottle and again had a pretty good night's sleep, but his head ached like the furies the next morning. A lethal pattern was beginning to form: a hard day's riding, then a quick meal, followed by a grieving surrender to sweet memories of Meg and little Matt, then enough whiskey to dull his mind into a dreamless sleep. And always on the next morning, an aching head, dullness of thought, and the dreariness of the lonely trail.

CHAPTER 13
A NEW
HUNT BEGINS

Marty spent a day confirming his worst fears. Hulett and his men had definitely left Wichita on the same day as the Lazy 6 crew. Unfortunately, they did not ride to the same destination. Where Hulett's gang did go was a matter of conjecture. Marty talked it over with the sheriff, an early settler of Wichita named George Sedgwick, who listened sympathetically.

"I don't doubt that's exactly what happened, Ranger Keller. A gent on the dodge seems to get a sixth sense about someone a'chasin' him. The average outlaw may be dumb, and most are, but they're usually sly as foxes."

"I'm at a loss as to what to do now," Marty complained.

"You got a few options, none of them very good, I'm afraid. One, you can go home and wait to hear about the outlaws from some lawman who's seen or run into 'em. Two, you can start lookin' for 'em blind — that is, you can just sort of wander around, hopin' you'll run into 'em somewhere — or three, find out from someone where they're headed and light out after 'em." The sheriff pushed some papers around on his desk, then looked up at Marty. "I reckon you're not interested in trying option one, are ya?"

"Nope. I'm gonna keep looking for the vermin."

"You have a plan?"

"I'd like you to send out some inquiries for me, if you will. If you hear anything, please contact Captain Self at the Dallas Ranger Headquarters. I'll keep in touch with him as I hunt."

"I'll do that for ya. I'll get telegrams and letters out right away. Any word, I'll wire it down to Captain Self. Where'll you be headin'?"

"I think I'll start out in a big circle around Wichita, say maybe out a hundred miles around or so. I'll ask if folks have seen anything, and see if I can cut their trail anywhere. I'll stay in touch with you and Captain Self, in case anything gets passed on to you."

"Fine by me. This business is bad enough that I'll bend over backards to help you find them no-good skunks. You can count on it."

"Thanks, Sheriff. I guess I'd better get over and stock up on trail goods. It might be a time before I can count on seeing another store."

"You think, too, boy. The Injuns are on the prod right now. You ride careful and stay off the ridgeline. A man alone is a mighty tempting target fer a redskin war party."

"Your point is taken. Thanks, Sheriff Sedgwick. You've been a big help."

The next three weeks saw Marty passing dreary days of riding, questioning ranchers, hide hunters, and residents of the tiny towns scattered within the one hundred mile circumference around Wichita. Finally, on the twenty-third day, he got his first tidbit of information.

He had stopped in the small trading post at Wilmott Station, over a hundred miles east of Wichita. The owner, a grizzled old-timer named Grossman, scratched his white beard and tapped a grimy fingernail on the bar top.

" 'Pears to me I heard about a robbery over to Missouri recently. Neosho or Carthage, which was it? Carthage, that's where it were. Five men held up the bank thar. Kilt the manager and set the danged place on fire to cover their gitaway. Damned near kilt several others as well. They was

145

near dead from smoke when the townsfolk got the blaze out. Some cowpokes who rode on the posse came by a couple of weeks ago and tolt me 'bout it all. Two a' the robbers looked 'xactly alike, so they said. Coulda been the fellas yur lookin' fer." He looked at Marty, trail-worn and grimy. "I got a tub and some soap out back fer four bits. All the hot water you can stand. My boy'll pour fer ya. After ya clean up, I'll feed ya a good, home-cooked meal fer another four bits and point ya on yur way to Carthage."

"All right," Marty agreed. "Did the posse have any luck trailing the five robbers?"

"Nope. According to the fellas I talked with, they think the outlaws split up. Anyhow, they lost the trail pretty quick."

"Well, it's the best lead I've had in more'n a month. Get the water started for the bath. As soon as I'm done eating, I'm headed for Carthage."

Marty pushed his horse and reached the small town in southwest Missouri in four days. He immediately saw the ruined shell of the bank. Several carpenters were at work rebuilding the damaged structure. A pile of half-burned wooden beams had been stacked on the sidewalk. He pulled his horse over to the town marshal's office and tied off his tired mount before entering the office. A husky, dark-haired man looked up from a letter he was writing at a scarred desk, a question in his eyes. "Can I help you, stranger?"

"Marshall er, Greenfield, is it?" Marty glanced at the nameplate on the desk.

"Yep, that's me. And you're?"

"Marty Keller. Texas Rangers." Marty held out his hand with his Ranger star cupped inside. It had been cut from a Mexican silver five-peso coin by a silver-smith in Austin over a year earlier, when Captain Self ordered all the rangers in his company to carry one. Marty counted the two dollars it had cost him as one of the best investments he had ever made. The lawman's star opened up dialogue with local law enforcement officers faster than any verbal explanation Marty could have given.

"Yur a long way from home, Ranger Keller. You come here about the bank holdup?"

"That's right. I'm wondering if the men I'm chasing might have done it." Marty pointed at the chair by the marshal's desk. "May I sit down?"

"Shore, have a seat. What do you know about the dirty, rotten jaspers who held up our bank?"

Marty related the short version of why he

was searching for the five men, omitting exactly whom they had killed. The pitying expressions he'd received from listeners once they knew the full story were annoying him. "I'm pretty certain the men I'm looking for were in this general area a few weeks ago." Marty described his fugitives for Marshal Greenfield.

"Well, I ain't too sure about no Mexican bein' involved. According to the eyewitnesses, there was only four men involved. But two of 'em were fer certain the blond-haired twins you described. Everyone agreed the two of 'em was as alike as peas in a pod. The dark, skinny one could have been the leader. He stayed by the door, coverin' the whole bank, while the twins looted the cash drawers and the vault." Greenfield lit a well-used pipe, puffing clouds of smoke out of his mouth as he fired the tobacco up good and hot. He blew a stream of smoke up toward the ceiling.

"One of the blond fellas shot poor Tom Enwright, the bank manager, as he come runnin' out of his office. Pressed the pistol right up to him, which muffled the shot so's nobody outside heard nothin'."

The marshal shook his head. "We was busy fer an hour or more, puttin' out the fire they started. Almost lost the five folks they put in the vault. Poor ole Tom was dead and half burned by the time we got the fire took care of. We put a posse together right quick and followed 'em to the spot where they split up. We followed three trails outta there, but soon lost 'em. I'm pretty certain there was five of 'em. Two trails of two men each, one trail goin' north, and one goin' west, and a single man ridin' toward the south. I split the posse, but it weren't no good.

"You couldn't stay on any of them?" Marty queried, disappointment in the tone of his voice.

"Nope. There's lots of streams and such north and south of here, and the wind wiped out the westerly trail. I followed the two men headed north. They was on a straight line fer Kansas City, if you ask me. That's where I'd try and pick the trail up agin. I just couldn't be gone that long from my duties here. I don't have a deputy or nothin'."

"What about the one man headed south?"

"The fellas that went after him said it seemed like he was headed back to Texas. I sent out alerts to the Texas Rangers and some of the sheriffs in East Texas."

"And the two that headed west?"

"I couldn't say. They lost the trail just a

few miles to the west. They could've gone most anywhere. The gang probably planned to meet up somewhere as soon as they slipped my men."

Marty nodded in agreement. "The gang seems to have stayed together up to now. They go through their stolen money pretty quickly. They'll most likely strike again before long. I wonder if you would point me toward the spot where they split up?"

The marshal pulled a small map from a desk drawer. "Shore can. Here's the south road to Joplin. Turn left at the edge of town and follow it fer about two miles. You'll come to a small creek, Spring Creek. There's a grove of oak trees there. Right in the middle is a spot where Bloody Bill Anderson's band hid out during the war, afore they had a big fight with the Union cavalry, just north of here." Greenfield tapped the map with his forefinger. "They laid over there afore they came into town, and met up there after. That's where we tracked 'em, and that's where they split up." Greenfield paused. "I wonder if one of them fellas might have been in that bunch. They was bushwhackers and killers, to a man. The Union whipped 'em good and proper, thank goodness. They might've tried to sack the town iffen they had won the fight."

Marty learned very little more while he was in the town. The victims at the bank were not much help. They had all been too terrified to make note of much, except that two of the robbers were twins, and the leader was tall and skinny with dark hair. No one seemed to have seen the Mexican, Sanchez, or the gambler, Ace. Marty left Carthage and rode to the rendezvous location described by Marshal Greenfield. The signs were still there suggesting someone had spent time at the natural campsite, but there was nothing to point Marty in any specific direction, nor tracks for him to study. He eventually rode away and pointed his horse north, deciding to go to Kansas City and take up the hunt there.

"One thing is certain," he grumbled to his horse as they made their way along the road. "These scum can't stay out of trouble. Once they hit a town, it's only a matter of time before they cause enough commotion to get noticed. I reckon if I stay close behind them long enough, we'll meet up with them before they can get away. Then, ole hoss, I'll make certain there's blood spilled. Meg, my darlin' wife, that I promise you. Their blood will spill in the dirt before I quit looking for them. They can run, but they can't hide from my retribution. They will pay, so help me God!"

Marty's trip up the western border of Missouri was uneventful and unproductive. He rode into Kansas City just before sunset. His head still throbbed from the whiskey he had consumed the night before. While he did not dwell on it, he knew that it was taking more alcohol to put him to sleep than it once did. He accepted his growing dependency on the amber head-buster to dull his dreams and allow him to sleep through the night.

He stopped at the first saloon to cut the trail dust from his throat. He called to the barkeep, a beefy man with a curled moustache covering his upper lip. "A whiskey and a beer chaser." As he raised the first drink to his lips, his elbow brushed the arm of the man next to him. "Pardon me," Marty apologized. He started to ask the bartender his standard questions about Hulett and his gang, when the man next to him grabbed his arm and swung him around until they were face-to-face.

"Bucko, you made me spill me drink. Nothin' makes me madder than a nosey busybody who makes me spill me whiskey."

Marty shrugged off the offending arm. "Mister, you're mistaken. I didn't make you spill your drink. I barely touched you. But

I'm happy to buy you a drink just the same. As to my questions, they don't concern you, so butt out. Now, what were you drinking?"

The man, a heavy, work-hardened laborer, was likely from a riverboat or the railroad gangs that were forming up to build the transcontinental railroad, already halfway through Nebraska, building toward the Wyoming Territory.

The man wiped a meaty hand across his smashed nose, and grinned wickedly, his blue eyes peering out from under tangled eyebrows. "Me bucko, now you've gone and made me day fer me. I'm gonna wipe yur pretty mug all over the floor, just fer the joy of it."

Marty's eyes drilled into the man, who was spoiling for a fight. Suddenly his adrenaline kicked in and he relished the coming brawl with boyish enthusiasm. He needed the emotional release a good, old-fashioned butt-kicking could give. "My ugly friend, I'm happy to oblige you. You're just the exercise I've been cravin'. I just hope you're not as tough as you look, otherwise I may have bitten off more than I can chew."

"Bucko, you've not only bitten off more, yur gonna lose yur teeth tryin'." The Irish brawler shuffled away from Marty, his hammerlike fists hanging loosely at his sides.

"Since yur such a polite bloke, I'm gonna give you first swing. Take yur best shot."

Marty moved away from the bar, measuring his opponent. The man was an experienced barroom brawler, that was very clear. He was also not a fighter, just a slammer. His strategy would be to move in close and hammer away until one man fell. He probably also gouged eyes, bit ears, and did anything else he could do to win. Marty would have to be very careful, else he could be seriously hurt, and that would not suit his purpose.

Marty considered the man carefully. "My pugnacious friend, my name is Marty Keller. Before you wipe my face, would you be so kind as to tell me your name, so I can explain to my friends why my nose is parked next to my ear?"

"Me name?" The man laughed. "Yur the queer duck, Mr. Marty Keller. Very well, Shamus O'Rourke is the name o' the man who's gonna whip yur butt to soft butter. That is, iffen you'll stop jabberin' and start fightin'."

Marty sighed and faked a left before hammering a quick right to O'Rourke's jaw. He had a solid connection, and it almost broke his hand. O'Rourke merely blinked, shook his head and moved to his left, a slight grin still plastered on his homely mug. Marty knew he was in trouble. Big trouble.

CHAPTER 14
THE NEW TRAIL

Marty and the burly Irishman cautiously circled one another, the self-assured grin never leaving the Irishman's fight-scarred face. "Oh, come now, me bucko. Is it a fight you want or is it a waltz?"

Marty jabbed a hard left against O'Rourke's iron jaw and hammered a quick right to his cheek. He took a roundhouse right in return that sent him spinning down the length of the bar, his head ringing and his eyes seeing stars. Shaking the cobwebs out of his rattled brain, he stepped back toward O'Rourke and drove his fist into the Irishman's stomach, in the hopes that it might be the man's Achilles heel. It was not to be.

O'Rourke barely winced, and moved in on Marty like a grizzly bear, absorbing punishment in exchange for the opportunity to give a couple of massive blows to Marty's noggin. It worked. On the second blow,

Marty backpedaled into a table, flipping over it and ending up on his face in the gritty sawdust spread on the floor.

Marty struggled to his feet, wiping sweat, sawdust, and blood from his face as he moved back toward O'Rourke. "Are you certain you're not hitting me with ten-pound sledgehammers instead of just your fists, Mr. O'Rourke?"

O'Rourke laughed and swung a wicked right, which Marty managed to duck. He then moved in quickly and delivered two hard rights and a looping left to O'Rourke's head.

"Don't make me laugh, bucko. It just postpones the inevitable, for which may you be properly grateful."

"Oh, I'm grateful, Mr. O'Rourke," Marty gasped as the wind whistled in and out between his bruised lips. "So much that I'd rather be in church right now."

O'Rourke laughed even louder and delivered a stunning blow to Marty's chest, paralyzing him for an instant. That was all it took. The crafty barroom brawler measured a right cross that spun Marty's head nearly off his shoulders and deposited him unconscious into a chair, which then tipped over backward. Marty lay there still and silent, his feet up in the air, blood seeping from the corner of his mouth and nose onto his shirt.

O'Rourke whooped in satisfaction. "By the saints, that was a good un. Drinks on me, lads. Barkeeper, a beer. Me mouth is as dry a potato bug's arse."

The onlookers all rushed to the bar, a couple slowing down to check out Marty's still form before stepping over him and bellying up to the bar. O'Rourke raised his beer in a toast, "To the auld sod, me Ireland, may God bless 'er." He guzzled down his drink and ordered another, accepting the slaps on the back from the many well-wishers drinking on his money. As he drained his glass, he wiped the foam from his lips and ordered a third. Taking the glass over to where Marty lay quietly, still in an induced slumberland, he considered the man's slack form and smiled. "You made it a good fight, bucko. Time to wake up now." O'Rourke poured half the glass on Marty's face.

Marty came to, sputtering and swinging his fists even though he lay flat on his back. O'Rourke held out a meaty paw and grabbed Marty's hand. "Up you go, bucko. How ya feelin'?"

"Like I was kicked by a mule. Am I still among the living?"

O'Rourke roared his pleasure at the joke, handing Marty what remained of the beer. "Here, wet yur whistle. A good tussle is drying work."

"Thank you, Mr. O'Rourke. I needed that. Ooh, my poor jaw. I may never chew on a steak again."

O'Rourke slapped Marty between the shoulder blades, nearly knocking him over. "Come on, have another drink on me. Make way, ya louts. A real man needs to git some whiskey." He pounded Marty some more. "Call me Big Mick, bucko. All my friends do."

"Thank you. Please, call me Marty."

The bartender slid two glasses of amber whiskey in front of the men. O'Rourke gulped his down in one swallow. Marty swished his around the inside of his mouth, trying to cauterize the cuts he had incurred. Finally he swallowed most of the stuff, shuddering at the impact on his stomach.

"I need a meal, Big Mick. Would you be interested in breaking bread with me?"

"I could be persuaded, Marty, me friend. I know just the place, if yur so inclined."

"Lead on," Marty chuckled. "If I don't eat something quick, that rotgut we just drank is going to burn through my stomach straight to my feet."

O'Rourke threw his arm over Marty's shoulders and escorted him out of the bar. Marty needed the help. His feet did not seem to accept his brain's signals. Supported by O'Rourke, they semistaggered down the wooden sidewalk to a café, where O'Rourke steered Marty inside. The waitress, a shy girl still in her teens, greeted the sturdy Irishman as an old friend and sat them at a table overlooking the street.

"Shepherd's pie and coffee, me fine lass. And lots of fresh biscuits and honey. How 'bout you, Marty?"

"Sounds good to me, Mick. Whatever you say."

"Two orders then, me darlin'. And tell that ole reprobate you call a cook to hurry it up. Some real men are hungry out here."

While they were eating, the cook came out and returned O'Rourke's insults. Marty laughed as the two friends out-lied one another as to whom was the best, be it drinker, lover, or cook.

After the meal, over steaming cups of coffee, O'Rourke drew out from Marty the reason for his visit to Kansas City. "Hell's bells, Marty. You jus' leave everything to Big Mick. I'll pass the word among my road gang, and by tomorrow night, iffen these men are in Kansas City, we'll have found 'em. You can count on it."

"You can get some men to help you?"

"By the saints, me bucko, I'm the big mucky for the Union Pacific roadbed gang. I've got four hundred Irish lads workin' under me. We grade and lay the roadbed fer the railroad to put its tracks on. We're here fer three days off after working thirty straight. We almost got roadbed laid to Omaha."

When they reentered the saloon where the evening's fun all started, O'Rourke called together as many of his men as he could muster, and passed the word. Within an hour, the men were all over the town, looking for any sign of Hulett and his gang. Marty and Big Mick spent the evening listening to reports, drinking, and regaling themselves and the onlookers with outrageous tales of their lives, some possibly even true.

By midnight, Marty was as wiped out as he had ever been in his life. Big Mick was only getting started, his face a bit redder, his voice louder, but still able to steer a straight line from table to bar and back with his hands full of filled glasses of whiskey.

Marty finally pushed away, his voice slurred. "I'm a goner, Big Mick. I've gotta find a bed and get some sleep."

"*What!* You runnin' out on me, Bucko? Where's yur pride? Yur not gonna let little ole me outdrink ya, are ya?"

"Outdrink, out-lie, outfight." Marty gasped. "I'm goin' to bed before I pass out and sleep the night on the floor. Where's a hotel?"

"Turn right out the door and go down two blocks. The nicest one in town," O'Rourke instructed. "Me, I'm here fer a while yet. There's more whiskey to drink, and more fellas to fight, if I'm lucky."

"See you in the morning," Marty mumbled as he staggered toward the door.

"I'll be here, bucko. Tomorrow day and tomorrow night. Then it's back to end of track fer me and me lads."

Marty stumbled out of the saloon and turned left, his head spinning, barely able to walk. He shuffled down the street, coming to an alley that led to the livery where he had stabled his horse. Confused as to where the hotel was that Big Mick had recommended, he decided to go to the stable instead and sleep in the hay.

He never made it. Marty never saw nor heard the person who thumped his noggin with a heavy sap. He only knew that he awoke as the sun was rising, his head aching, both from drink and the cowardly blow, and minus his boots, gun, and the nearly two hundred dollars he had in his shirt pocket. The mugger had mistakenly left him the three silver dollars he carried in his pants pocket.

Marty made his way to the Kansas City Police office and made his woeful complaint. The officer on duty was barely sympathetic, but took Marty's name and where he would be staying.

"We had a lot of footpads in town, Mister. The railroad workers draw 'em like flies to cow piles. You're better off not drinking so much and keeping your eyes open when you walk down dark alleys."

Marty left the office, his face lowered in shame. He'd certainly walked into this manure pile on his own. He had nobody to blame but himself. He headed for the telegraph office to wire his bank in Dallas for more funds. Afterward he went to meet Big Mick, and told his sad tale one more time. The big Irishman was remorseful and vowed to extract bloody justice if the scoundrel was ever caught. Marty thanked him but noted wryly, "Our chances of ever finding the sumbitch are probably slim to none."

O'Rourke looked down at Marty's bootless feet. "You gonna go barefoot till yur money comes up from Texas?"

"I'm afraid I'll have to. All I've got left is a dollar after I sent off the telegram to my bank."

"Would you be offended iffen I was to offer ya fifty dollars to tide you over?" O'Rourke dug his knurly hand into a pants pocket.

"Would that set you back until I could pay you off?"

"Not a bit. I won some money last night at faro after you left. Me and money never git along noways. Better you use it than I drink it up or gamble it away."

"It might be some three or four days until the bank clears the draft from Dallas, Mick. Are you sure?"

"Faith and begorra, didn't I just say so? Here's the money. Go get yurself some decent coverin' fer yur feets."

Marty took the money and bought himself new boots and a new pistol, a Remington six-shooter chambered for the new brass .44-40 cartridge. He picked up a new shirt and pants and some food for wherever the trail might take him next. Refurbished and feeling better, he walked back to rejoin his new friend.

"Any word from your boys?" were the first words out of his mouth as he sat down beside O'Rourke.

"We've been waitin' fer ya to return. Sean, this here's me friend Marty Keller. Marty, Sean here has some news ya might find interestin'."

Sean was slight of build, blond-haired, with a face worn by hard work and harder living beyond his years, the clothes he wore simple and threadbare. "I played ochre with a gent who might be one of them you was a'huntin'. He called hisself Al. Said he was tryin' to make money to git to Californie. He was in town about two weeks ago, but I ain't seen him since that night."

"How long ago was it exactly?" Marty urged.

Sean counted back on his fingers. "Eleven days ago."

"You're certain he looked like one of the men I am seeking? Had he lost some of the fingers on his left hand?"

"Yep. He even wore a glove while we played cards. Never took it off, but the last two fingers never moved. I reckon they was jus' some stuffin' in the glove. He had a Mexican a'watchin' him play. I never knowed what his name was or nothin'."

Marty nodded. "Thanks, Sean. You've been very helpful."

The young man looked anxiously at Big Mick.

"All right, boy. You're hired. Be at the station tomorry at sunrise. We leave fer end of track at seven a.m. sharp." With that, Sean scurried off.

"You promised him a job?"

"Sure. It's good money and hard to git. I told me lads to pass it around that anyone had some good info, he could have a job with my road gang iffen he wanted it."

"Thank you, Mick. You've been very kind to me."

Mick waved his hand casually. "Aren't nuttin'. Big Mick takes care o' his friends. You'll be comin' with me to end of track, I reckon?"

"I will have to wait until my money comes. I'm busted, remember?"

"You can git it sent out by the station master. I'll speak to Mr. Glenville. He's head of layin' fer the Union Pacific. I'll git you some work whilst yur a'waitin' fer yur money to show up."

"I don't think I'd be a very good track layer."

"You can shoot can't ya?"

"Quite well, actually."

"Bill Cody is our chief hunter. He brings in fifty head of buffalo a day fer the cooks. I imagine he could use some help. I know the hunter who delivered the meat fer the road gang came down sick and ain't going out this month. I reckon I could get Mr. Glenville to let you be the hunter fer me lads and me. I think the hunters git a hundred a month."

"My goodness."

"It's dangerous work. The Injuns don't like us shootin' all their buffalo. We've already lost a few hunters to scalp takers."

"I don't know if I can wait a month before I continue after the men I'm chasing."

"You might catch up with 'em at end of track. If so, you can conclude yur business and ride straight back here. If not, it'll give ya some spendin' money till yur own gits here."

"All right, I'll give it a try."

"Good fer you, Marty Keller. Have a drink. I'll make a railroad man outta you yet."

CHAPTER 15
MEET BUFFALO BILL

Marty dragged himself out of bed the next morning, his head pounding like a gold miner's jackhammer. "I've got to cut back on the skull-poppers," he grumbled to himself. "I guess I'll not see much of it out on the prairie, thank goodness."

He barely made it to the train station on time to catch the transport taking Big Mick O'Rourke and his work crews out to end of track. Marty got his horse loaded in the stock car at the front of the train, then joined Mick at the station office. The happy-go-lucky Irishman introduced Marty to the stationmaster who promised, "I'll send your money out just as soon as it arrives. Mail gets delivered twice a week to the track gang."

Marty nodded his thanks and mounted the single passenger car hooked behind a long line of flat cars carrying iron rails, wooden ties and hungover workers in jammed confusion.

O'Rourke stopped Marty from entering the passenger car. "Let's ride in the caboose, Marty, me bucko. It'll be a lot more comfortable. The lads in the car will soon stink it up with smokin' and drinkin'."

"You allow that?"

"Until we reach end of track. From then on, any drinkin' and yur run outta camp. You'd have to walk back to Kansas City. It's a good rule, and steadfastly enforced."

"What about the gambling tents and such I've heard about at end of track?"

"Me lads rarely git in to see 'em. If they do, they can get as pie-eyed as they want, they just can't bring it back to grader's camp."

Marty small-talked with Mick and the conductor, until he eventually fell asleep in his chair and did not awaken for nearly three hours. He blinked his eyes into focus and walked outside to join Mick on the rear transom. Mick was smoking a black cigar and watching the scenery flow past. Marty listened to the *clickity-clack* of the wheels on the rails for a few minutes, then spoke to the silent Irishman.

"Sorry there, Mick. Riding the rails always makes me sleepy."

"Not me. I'm jus' the opposite. I love

watchin' the ground rush by. It's like sailin' on the sea only faster. Hell, we must be goin' twenty-five miles an hour or more."

Marty stared at the waving sea of prairie grass flowing in undulating ribbons as the wind pushed it about. "It does sort of look like water, doesn't it? Kind of a golden sea ebbing and surging."

"I love it," the big man answered. "We're really buildin' somethin' grand here. Somethin' to be proud of and to tell yur grandkids about when yur an old, toothless grandpa."

"Mick, you'll never be toothless, you big Irish mug."

"Who knows. Somedays I think I'm gettin' too old too fast." He flipped his smoked-out butt off the transom and turned to grin at Marty, the sparkle back in his eyes. "Not that I can't wipe the floor with you, bucko, anytime I want to."

Marty rubbed his jaw ruefully. "No need to prove that again. My jaw is still achin' from your last demonstration."

"Good enough," Mick answered and slapped Marty on the shoulder. "Let's go in and play some cards. I might win back some of the money I lent you."

Marty laughed. "And you might end up broke, my friend. I can fan a deck some myself."

"Good enough. Either way, I'll be satisfied." O'Rourke headed inside, Marty trailing behind.

By the time they reached end of track, Marty's bill to Mick had been cut to nineteen dollars.

When they arrived, Marty was mesmerized by the activity. Sweating work gangs were busy setting ties in the roadbed, while track layers were just as busy laying iron rails on top and spiking them down. Blacksmiths hammered away, shoeing mules and horses or repairing work tools. No man was idle. Smoke poured out of cook tents, and men walked to and from sleeping tents set up in a semicircle around the cooking tents. Farther out at the periphery of the temporary city were sutler's tents, whiskey tents, and whorehouse tents.

Mick took Marty to meet George Glenville, the track boss. "So you want to be the road gang meat hunter until Clay Robards comes off sick status."

"Yes, sir. I'd do you the job, I reckon."

"Ever hunt buffalo afore?"

"Just for sport. I used to hunt Yankee officers from long-distance, though."

"Well, I guess you can shoot, then. If Mick wants you, it's okay with me. Bill Cody is our chief hunter. When he gets in tonight, go meet up with him. He'll give you the particulars. You'll draw a hundred a month from the railroad, and if you want, you can sell the hides yourself. They bring three dollars apiece in Omaha. We'll ship 'em for ya for twenty dollars a hundred." Glenville held out his hand. Marty noted that it was as hard as any spike pounder's. "Bill will set you up. Just get the meat to Mick's cooks. I want the graders and roadbedders to keep on movin' out. We're up to better'n ten miles a day now. I want to double it before long."

They left the track boss's tent and walked back. Marty's gaze turned toward the tents where the gamblers and whiskey awaited bored and thirsty laborers. Mick followed his gaze.

"Don't fret, bucko. I'll put the word out tonight. Iffen yur skunks are here, we'll know about it this time tomorrow. They won't go nowhere."

Marty and Mick walked over to the tent where the chief hunter resided when he was in camp. Mick made the introductions, then begged off, saying he had things to get done before his road gang left the camp at first light.

Marty sized up the man who was already

becoming famous as a buffalo hunter. Mick said some people were even calling him "Buffalo Bill." He was tall, with shining, curly blond locks hanging down to his shoulders. A sweeping handlebar moustache perched on his upper lip. Deep, piercing blue eyes twinkled from under light, bushy eyebrows. He was dressed in buckskin from head to toe, including knee-high moccasins.

He twirled the corners of his moustache after Marty finished recounting his experience with long-range shooting during the war. "Sounds like you can hit what you aim at, Marty. Huntin' buffer isn't all that hard. A couple of things to watch, then it's Katy bar the door. Them animals is so dumb they just stand there until you've killed 'em all. I've done it a time or two, I know."

Bill motioned for Marty to follow him. "Come on, let me introduce you to your skinners, wagon drivers, and protection riders."

"Protection?"

"Yep. The Injuns don't like us killin' all their meat. Think the buffer all belong to them. The braves won't take on a hunter. They know what a Sharps .50-caliber bullet will do to them at a longer range than any of their guns can reach. However, they will attack a wagon filled with meat. That's what the protection riders protect. As you fill up a wagon and send it back to camp, them savages are always lookin' for a chance to jump it."

"So you stay out, some of the time?"

"Yeah, until I run outta wagons. Then I come in for a couple of days. I got to wash the stink of blood offa me by then." Bill Cody walked with Marty to the hunter's camp at the far edge of the tent city. Marty could see why it was so far out. The wagons and even the men reeked of death. The cloying smell of blood and rotting flesh assaulted his nostrils as they walked up to several men squatting around a campfire drinking cups of coffee.

"Boys, this here is Marty Keller. He'll be huntin' until Clay gets back on his feet. Marty, Francisco and One-Eye are your skinners. Pete and Herb drive your wagons. Ray and five of his men are the guards. We'll all go out tomorrow together. You and me'll shoot some, and iffen I think you're ready, you can light off on your own after that."

"Pleased to meet you fellas," Marty announced. They all nodded, stood and shook hands or not, depending on their manners or lack thereof.

As Marty followed Cody back toward the hunter's tent, he asked, "Why would I want to do that? Go off on my own, I mean."

"The road gang gets way ahead of the track gang. It's too far to make both trips with the same wagon. On the good side, you'll only need to get fifteen or twenty buffer a day. I gotta do sixty to have enough for the track crew. Sometimes we have to go a might spell to find enough animals for our needs."

Cody stopped at the door flap of his tent. "You have a huntin' rifle?"

"I've got a Winchester .44-40. I've taken buffalo down with it before."

"Naw, you'll need a Sharps .50–70 with vernier sights. I got one inside you can use."

Cody passed the heavy rifle over to Marty. "It belonged to a hunter who took an arrow in his arm. When they cut it off, he died. You're welcome to it."

Marty hefted the single-shot hunting rifle. "Wow, it's heavy."

"Has a thirty-four-inch octagon barrel. The barrel is an extra four inches longer to improve accuracy." Cody passed a sack of shells to Marty. The heavy bullet looked like a small log in Marty's hand.

"Looks like this round could knock down a sizable tree."

"Damned near can. It'll sure enough drop a buffer bull dead in his tracks, you hit him right. I'll show you tomorrow."

The next morning, Marty rode out on the plains behind Cody and the meat wagons. He stopped at the top of a small rise and looked back. Big Mick was just leading his road gang out of camp, trooping toward where the surveyors had marked the trail. Marty waved and Mick waved back. The big Irishman had instructed that any information concerning the men Marty was chasing after be forwarded to him at the road gang campsite.

"You come in with the meat wagons tomorrow or the next day. We'll know by then, fer certain." The burly foreman pounded a clenched fist into a hard palm with a satisfying smack.

For several hours Marty rode to the north with Cody and his men. "I seen a big herd this way a couple of days ago. We should find 'em soon. Once you killed your quota for the day, you need to be thinking about tomorrow's hunt. Always be lookin' for fresh herds. That way you can keep the critters from running out too quick."

"What about deer or antelope or such we might run across?"

"Anything that's meat, you take it. The cooks'll make somethin' out of it. Stew or roast or somethin'."

They were just topping a small rise. Cody stopped and turned to the drivers. Take a breather, boys. Me and Marty need to zero his rifle. We'll be back in a few minutes."

Cody turned to Marty. "Follow me. We'll get you a good zero, so's you can hit what you aim at."

He led Marty to a spot where they could see a small bluff, about two hundred yards to their front. He climbed down from his pony and took his heavy rifle from its scabbard. Marty did the same and waited for Cody's next instruction.

Cody took a pair of army binoculars from his saddlebag and scanned the bluff. "You need to get some binocs if you can. They make spotting game a lot easier."

Marty nodded. "I'm carrying a telescope I took from a Yankee general a few years back. Gives me a good view out." He pulled the telescope from his saddlebag and took it out of its velvet-lined carrying case.

"What's its power?"

"I'm not certain. I think about four or so."

"Let me look?"

"Certainly." Marty passed over the small cylinder and Cody looked through it at the bluff. He passed it back to Marty.

"See that rock about halfway up the slope over there?"

Marty could see the light rock against the darker earth without the telescope. "Yes."

"It's just about the size of a good buffer at two hundred yards. I like to work in from three to two hundred yards from a herd. Come up from downwind so they don't smell me. At that distance, the bullet has still got plenty of punch, the noise of the gun is less, and the buffer fer certain can't see you. Watch the rock."

Cody took a rod with a "U" the size of his rifle barrel on one end from his saddlebag. He screwed the other end into the ground and sat in a cross-legged position behind it, the stock of his rifle to his shoulder, the barrel resting in the steel "U." He sighted his weapon and fired a round. Marty saw the dust fly on the rock and looked through his scope. A fist-sized hunk of rock, had been pulverized by the impact of the heavy bullet. A pale scar stood out against the darker rock surrounding it.

"There's your target. Let's see you hit it." Cody took his rifle from the holding stake. "You want to use my steady rest?"

"Thanks. I wish I had one."

"You can make one from two small stakes. Tie 'em together about three-quarters of the way up, then split the two legs apart. Makes a nice steady rest."

"Good idea. I'll make one as soon as I can get myself some small stakes somewhere."

"I already thought of that. I brought you some from camp."

"Why thanks, Bill. That was considerate of you."

"Weren't nothing. Come on, let's see you hit the target, if ya can."

Marty set himself in a good firing position, the barrel of his rifle supported by the steel steady rest. He set the vernier scope to two hundred twenty yards, which was what he estimated the distance to be. He aimed through the small hole in the rear vernier and set the barrel's front post at the center of the scar. Gently, he pulled the trigger. The powerful rifle kicked like a mule against his shoulder. As soon as the white gun smoke drifted away, he focused his telescope at the target.

The second bullet had hit in the middle of the scar. Cody looked with his binoculars and nodded his head. "You don't need no help, Marty. Good shootin'."

Cody pulled the steady rest out of the ground. "What say we go find us some meat fer the table."

Soon Cody stopped the small party again. He shifted in the saddle until he was sideways to the direction they had been riding. "Hear 'em?" he asked Marty. "That's buffalo, jus' over that hill, if I'm hearin' right." Marty had not heard anything, but he nodded as if he had. They both got off their horses and tied them to the rear of one of the wagons. "Don't want 'em running off when the blood starts to stink," Cody advised.

Marty and Cody slipped up to the top of the hill. In a small valley below, hundreds, perhaps thousands of buffalo milled about, some munching the prairie grass, some lying down, chewing their cud and bellowing the contented snorts and grunts of buffalo talk.

The dark, teeming mass of heavy animals seemed to go on forever. Cody pointed to a small hillock to the south of the herd.

"Lookie there. A perfect spot to set up the shoot. About two hundred yards from the edge of the herd and downwind. Let's take a look-see."

Marty followed Cody around the hill from the herd to the small bump in the earth. Cody climbed to the top and peered over the edge at the buffalo below him. "Almost perfect. About two-thirty yards and right downwind. Marty, we gotta get near seventy total. Aim just behind their foreleg. You don't wanna hit the leg bone, but if you go right behind, you'll cut the lungs and heart. It'll drop them on the spot most of the time. I'll get settled in here, you go over to the far side as soon as you see me shoot a couple. Watch where I put the bullet."

Cody screwed in his steady rest and took careful aim. His heavy rifle went off with a loud boom. As soon as the smoke cleared, Marty looked at the herd. Nothing seemed amiss, yet one mature cow was slowly sinking to her side. None of the other buffalo seemed to pay any mind to the incident.

Cody sighted another target. "See that big bull off to the side there, by himself? Watch where I hit him."

Marty put the telescope on the target and saw the puff of dust as the round went in just behind the right foreleg. The big animal dropped to his knees, his mighty chest slamming against the ground, and did not move again.

Cody looked at Marty. "You get the idea?"

"Yeah."

"Take your time. Aim at animals on the edge of the herd, never in the middle. Reload quickly, in case you only wound an animal. Nothing spooks a herd quicker than the cries of a wounded buffer. They're as liable to run right over you as not. Go get

your steady rest made and come on back.
We got some buffer to shoot."

CHAPTER 16
HUNTING ON
THE PLAINS

Marty returned to Bill Cody's side and tied off the two stakes to make his steady rest. He bound the stakes together about six inches from the top with a rawhide thong, then spread the lower legs about eighteen inches apart. The finished product formed an odd-shaped "X" with the short legs at the top.

Cody had stopped shooting and watched while Marty finished the steady rest. He explained, "The herd is gettin' a mite restive. I'm lettin' 'em calm down some before startin' again."

Marty edged up to the crest of the hill. Eight buffalo were down. The herd had slowly moved away from the fallen animals, but continued to graze and snort, seemingly oblivious to their dead companions.

Cody spoke up, "Funny about shootin' buffer. Sometimes you can kill 'em all day and they never move an inch. Other times they get spooked by something, maybe the smell of blood, and off they go. If I see 'em gettin' restive, I stop until they settle down and then start up again. Looks like they're calmin' down now. You ready to take one?"

"I think so." Marty sat down and rested the barrel of his rifle in the upper 'V' of his steady rest. He took aim at his first target.

"Which one you shootin' at?" Bill Cody asked.

"The one on the far left of the bunch right in front of us. She's the big cow with the dirt spot on her flank." The animal had obviously rolled in a mud wallow recently, leaving a large mud clot on her dark hide.

"Right behind the front shoulder," Bill murmured.

Marty nodded, set his vernier rear sight up to two hundred yards and aimed at his first buffalo. His shot kicked up dust right behind the animal's shoulder and the big cow dropped flat on her stomach as if some invisible giant had kicked the legs right out from under her.

Cody patted Marty on the arm. "Good shot. That's all there is to it. Take your time, hit 'em dead center, and work the edges of the herd. You'll see when they become restive. Stop shootin' for a spell, and then you can start up again. If the herd bolts, shoot as many as you can before they run outta range, then trail 'em until they quit runnin' and stop to feed. They spend most of the day eatin', so it won't be long."

"You only need about twenty a day to feed the road gang. If I was you, I'd shoot forty. The hides will make you more than the meat will, anyway."

"And just leave the meat to rot on the prairie?"

"Sure."

"No wonder the Indians hate what we're doing."

"Yeah, it's a shame. But the Injuns are gonna have to move over for the American settler. The sooner we kill off the buffalo, the quicker they're gonna move to the government reservation set aside for 'em and settle down. When they have to grow their food and raise their own cattle for meat, they'll have a lot less time for raidin' and scalpin'. It's too bad, but life's tougher for some than others, and that's a fact."

In less than two hours the two hunters had killed the day's quota plus twenty more for Marty's hide collection. As the hunt progressed, they slipped down the hill until they reached the first victims, following the massive buffalo herd while it drifted to the north. As soon as Cody called the hunt over, he fired three quick shots with his pistol. The skinners and wagons came over the hill while he and Marty cleaned their rifles where they sat.

"We always clean the rifles first off, in case we need 'em later. Then you and I will ride out to check the direction the herd is going, or to see if we can find some more for tomorrow's hunt. The hunters don't do none of the skinnin' or meat collectin'. The wagons will go on back to the cook tents as soon as they finish. We'll come in on our own."

Marty watched as the skinners arrived and started their grisly job of skinning and cutting up the animals. Crows and buzzards circled overhead, awaiting their chance at the offal left behind. Marty spotted two coyotes skulking further out, the smell of fresh blood drawing them toward the recent slaughter.

Cody followed Marty's glance. "You'll see wolves, maybe even bears hangin' around while the skinners do their work. And now and then you'll see some Injuns. You can tell they're madder than wet hornets, but usually they'll leave you alone. Just don't get careless. That's what they're anglin' for. That's how you lose your hair."

Cody shoved his freshly cleaned rifle in its

saddle scabbard, and swung onto his horse. "By the way, you'll owe your skinners a dollar a hide, once you sell 'em."

Marty followed, mentally calculating his potential profit. In a month, he could kill twelve hundred buffalo. If he could clear one dollar and eighty cents apiece for the hides, after expenses, he would have nearly two thousand dollars to refinance his search for the killers.

Marty and his mentor rode west. He was a fortunate benefactor of Cody's expertise hunting the shaggy American bison. They rode toward a small stream with several red oak trees growing along its meandering banks. "Sometimes we can scare up some venison along that stream. Let's ease up slow like and see what develops," Cody whispered.

"Why? We've got plenty of meat already."

"Ole Francisco is a first-class cook. He can do wonders with venison. Eatin' buffalo gets mighty tiresome after awhile. Any time you can get him something else, do it."

Cody slipped off his horse, grabbing his Sharps buffalo rifle. "Come on," he whispered.

Marty followed Cody into the grove of trees, his rifle at the ready. "There's a bunch," Cody whispered, pointing upstream. Marty had already seen them, and was slowly bringing his rifle to his shoulder. Cody whispered, "You take the one farthest to the north, I'll take the one farthest to the south. On three. One, two, three!" The two rifles boomed out simultaneously, and two fat deer fell where they stood. The heavy bullets had ripped through them with deadly accuracy.

"Hot damn," Cody exulted. "We eat good tonight."

They gathered the two dead animals, field gutted and skinned them, and then slung over a hundred pounds of the best portions of the fresh venison over the back of Marty's horse, tied in the two skins. Cody did not volunteer to help transport the venison behind his horse and Marty decided it was not worth the aggravation to complain about it.

Marty and Cody rode on, finding another buffalo herd a few miles further along. The milling mass of tawny buffalo grazed as they slowly followed a meandering stream. The two hunters rode behind the herd, stalking their pace.

The ground beneath Marty was torn and pulverized as if a farmer had prepared the field for planting. "These animals sure do chop up the ground, don't they?" he observed.

"I've seen it a lot in my time. What's even more interestin' is how good the grass comes up where they've grazed. It's like the hooves prepare the ground for plantin', and then the droppings and blown seed settle in the dirt and grow new grass."

"Makes a body wonder what will happen once all the buffalo are driven away by the white man," Marty mused.

"Maybe cows'll take over. I don't know. I do know it's time we headed back. Ole Francisco will need some time to make us his fine-tastin' venison roast."

"Should I go back to main camp with you?" Marty asked.

"Sure. Big Mick's gang can grade a mile or two a day more than Glenville's track gang can lay, so you may as well stay with me for a couple of weeks. If he gets too far ahead, you might want to move over to his camp later in the month." Cody pulled his horse to a halt, looking to the west at a low rise.

Marty followed his glance. Six Indians were sitting quietly on their ponies, watching the two men.

"Cheyenne," Cody announced. "Maybe Yellow Hand's band. That sumbitch has been after my hair for ten years now."

"Ten years?" Marty exclaimed. "How long you been out here?"

"Since '59. I rode with the Pony Express when I was sixteen. Ole Yellow Hand's been trying to take my scalp all that time and hasn't yet. He's gettin' plumb perverse over it."

"Do tell. That why you grow it so long? So he's got a real trophy when he does?" Marty chuckled.

"Something like that. I want him to want it bad. Hope it keeps him awake at night. He's done kilt a couple of my friends on the Express and in the army."

Marty's brows furrowed as he eyed the silent Indians. "We need to worry?" he asked.

"Naw, I don't think so. They know who we are. If they were up to something, they wouldn't have let us see them on the hill. They just want us to know that they know we're out, and now we know they're out." Cody slapped the stock of his rifle with the palm of his hand. "They don't want nothing to do with these long guns. But they'd love to catch us with our drawers down, so stay alert, like I said. Don't get careless."

Marty followed Cody back toward the railroad construction route. "I won't. I've got a good reason to stay healthy."

"Oh, what's that?"

Marty told Cody a short version of his vendetta and what he had accomplished to date. "I'm hoping they're in among the riffraff in the whiskey tents. Big Mick has his contacts nosin' around for me."

"Well, if they are, I'd count it a real favor if you'd allow me to back your play. Skunks like that don't deserve to live."

"Thanks, Bill. I appreciate your offer."

"I mean it, Marty. If they're around here, you and me'll go up agin 'em."

Marty spoke very little more as they rode back to the railhead. He turned over the venison to old Francisco, and hastily cleaned up. He was waiting at the graders' camp as Big Mick led his gang in for the evening meal.

"Hello, Marty," the burly foreman shouted. "How's it huntin', instead of poundin' rock all day like I did?"

"Hello, Mick. It's not too bad. Saw some red-hide Injuns, though. A body's got to watch himself out there, else he's liable to lose his hair."

Mick quickly crossed himself. "The bloody heathens. To tear the hair offa a man, why that's almost unholy."

Marty smiled. Mick was fearless, when it

191

came to fighting with his hands and feet. The idea of scalping made him squirm. "You hear anything about my outlaws?"

"Nope, nary a thing. I'll put out the word again tonight. Somebody's gotta have seen 'em if they came to end of track."

Marty swallowed his disappointment, and spent the evening in Mick's company, enjoying the happy-go-lucky Irishman's humor. Laughing was something he had not done much of lately.

He had a hard time sleeping that night, his desire for a drink to chase away the demons almost convincing him to go over to the sutler's tent to buy a bottle of whiskey. He willed himself to stay in his bed, even though he tossed and turned the entire night. At sunrise the next morning, he and Bill Cody were back in the saddle, headed for another day's butchery of buffalo to feed the sweating mass of men laying the iron ribbons of progress across America.

The days passed in a gruesome routine. Marty grew sick and tired of his job. "It's worse than being a bloody butcher," he groused to Big Mick. "I'm glad I'm done with it as soon as the month ends."

"You thinkin' of leavin' the railroad?" Mick asked. "I could get you a job as scout fer the surveyors, or maybe as my assistant here with the road gang, if you'd like to stay and do somethin' else."

"No, I need to move on, Mick. As soon as I get my money for the hides, I'm heading out. Those men I'm looking for came west from Kansas City. I'm hoping they didn't double back on me. I'll move on down toward Colorado, see if I can cut their tracks again."

"Faith, but I'll miss you, bucko. I've grown accustomed to havin' you around."

"I'll miss you, Big Mick. You're a true friend. But you know why I've got to go on."

"Yes, I know. It pains me, but yur right. The angels in Heaven will watch over you, since I can't."

"As long as they lead me to Hulett and the others, I'll be content."

It was soon evident that neither Hulett nor any of his men had come to end of track. Marty was disappointed, but was becoming accustomed to finding that trailing the outlaw was not going to be a simple task. He did his job, supplying Mick's crew with all the buffalo the hungry men could eat. He always filled the wagon with skins, until at the end of the month he had accumulated the twelve hundred skins he had set out to obtain. He shipped them off to Kansas City at the end of the month, and welcomed Clay back from his convalescent leave.

"Ya still leavin' us, Marty?" Bill Cody asked.

"Yep, just as soon as I get my money for the skins and pay off my skinners."

Marty was true to his promise. As soon as the supply train returned with the money he made from the buffalo skins, he packed his gear and rode away from the men laying the Union Pacific toward the setting sun. He felt like he was leaving a safe haven for the unknown, but his path was set and he had to stay true to his vow.

Big Mick and Bill Cody stood at the end of track, waving a last good-bye as Marty's pony carried him to the top of a low hill.

"So long," he murmured as he waved his hat toward the figures below. "I'll be seein' you both another time."

He chucked his horse with his spurs. "Come on, hoss. Let's go to Colorado, there's gold down there. And where there's gold, scum like Hulett can't be far away."

CHAPTER 17
MEXICAN BANK JOB

"Damnation, amigo. I sure hate it that I got so careless back there in Central City. I don't know how that stupid miner caught on that I was bottom-dealin' him. It looked to me like good pickin's were there fer the askin'."

"Por nada, Señor Al. We will just go to Mexico sooner than we intended. I am anxious to see my family, anyway. It was cold in those mountains. My bones ached for the warmth of Sonora."

"Yur a good pard, Sanchez. I'll make it up to ya, I promise. Them miners woulda blowed a hole in my gut iffen you hadn't backed me. I won't forget that."

Sanchez rode on silently, his pride nearly overflowing. Hulett was his patron, come hell or high water, and any praise he received from Hulett fell sweet on his ears. The two men rode on, putting long miles between them and the miner's court in

Central City. Hulett knew he had escaped hanging by the skin of his teeth. Their narrow escape from the Miners' Committee's favorite hanging tree had shaken him considerably. He was ready to get down to Mexico and lay low with Sanchez's family for a spell.

"It won't be too bad down yur way, pardner. I heared there's been a lot of silver showing up from the mines in that area. We might find a situation where we could lighten the load, so to speak, from one of their banks." He rode on silent for a while, then spoke again. "I've been feelin' that itch agin in my gut. Somehow, I know some jasper's on our trail. This detour into Mexico oughta put him off. I swear, I ain't gonna show my face in a single town twixt here and the border."

Hulett did just that, sending Sanchez into the towns when they needed more supplies, and contenting himself with a few sips of whiskey before he slept each night. The two fugitives made good time, avoided any contact on the trail with other travelers, and crossed the border into Mexico east of El Paso del Norte about the same time Marty took his leave of the railroad.

They were welcomed in the small village of Oputo by the many relatives of José

Sanchez. None mentioned that the returning relative had killed a Federale during a bank holdup in the neighboring town of Bavispe some five years earlier and subsequently had to flee for his life into the United States.

Instead, there were fiestas and banquets to celebrate the return of the prodigal son, and his lanky, but surly, Americano friend. In fact, Hulett could have relaxed and enjoyed himself for a long time in Mexico, except for the annoying fact that all of Sanchez's many relatives thought he and Hulett were flush with money.

After loaning small sums to many needy members of the Sanchez family, as well as paying for much of the expense involved in supplying the luxuries needed for the parties, plus the food and drink for the banquets, Al Hulett was eventually tapped out of funds.

He pulled his friend aside one afternoon and explained the facts to Sanchez.

"Amigo, we're about out of money. You've been going through it like snot through a goose. We can't go on like this much longer. You got any plans to make us some?"

Sanchez nodded his head. "Sí, Señor Al. My cousin, Fernando, tells of a bank in Tonichi, about one hundred fifty miles west of here. He says it is filled with money from the silver mines in the Sonora Mountains. He says he has seen this bank many times. It is in a small town with few Federales guarding it. I was thinking we could take my cousin and two of his friends, and go help ourselves to some of this money."

"Ya trust yur cousin? I don't wanna step into no hornets' nest."

"Let us go see for ourselves, Señor Al. We can take Hector with us. He can show us routes for our gitaway. If it is not good, we can come back to Oputo and look for other opportunities."

"Sounds good, amigo. When can yur cousin and his friends be ready to ride? I'm anxious to get my hands on some hard cash."

"I will contact Fernando and find out. It should not be long. We will need to buy some supplies, of course."

"Of course. And you ask where our money went."

By the end of the week, Hulett, Sanchez, Fernando and two hard cases were riding west, crossing the mountains of central Mexico and heading on to the eastern region of the great Sonoran Desert, which spread north into the southwest United States. It was high desert, with cactus, rocks, sand, and very, very little water.

The landscape changed from trees and grass to rocks and sand. Shades of green turned to tans and yellows. The climate went from temperate to desert, all within a few miles.

Hulett wiped his brow with a ragged kerchief, shifting irritably on his saddle. "Damn, it's hot. How much longer we got to go, Fernando?"

"I think about two, three days, Señor Al. It is beyond those mountains to our front, and they are fifty miles away or more."

"I'm all dirty and sweaty. I sure hope you can find that spot you promised by the river."

"Oh, sí, I can find it. I herded sheep here for two years. I know all the mountain streams and trails. I will show you. It is a good place to rest up and camp while we look over the town and its rich bank."

"Well, it can't be too soon fer me. This damned sand and grit is all over me like fleas on a mongrel dog. I jus' want to wash it off."

Fernando glanced at his cousin. The gringo was never happy. How could José devote himself to such a whiny gringo, anyway? Fernando shook his head, unable to understand his cousin's loyalty.

When they finally reached the little river and the tall trees growing along its banks, Hulett sighed in relief. He hopped off his horse and gave it to Sanchez to care for, while he headed for the water, tugging off his boots en route. He sat down in the middle of the river, up to his neck in the cool current, clothes and all.

"Boy, oh boy, does that feel good. I may just spend the rest of the day in here."

By the time Sanchez and Fernando had the camp established and a slab of meat frying over a small campfire, Hulett was satisfied and finally left the water. He stripped off his clothing down to his long handles and shook the water from his dark, greasy hair before raking it back with his fingers.

"Well, that damned well feels a lot better," he happily announced. "What we got fer supper, Fernando?"

"Frijoles, Señor Al, with fried salt pork."

"Good enough. I could eat a horse."

After the meal, Al proceeded to instruct his men. "Sanchez and Fernando, you two ride into town tomorrow. Buy some food fer us. You two," he nodded at the two surly extras that Fernando had hired, "plan on going in about midday. I'll go in last, just about four in the afternoon. You fellas don't stop at the same cantina, we don't want nobody thinkin' we're all together. Ask around. How many Federales? Any guards at the bank? How many? When does the bank got the most cash on hand? Was the bank ever robbed? What happened then?"

He poured himself another cup of the bitter coffee Sanchez brewed. "Y'all know what we need to know. We'll meet back here around dark and compare what we seen. No gettin' drunk nor whorin' around or gamblin'. We got a job to do, and that comes first. Everybody clear on that?"

Al heard no arguments. He nodded, and wandered off to the stream, where he had set up a line, hoping to catch some fish. Sanchez tagged along, having spotted Al's slight signal given to him as they broke up the planning meeting.

Hulett sat down on the grassy bank, fiddling with the string, rebaiting the hook and killing time until he was certain his discussion with Sanchez held no interest to the others.

He spoke softly to Sanchez, "Them two yahoos Fernando got. They any of yur kin?"

"No, Señor Al."

"You got any special feelin' fer 'em?"

"No, señor."

"I was thinkin'. When we git the money, maybe we oughta leave them in the desert, to feed the buzzards. Jus' split the take among the three of us."

"Sí, Señor Al. I agree." Sanchez's face broke into a grin as he calculated the extra money he would earn simply by killing two worthless, peon outlaws.

Hulett's expression was evil personified. "That's settled, then. Git on back, so's they won't see us conspirin' together."

Al rode into the town of Tonichi at precisely four o'clock the next afternoon. He tied his horse in front of the first cantina he saw, the Casa Mecedoa, or Rocking Chair Saloon, and made his way inside. The few customers scarcely paid him any attention. They concerned themselves with the tequila or beer in front of them. Hulett was just another gringo looking for work in the silver mines opening up in the dry mountains outside the town.

Al stepped to the bar. "Una botella de tequila, por favor."

"Sí, Señor. Tres pesos."

Al slapped a five-peso silver coin on the bar, took his change and bottle and sat down in a corner. He sipped the fiery liquid and watched as the customers drank and left, to be replaced by others. He motioned to a bar girl who was circulating the room. "Have a drink, señorita?"

"Gracias. My name is Lupe. What is yours?"

"Call me Al."

"You like me, Señor Al? You want come up my room for good time? Only cinco pesos?"

Al could barely understand her English, it was so heavily accented. "Maybe later, Lupe. Now, I want to drink."

"Okay. I drink with you." She motioned to the bar. "I drink a special tequila. Is fifty centavos a glass. Okay?"

"Sure. You drink some of yurs, then some of mine. I'll be happy."

Hulett plied the floozy with plenty of tequila. With her tongue loosened by the liquor, he started pumping her for information. After he was satisfied he had all the answers she could provide him, he allowed her to escort him upstairs, where he had a quick poke, gave her enough tequila to leave her snoring softly in her bed and then rode back to his camp.

With what he had learned from Lupe and what the others had obtained, Al had a pretty good idea of the bank's routine, the afternoon sleeping habits of the six Federales guarding the town, and the fact that the bank would have the mines' payrolls on deposit the following Friday.

The next day Al stayed in camp. "We don't need to be in town too much, especially me. You boys can go in, but don't visit the same places you was at yesterday. See if you can find out anything more we can use."

Al slept, fished, and relaxed while the other men went into the town. It was a big mistake. One of the patrons at the bar where Fernando was drinking was the son of the bank manager. He listened intently as Fernando pushed a drunken townsman for information about the bank's routine.

As soon as Fernando rode off, the young man hurried to his father and told him what he had overheard. The worried manager immediately sent for the sergeant in charge of the Federales responsible for law enforcement in the town.

"It may be nothing, Señor Morales," the grizzled sergeant observed, "but it may foretell of an attempt to rob the bank. Tomorrow, I shall send out my best trackers to see if any strangers are around."

"Tomorrow? No, Sergeant Tomás. Tonight. See if they can spot the campfires of the villains. We must know. Tomorrow is Friday. The mine payroll will arrive on the afternoon train."

"Very well. But I cannot do anything until they break the law. All we can do is be ready, if they are robbers."

The sergeant was a man of his word. He put his best trackers out immediately and was rewarded the next morning with a report that several men were staying at the old shepherd's camp by the steep curve that gave Codo Arroyo, or Elbow Creek its name.

"Bueno. If they are banditos, they will have to go through Arroyo Seco to get away to the east. We can set up an ambush there ahead of time. Corporal Castilla, take three men and make the necessary preparations. If they rob the bank tomorrow, we will have them."

Hulett led his men to the edge of town around midday. He knew most of the citizens and Federales would be taking a siesta around this time. He sent Sanchez into the town to look things over. Sanchez was back in just moments.

"Señor Al. There are two Federales at the door to the bank."

"Got some guards, do they?" Al thought for a moment. "Fernando, go to the stables at the far end of town. Start a fire. Make a lot of commotion, like the world was comin' to an end. As soon as the townsfolk start coming to the fire, light out fer the camp. We'll meet ya there after we clean out the bank. We'll wait until the Federales go to the fire, then hit the bank quick. Me and Sanchez will go in. You two" — he pointed at the two extra outlaws — "guard the door and keep anybody from interferin'."

They did not have long to wait. The commotion from the fire had most of the town responding to the alarm. Few people remained on the streets as the outlaws rode up to the bank. Al and Sanchez hurried up the steps to the door and went inside. The other two men took up positions on either side of the door.

Inside the bank, the two outlaws quickly filled four canvas sacks with gold and silver pesos. Nearly staggering under the weight of their booty, they hurried out and leaped on their horses and galloped out of town, headed for the campsite where Fernando anxiously awaited them.

"Come on," Al urged, as they galloped into the camp. "Git yur gear and let's ride. I wanna be long gone afore the posse gits organized."

Al led the others away from the camp, toward the mountains to the east. He knew that once they crossed them, he was home free. Sanchez pointed out the dust cloud coming up the road behind them. "The posse, Señor Al."

Al slowed, allowing the two outlaws and Fernando to pass him. He looked to the rear, gauging the time between himself and the oncoming posse. "Damn, they shore got on our trail quick. It's all right. Once we git through this dry arroyo, it's a straight shot to the mountain pass. The ground up there is so rough, we can shake them fellas real easy."

Hulett and Sanchez followed the other three outlaws up the winding trail that ran through the dry arroyo, casting hasty looks to their rear. The posse was very close. Too close. Suddenly, gunfire ripped the air and the two outlaws in the lead went tumbling from their horses. Fernando slid his pony to a sudden stop and turned to ride back toward his cousin, when his animal pitched forward, hit by a bullet from one of the hidden ambushers. Fernando flopped to the ground, then lay still, either dead or unconscious.

Hulett jerked hard on the reins of his horse, spinning it around and spurring it back toward the entrance to the arroyo, just in time to see a dozen men riding up, guns drawn and vengeance in their eyes.

"All right, I quit," he shouted, throwing his pistol on the ground. He turned to Sanchez, still looking wildly around, seeking some way to get out of the fix they found themselves in. "We've hit a dry well, amigo. Don't give 'em any excuse to shoot you down." Hulett sat on his horse with his hands raised high in the air. "We give up, we give up."

"Señor Al," Sanchez muttered. "We can't surrender. Do you know what the prison is like in Sonora? We are doomed to a hell on earth, Señor."

CHAPTER 18
MEXICAN HARD TIME

The laughing posse of Federales rode into Tonichi at a gallop, dust and dirt flying, chickens scattering with frantic squawks, the local dogs adding their frenzied barks to the general confusion. The exuberant soldiers reined to a stop in front of the bank, proudly displaying the results of their ambush. Hulett and Sanchez were securely tied to their saddles, the two dead outlaws and the unconscious Fernando lying facedown over their horses.

Amid the hubbub, the three living bank robbers were summarily deposited in the local hoosegow, but only after enduring a good bit of poking, being cursed at and spit upon, along with a couple of painful cuffs to the head by one of their capturers, just to remind them who was in charge.

The outlaws were shoved into the dank cell by one of the jailors, a fat, slovenly man with a full, unkempt beard and a mouthful of broken, rotting teeth. He hungrily eyed Alva's boots.

"Give me the boots, Señor," he croaked.

"Nothin' doin', ya dirty greaser," Hulett snarled. "Stay away from me."

The obese jailor did not respond, he simply glared at Alva and walked away.

"That's how you treat these simple bastards," Alva smirked to Sanchez.

The wily Mexican did not respond, he merely retreated to the corner bunk and sat quietly. He had been in a Mexican jail before. He waited silently, his obsidian-colored eyes wary.

Within minutes the jailor returned, accompanied by three other disreputable-looking men. They stepped inside the cell and proceeded to beat and stomp the living hell out of Al Hulett. He ended up losing not only his boots, but also his shirt and a fine silk kerchief.

When the larcenous jailors left with their booty, Sanchez scurried over to Hulett and helped him into his bunk, where the aching outlaw lay still, moaning softly now and then. Sanchez murmured a quiet piece of advice to the unhappy outlaw.

"Don't ever argue with the jailors, Señor Al. They have the power in here. They can kill you if they want, and nobody will care.

Listen to me on this, señor. We're going to be here for a long time, I think."

Fernando finally awakened. He had been grievously hurt when thrown from his horse. He drifted in and out of true awareness of his situation, and spent a majority of the days lying on his cot, asleep. Twice a day, he docilely ate the slop delivered to the three men by the grinning slob of a jailor, who never failed to show off his fine pair of boots to the barefoot Hulett.

"Not only do we have to eat this swill they call food," Hulett groused to Sanchez, "but I've gotta put up with that fat bastard's acting like he's king of the walk in my boots." Hulett smacked a fist into his palm. "Well, wait till I git in front of the judge. I'll let him know what kind of thievin' scum they got workin' here."

Sanchez stomped on a thick, black cockroach scurrying past. He wiped his boot on the floor and shook his head. "You will be wasting your breath, Señor Al. The judge will not care. He is as bad as the fat jailor, perhaps he is his uncle."

"I'm still gonna vent my spleen when I see that judge," Hulett vowed.

It took fours days before they were hauled up in front of the local judge. Their visit was as bad as Sanchez predicted. Hulett's

211

impassioned plea concerning the theft of his boots brought immediate action from the judge.

"Señor Jailor," he admonished the white-haired chief jailor of the town, "this gringo bandito is barefoot. Please insure that he has shoes the next time he comes into my court."

"Sí, Your Honor," the old man promised.

That evening, after another solid butt-whuppin' by the fat jailor and his buddies, a pair of peon's sandals were dropped by Hulett's prostrate form. "Your shoes, señor. Wear them tomorrow for the judge. Say nothing more or I will cut your lyin' tongue from your mouth."

Hulett looked with disdain at the worn sandals, the leather dried and cracking, the soles worn thin as paper. They were a poor exchange for his fancy boots, but they were on his feet the next time he stood in front of the judge.

The rest of their trial was cut and dried. After sitting mutely through several witnesses' renditions of the same story of the evil threat to their person's, and how the bank employees heroically resisted the bank holdup, until at last the money was rested from their unyielding grasp, Hulett was brought to the stand and asked his version of the events.

He tried to place the blame for the robbery on the two dead outlaws, claiming he and Sanchez were coerced into the scheme through fear of their lives. "We didn' even know what them hombres was up to, yur honor, till they come outta of the bank with the money. Then we was too scared not to run away."

The witnesses immediately refuted Hulett's story, and the rest of the trial was uneventful. The judge stood the three men in front of the judgment bench, Hulett in arrogant defiance, Sanchez staring at the floor impassive and resigned, and Fernando somewhere else in his confused mind.

"You are all banditos, liars, and murderers. Everyone agrees that you, gringo, were the man in charge at the holdup. Your lies are rejected. I hereby sentence you to cinco" — he glared at Hulett — "five years in the prison at Sonora. Perhaps a few years breaking rock will convince you to forsake the bandito way of life. Sergeant Bernal, deliver them to the prison on the next train to Hermosilla."

"Sí, Your Honor. It will be my pleasure."

Hulett, Sanchez, and Fernando were delivered to the Sonora Prison just as the day drew to a close for the several hundred unfortunate souls incarcerated there. The forlorn trio watched morosely as the ragged, half-starved prisoners shuffled in to the main yard from a day spent busting rock in the quarry located in the back of the compound. The entire rear half of the prison was formed by the sheer walls of the stone quarry. The confining walls butted tightly against the rock sides of the quarry. The rocks quarried from the convicts' labors were used to make more cells and support buildings of the prison.

The walls were twenty feet high, and twelve feet thick at the bottom, with a guard's walkway at the top. Armed guards roamed the top, moving between the four guard towers, one at each end of the walls and two flanking the massive twin wooden doors that opened to the outside world.

Hulett surveyed his future home as they waited for the prisoners to shuffle into the central dining hall. He spotted a small rope strung between one-foot-high stakes that paralleled the rock walls and was positioned five feet from the base of the wall.

Sanchez whispered an explanation. "Dead man's line, Señor Al. Cross the rope and the guards will shoot you from above."

Hulett glanced up. The guards stood on the walkway, eyes on the convicts, rifles cradled in their arms. He shivered; they reminded him of vultures, looking for carrion. The prison appeared to be a difficult place to bust out of, once a body was locked inside. "Anyone ever git outta here?" he whispered.

"Only feet first, Señor Al. Only feet first."

After processing, Hulett, Sanchez, and Fernando were delivered to the mess hall. The foul-looking slop poured on his plate sickened the outlaw just to smell it. Its taste was even worse. Hulett forced a few swallows, then drank the tepid water and ate the single enchilada wrapped around some rancid beans. They were then escorted to their cell by a sullen guard. He pushed them inside and slammed the door with a resounding clang. An old man sat on one of the bunks in the four-man cell, moodily picking his teeth with a dirt-encrusted fingernail.

"Welcome to Sonora, señors. I am Felipe Gonsolvas, and you are now my bunkies. How long will you be my guests?" He chuckled.

"Cinco años," Sanchez answered.

"Not likely," Al seconded. "We'll be gone long afore that."

"Not unless you let these swine kill you, señor. Nobody escapes from Sonora. You are fifty miles from water, further from any town. Those that escape over the walls die in the desert. Be grateful you have only five years to enjoy this pigsty. I am here for the rest of my life, thanks to the pig of a Federale I had to kill for abusing my wife."

"How long you been here, amigo?" Hulett asked.

"Quince anos, señor."

"Fifteen years, Señor Al," Sanchez translated the old man's Spanish.

"And how old are you?" Hulett estimated the man was close to sixty, maybe more.

"I am cuarenta y tres," he answered.

"Forty-three, Señor Al," Sanchez translated.

"Holy Mother of God," Hulett whispered. He had come into the prison just a little older than Hulett now was. If Hulett stayed in for the five years of his sentence, what would he look like?

Their daily routine was quickly established. In the morning they awoke to an assembly where they were counted by their guards. After a quick breakfast of some tasteless gruel, they marched out to the quarry where they broke rock with twelve-pound sledgehammers for twelve hours. They were subject to whatever abuse their guards chose to dish out. Any resistance to orders was swiftly and violently disposed of. Hulett learned how painful the lash could be, on the punishment afternoon scheduled the last day of every month. He learned the hard way to keep his mouth shut. Take the abuse and insults and keep swinging the sledgehammer, his tool of labor.

Six days a week, the routine never changed. Only on Sunday was their schedule altered. That day, they marched in from the quarry at two p.m. instead of at six. They had the opportunity to wash their stinking bodies and their threadbare, filthy clothing in the same bathwater. After mandatory church services, they marched to the Sunday meal. Sometimes they had meat of an unknown origin mixed in the bean gruel and hog slop that passed for food in the prison. Those men who had a source of outside funds could buy items to make their life easier, but for those like Hulett and Sanchez, they had to survive on what the prison system provided.

They did survive, even prosper in a minor way, since neither Hulett nor Sanchez had any compulsion about robbing those less powerful than they, or stealing from the dead as they expired, sometimes before the unfortunate one had even breathed his last desperate gasp. For the hapless Fernando, the story was different. He never fully recovered from the head injury he received the day of the bank robbery. One morning, he simply did not wake up. He was buried, wrapped in a dirty sheet, in the prison graveyard. It was the first time Hulett and Sanchez saw the world from outside the prison walls since they entered the foreboding enclosure many months earlier. They were the only mourners at the burial, and even then only because they volunteered to dig the grave. Four armed guards made certain they did not try anything while outside the prison walls.

As Al lay on his bunk one hot, sweltering night, suffering in the relentless heat and grim airlessness of his cell, he vowed for about the ten thousandth time. "Once I git outta here, I'll live the good life. I swear it."

"Sí, Señor Al. We will." Sanchez turned over to sleep. It was too hot to talk.

Chapter 19
The Long Trail

"So, Pat, that's my sad story." Marty sat next to the desk of his old friend, and sheriff of Corpus Christi, Texas, Pat Henderson. "I followed them to Central City, Colorado, easily enough, then they just disappeared. I thought they might head for the diggings at Virginia City, Nevada Territory, but they didn't. I went on to California and poked around some, then started back east. When I heard a story about two men holding up a bank here in Corpus and killing an innocent bystander for no reason, I headed this way from New Mexico Territory."

"Well, it sure wasn't your men. We caught them two, tried 'em, hung 'em, and planted 'em in boot hill within a week. And that was nearly ten months ago — that you lost their trail, I mean?"

"Yep. Nary a sign in all that time. I'm at my wit's end."

Sheriff Henderson leaned back in his

chair, thoughtfully stroking his McClellan-style goatee. "You wanna know what I think, Marty?"

"Sure do, Pat."

"I say stop lookin' fer the two you were chasin', Hulett and the Mexican, and look for the others. If you find them, they may put you on the track fer the one you want the worst."

"Yeah, that's a possibility. They may have got back together again sometime after I tracked 'em to Colorado."

"I sort of doubt it, Marty. Scum like that gits on one another's nerves after a spell. They split and go their separate ways, fer the most part."

"Well then, what makes you think any of 'em will know where Hulett has gone?"

"I ain't certain they will know. But there's no sense in jus' keepin' on pokin' around the West lookin' for two men who seemed to have dropped off the face of the earth." Henderson pulled a map of the United States from a desk drawer. "You had a plan and it didn't pan out. So, let's put together another plan."

Henderson pulled another paper from his desk. "By the way, did you know the town of Athens has put out a five-hundred-dollar reward fer the capture of any of the holdup

220

men you're a'chasin'?'"

Marty took the WANTED poster. "I want them for more than the reward money."

"Sure you do, but it's nice to git paid fer takin' care of God's work, ain't it?"

"What do you mean?"

" 'Vengeance is mine, sayeth the Lord.' "

"The Lord never meant for godless killers like I'm hunting to make it to the Pearly Gates to get judged. They're on a direct route to Hell."

"How 'bout you, Marty? You're drinkin' too much, sleepin' too little, and runnin' yourself ragged traipsin' all over the country after these scumbags — killers that they are, and even though you certainly have revenge due ya."

"What makes you think I'm drinking too much?"

"You put down three shots of whiskey whilst I was drinkin' one beer at the saloon. You seem as sober as a judge and you sure couldn't do that unless you were hittin' the sauce hard. You're used to booze in your gut, burnin' and boilin' your insides."

"Well, I can quit any time I want."

"Fine. Quit. You're gittin' ready to take on vicious killers, men without remorse or scruples. You have to be better than them. Are you? Or did you plan to just kill them with the purity of your purpose?"

"I'll make do." Marty's face was set. He did not like the way his friend was tongue-lashing him.

"Let's find out. Unload your pistol."

"What?"

"Go on, unload it. I want to see you draw your pistol. I don't want you to plug me by mistake. I rode with you in Forrest's command. I know you're brave, a damned good rifle shot, tough, and smart. How do you handle your pistol? You may have to use it against one or more of your fugitives."

Grumbling but determined to shut his friend up, Marty did as he was asked. Sheriff Henderson did the same, both men unloading their six-shot revolvers of their brass cartridges. Marty spun the empty cylinder of his pistol against his forearm. "Now what?"

"Let's see you draw. Wait until I snap my fingers."

The sheriff suddenly snapped his fingers. Marty drew his pistol and snapped the hammer down on an empty chamber.

"Again."

"Again."

"Now," he instructed. "Come up closer to me. I'm gonna draw. When I do, you draw, but not before. Ready?"

Marty took a gunfighter's stance, his hand poised over the butt of his pistol, his feet spread. "Ready."

Henderson drew and Marty drew in return. Henderson's pistol snapped twice before Marty's did once.

"Let's do that again, Pat. I can do it faster than that."

"Okay. This time you go first — I'll react to your move." Henderson went into a slight crouch, his hand poised.

Marty drew his pistol. Henderson's gun was aimed at Marty's gut and snapped once before Marty answered. Henderson held out his hand, stopping Marty from moving his pistol. "Look where you shot. You may have hit me in the foot, but my pistol was aimed right at your gut. See what I mean? Tomorrow, let's go outta town and do some work. I think I'm gonna help save your life afore I'm done. Meanwhile, you ready for some supper?"

The next morning Marty accompanied Henderson out of town where a high bank offered a backstop for target practice. Henderson had several boxes of .44 brass cartridges with him. He stood back while Marty fired at a man-sized rock from several different distances and positions.

"You're a right fair shot, Marty, I'll grant

you that. The problem is, you may not have time to aim and fire. That's what you need to work on, and once you get as good as you can git, you'll have to practice often and regularly. It's not like ridin' a pony: stay off a month or two and just jump back on and start ridin' again. Plan on three times a week, religiously. Now here's your first lesson. How to pull, cock your hammer, and aim in one motion."

Marty eagerly trained for two weeks under the expert tutelage of Sheriff Henderson. He learned fast and practiced religiously. In time, Henderson was fairly satisfied with Marty's progress.

"You're fast. Not blazing fast, but fast enough. You hit what you aim at. I reckon you can take most men you'll go up against. Outlaws ain't stupid, at least not entirely. They know they need to be good with a gun to survive, so they'll be fast and aim good too. Learn to read your opponent's eyes like I showed ya. He'll give away his intention every time."

Henderson slapped Marty on the shoulder. "Your .44 Remington ain't too bad a handgun, but keep your eyes on what's new. Colt and the other gun makers are comin' up with new things all the time. Find a quality gun that works for you, and learn how to use it."

"I owe you a lot, Pat. I'll never be able to thank you enough."

"Jus' don't git yourself kilt by some no-good outlaw. That'll be thanks enough. You headed to Galveston, like I suggested?"

"Yep. I agree with you that a gambler like Richland might head over to try the river-boats on the Mississip' if he had some money in his pocket."

Marty rode away from Corpus Christi with true regret. He had enjoyed the company of Henderson. It was the first time he had relaxed with a friend since his month with the railroad, the previous year. He rode into Galveston and immediately booked a trip to New Orleans on the next packet steamer. He sold his faithful stallion and tack for less than they were worth, but he would not need them where he was going. He kept his pistol and two rifles. Those he would need.

At New Orleans, he strolled around the city for a couple of days until he was satisfied Ace Richland was not there, then booked a trip to St. Louis on a riverboat.

During the next few weeks, Marty traveled up and down the river, constantly searching for any clue as to the whereabouts of his prey. He found that he gathered the most useful information while he played cards with the professional gamblers that plied their trade along the Mississippi. To his dismay, his funds dwindled even faster, though he tried hard to play the minimum and question the maximum.

Finally, he hit pay dirt. He was gambling on the *Cairo Belle,* steaming north just south of Vicksburg when he got a lead that looked promising. He was at a poker table with a pasty-faced gambler who coughed a lot. Even so, the man smoked cigars from the moment he sat down at the table until he left, be it two or twenty-two hours later.

"A fella named Ace, huh? Might wear sleeve garters with Injun scalps on 'em? Yeah, I played with him a time or two. He worked the boats for a while, then got off. Said he had a gal in, where was it? Oh yeah, Ft. Scott, in Kansas. He got off in Prentiss, about six months ago. Said he was gonna take the riverboat up the Arkansas River to Ft. Smith and then ride over to Ft. Scott, in Kansas. Planned on gettin' a job dealin' in one of the bars there. Said he wanted to settle down with his gal."

The gambler covered Marty's raise and turned over a small straight. "Two pair? Looks like you lose, Mister."

"No," Marty replied, "I win, thanks to the information you just gave me. Cash me in."

Marty disembarked the boat at Prentiss, Mississippi, and waited impatiently until the *Arkansas Queen* arrived on its weekly run from the mouth of the Arkansas River up to Ft. Smith and back, which was as far as it could safely navigate.

Marty walked off the boat in Ft. Smith and took a stagecoach on to Ft. Scott, just inside the southwest state line of Kansas. When he arrived, he appraised his surroundings. The town was raw, growing too fast to provide streets, sanitation, and other basic services. Green-wood stores, some nothing more than tents of canvas but with fancy façades, lined the muddy thoroughfare. Thirsty men filled the many saloons, anxious to drink, gamble, and whore away what little money they had in their pockets, before the sun rose on the morrow.

Marty took a room in the nearest hotel and ate a decent meal, as had been his practice since his time in the Rangers. He strolled down the wooden sidewalk to the nearest saloon and stepped inside. The room was packed with men; cigar smoke obscured the tin ceiling, and the smell of booze, beer, and unwashed bodies permeated the stale air.

He stepped to the bar and carefully scanned the room. "Beer, please." He ordered from a gray-haired man with a large, pox-scarred nose. Several tables were filled with men gambling, but none of the players seemed to match the description of the man he was seeking. He put a silver dollar on the bar and faced the bartender who had delivered his beer. "I'm looking for a gambler. Name's Ace Richland. Sometimes wears sleeve garters with Injun scalps hanging from them. You know him?"

The bartender took the dollar and glanced around to insure nobody was interested in what he had to say to the stranger quizzing him. "Yeah, I do. Works over to the Red Door Saloon. That's on Rogers Street, just before you git to the cattle pens. Ace has been thar fer a few weeks now. I personally think he cheats. He won't never play in here if I have anything to say about it."

"You can count on it, pard," Marty answered. "Thanks for the information."

The bartender looked into Marty's eyes, nodding at something he saw there. "You goin' over there right now?"

"Yep."

"Sam," the bartender shouted to a man standing by the faro table. "Take over fer me fer a few minutes. There's somethin' I

228

wanna see."

"Okay, Jess."

"Follow me, Mister. I'm a'headin' fer the Red Door fer a short beer."

Marty followed along, his adrenaline kicking up as he mentally prepared for the impending encounter. He remembered his lessons with Sheriff Henderson and breathed deeply, but his heart beat like a trip-hammer. He followed the man into the saloon, pushing aside the batwing doors and peering through the smoky haze at the men inside. He trailed the informer to the bar.

"Hello, Jess. You lost?" the man behind the bar asked Marty's companion.

"Jus checkin' out the competition," Jess answered. "Gimme a beer." He gestured with his chin and whispered low to Marty. "That's him, dealing at the far table yonder."

Marty looked at the table. He spotted the sleeve garters immediately. His hands were clammy with nervous sweat. The husky gray-haired man dealing the cards was his quarry, one of the men he had relentlessly sought for so long and hard. He pushed away from the bar, and slowly walked through the crowd to the table. There was an empty chair across from the man known as Ace. "Mind if I sit in?"

"Glad to have ya, Mister. Name's Ace. This here is Charlie and that's Mais." He pointed to the two other men at the table. "Game is draw poker. Dollar ante and table stakes. All right with you?"

"Sure. I'm in. Name's Marty." Marty flipped a silver dollar on the green felt stretched across the top of the playing table. Ace dealt the hand. Marty opened with a pair of queens and stayed as Ace forced out the other two players with a dollar raise. Marty drew a pair of threes on the draw and showed his hand, losing to Ace's three jacks. Ace raked in the ten dollars in the pot and smiled at Marty, his eyes indifferent.

"Stayin' in Ft. Scott long?"

"Only as long as it takes to conclude my business."

"What's that?"

"Lately I've been a hunter."

"Buffalo?"

"Men."

A wary expression crossed Ace's face. "You lookin' for someone in particular?"

"A man. A cowardly, murdering son of a bitch who killed my wife and little boy back in Texas last year. He and four others raped her and cut her throat, then smashed my son's head in on the fireplace hearth. I swore I'd hunt them down and kill every mother's son of them. One of them was wearing sleeve garters with Injun scalps on 'em. Just like those on your arms. You the man I'm looking for, Ace? You a dirty, cowardly, murdering rapist and baby-killing son of a bitch?"

Ace pushed back from the table, knocking over his chair and scattering chips and the drink in front of him. He clawed for the pistol in the holster under his arm. His face blanched with fear. As his weapon cleared leather, Marty fired. His pistol was already out under the table, centered on the gambler's belt buckle. Marty hammered three quick shots in Ace's stomach from five feet, knocking the gambler back against the wall of the saloon. Ace stood there for an instant, shock on his face, holding his guts in with both hands while bright red blood seeped out between his fingers, staining his white shirt.

With a soft moan, he slowly slid down to the floor until he sat with his back against the wall, his legs splayed out in front of him. Marty stood and put his smoking pistol back into its holster. He walked over to stand between Ace's outstretched feet, and knelt to one knee.

"Where are the others, Ace?"

"I'm hurt. Git me a doc, quick."

"Too late for you, Ace. Where are the others?"

"I didn't wanna hurt yur family, Mister. I didn't even have my way with yur wife. I was outside on guard and didn't know they was gonna kill 'em, I swear."

"You were there. You rode in with them. You share the blame. Where are they, Ace?"

"I don't know, I swear. We split up after the bank job in Carthage. We were supposed to meet in Wichita, but I never went there. I headed for here, and then on to the riverboats. Hulett is insane. He likes to kill, and I was scared of him. I wish to God I'd never met him."

"Where are the twins, Ace? The blond brothers, Bob and Andy?"

Ace moaned, the sound coming from deep within him. The gambler was fading fast. Blood trickled from a corner of his mouth, dripping off his chin onto his white shirt collar. "Come on, Ace," Marty urged. "You don't want to meet your maker with blood on your hands. Help me find the men who killed my family. Where are they?"

Ace grimaced; his teeth were stained frothy red. Marty could barely hear him. "I don't know, I don't know. Oh, it hurts, it hurts. Sally, Sally, where are you?"

Ace's head fell over. He left this life for

the long trail to the next. Marty sighed and backed away. He had learned nothing from the man. He started to turn when he felt a gun rammed into his back and a deep voice spoke into his ear.

"Don't even twitch, Mister. I'll blow yur spine out. Raise yur hands, and be quick about it."

Marty did as he was told. The man behind him relieved him of his weapons, and pushed him aside to look down at the recently departed gambler. "See if he's dead," he ordered someone standing with him.

A young man wearing a deputy's badge knelt by Ace and put his ear to Ace's chest.

"I think so, Sheriff. Don't hear no heart-beat."

"So, Ace, ya finally got yurs, huh?" He prodded Marty with the barrel of his pistol. "Come on, Bub. You've got some explainin' to do."

"I'm coming, Sheriff. Question the two men at the table with me. They'll tell you it was self-defense."

"It'd better be, Bub. Otherwise, you'll be dancin' the stretch-rope polka at the next necktie party the town throws."

CHAPTER 20
THE MAKING OF A BOUNTY HUNTER

Marty sat on the crude bunk in the jail cell examining the absence of his feelings. He expected to feel vindication, satisfaction, and revenge — anything but the slightly nauseous sinking in the pit of his stomach. The gambler's death had done nothing to reduce the lump of ice in his heart, the numbness of his soul, the depth of his sorrow.

He idly picked at a thumbnail as he wondered about the sensation in his gut. Would all the others affect him so? Would the death of any of them purge the hatred that burned within him? He glanced up as the outer door squeaked open and the sheriff walked into the room where the holding cells were located.

"Well, Keller, yur in luck. The two men at yur table backed up yur statement. Richland did draw first. At least they think he drew first. I'm bettin' you already had yur gun out and just goaded him into drawing so's you could execute him, but I can't prove it."

"Believe me, Sheriff Harcourt, I didn't want him dead so quick. I wanted to question him about the other vermin he rode with when they killed my family. He forced the issue when he drew his gun as soon as I braced him. I wanted him alive, I honestly did."

"Well, it shore didn't work out that way. Yur lucky ole Ace wasn't very well liked in Ft. Scott. He been a'livin' with Sally Hemmings until he got drunk and beat her up real bad. She was so mad she run off with a drummer from St. Louis a few weeks ago. Ole Sally was a floozy, but everyone in town liked her. Ace had a lot to answer for, hurtin' her like he done."

The sheriff looked at Marty, who was sitting dejectedly on the bunk with his eyes staring at the floor. "I was inclined to believe yur story, anyways. I do think we'll have to hold ya here in jail until I git an answer from the Texas Rangers about what ya told me. Iffen it's the truth, I'll free ya up then." He shifted a toothpick he was working around his mouth. "Ft. Scott don't like fer folks to come into town and take the law into their own hands. Even someone who has as much right as you say you do. Iffen yur story holds up, I think I'll invite you to move on, as soon as I let ya go."

Marty looked up at the old sheriff, his eyes void of any expression. "You'll check on the reward for me? I know that Athens, Texas, had money out on the bank robbers, and perhaps Carthage did as well. I'm about tapped out and could use the money to continue my search."

"Yeah, I'll check on that, too. It peers to me you may have found yur callin'."

"Oh? What's that?"

"Bounty hunter. Trackin' down wanted men and bringin' 'em back to justice. You find 'em fer the money, not because the law requires it like an honest lawman. Fer certain it'll make you more money than any honest labor would. Git ya killed quicker, too. That's what ya really want, don't ya see?"

Marty's face set. He was too stubborn and too driven to pay any attention to talk like that.

A week later, proof of Marty's statements was received by the sheriff, along with five hundred dollars from the Athens WANTED poster and two hundred and fifty dollars from the city of Carthage.

The sheriff opened Marty's cell and

escorted him to the front office. "Here's yur money, Keller. I hope ya ain't plannin' to stay on in town very long. I have a feelin' yur gonna draw trouble, wherever you go."

"I would like to clean up, get a good night's sleep, and some supplies. I'll be gone tomorrow, if that's all right with you."

"Yep, that'll do." The sheriff handed Marty his pistol. "Your other stuff is at the Hotel Kansas, bein' held fer ya. Tell the clerk I said it was okay to give it to ya."

"I'll need to get a horse and such. I sold mine when I started riding the riverboats. Any suggestions?"

"Try Johansen's Stables, at the south end of town. Tell him I said to give you a good horse, not one of the swaybacked nags he usually tries to palm off on the tenderfoots." Harcourt chuckled. "Me and ole Swede go back quite a ways together. He'll do ya right, since I asked."

Marty looked at the stack of WANTED posters tacked to the board on the rear wall of the office. He quickly thumbed through the pile, seeking one with a large reward attached to it. He pulled it down. The person on it was wanted for robbery and murder. One thousand dollars was being offered, dead or alive, for the outlaw.

"What's the story on this fella, Sheriff?"

Harcourt took the WANTED poster and looked at it. "A bad one, Keller. Luke Brown is part Injun. Cherokee, I think. Kilt a man and his wife over near Bentonville, in Arkansas, and stole the poor fella's horses. He hightailed it back to Indian Territory quick enough. Everyone knows where he is, but nobody's dumb enough to go after him there. His Injun pals will put yur head on a stake iffen ya try."

"Where 'bouts does he hang out?"

"Over to the Washita Injun Reservation. You fer certain can't go into it and police him up. You'll just git scalped and left fer the coyotes to eat."

"If he's part white, he must go into town once in a while. Isn't Preston, Texas close to the south end of the reservation?"

"I ain't too certain."

"I am. How do I get from here to Boston, Texas? There's a road there that goes to Sherman, which is only thirty miles south of Preston."

"Take the south road to Fulton. That's about a hunnerd and twenty miles. Then git on the Little Rock Road. It goes to Boston, I think."

Marty thanked the sheriff and headed for the hotel and a hot bath. The next morning, he purchased a reasonably sound horse

238

from the livery, and a used but serviceable saddle. By noon, he had purchased the necessary supplies and was on the road south toward Fulton, Arkansas. As he rode he mulled over the gunfight with Richland.

"Well, Meg. One down and four to go. At least it's a start. Keep moving, hoss. We've got a long way to go and short time to get there."

Marty pushed hard and was in Preston a day earlier than he had anticipated. The small town was a one street, two saloon backwater place. It survived on thirsty soldiers from Ft. Townson and cowboys from the ranches along the Texas–Indian Territory border.

Marty settled in a room in a small hotel which consisted of only four bedrooms clustered behind a main room split into a restaurant on one side and a bar and gambling room on the other. A large room divider made of framed panels of silk screened oriental scenes separated the two areas.

Marty took the largest and most distant room from the front of the hotel. He unpacked his gear, ate a quick meal, and took a stroll along the only street in the small town. There were no sidewalks, so he walked along the edge of the road, stepping gingerly to avoid puddles of animal urine or piles of horse dung.

He visited both saloons in the town and the bar in the hotel. In all three locations, subtle conversation confirmed that Luke Brown did frequent the town from time to time. Because he had not been seen lately, Marty reconciled himself to a wait of indeterminate length. He ate, slept, and recovered from the strain of the last few months on a lonely trail. He made friends with the town's major businessman, Jeremy Wilkins, who owned the hotel, a dry goods store, and the livery.

"How long you plan to wait for this Brown fellow, Marty?"

"As long as it takes, Mr. Wilkins. He's gonna finance my search for Meg's killers for a few more months."

"And if you still don't succeed? Are you going to take up bounty hunting again?"

"Well, that's sort of hard to say. You have to admit, the pay is good if you get your man."

"And the penalty is pretty severe if you fail."

"There's that. But I'm pretty good at hunting men. I did it for General Forrest, and I can do it for myself."

They bantered back and forth, neither

man surrendering his position. Days passed slowly while Marty impatiently bided his time. He was confident that Brown would eventually get thirsty and come into town for the white man's whiskey. He would be waiting for him.

Marty was sitting in a rocking chair on the porch of the hotel, slowly rocking and thinking of happier times with Meg, when he saw Wilkins walking rapidly toward him.

"Evening, Mr. Wilkins."

"Hello, Marty. Well, he's here."

"Brown?"

"Yep. Just left my store after buying a new coffeepot. Said he was stopping off at the saloon for a drink before heading back to the reservation."

Marty stood, pushing the rocker with his legs. "Wait right here, Mr. Wilkins. I'll be right back." He rushed to his room and put on his pistol belt and slipped his .44 in and out a few times to insure it was easily drawn. He pulled on the heavy belt until it settled comfortably around his lean hips, then rejoined Wilkins on the front porch. "Well, I guess this is it. Thanks, Mr. Wilkins."

"Want me to come along and back your hand?"

"No, that's not necessary. I'll make out.

You head on home. There might be gunplay and who knows where the bullets will fly."

Marty walked casually into the cantina. A man wearing a red muslin shirt over buckskin pants was drinking at a table, moodily twirling the glass as he sat there. His dark, shining hair was parted into two long braids hanging nearly to his waist. Marty looked the room over. He had seen every man save the stranger before. The man he hoped was Luke Brown seemed to be there alone. Marty had an inspiration. He loudly ordered a drink.

"By the Almighty," he slurred his words as if he were already quite drunk. "I'm the strongest fella ever ya ever did see. I kin whup any man in here at arm wrestlin'. Ain't nobody can top me." He staggered over to the table where Brown was sitting. "How 'bout you, Mister? I'll bet ya a drink I can whup yur ass in arm wrestlin', hands down. Ya man enough to try me?"

"Go away." Brown responded with contempt. He hated white men, especially drunk white men. He had never been accepted as one of them, even though his mother was white. She had been kidnapped and raped as a young woman, and he was the result. She had died early, and his father's people had raised him. No matter how hard he tried to make it in the white man's world, he eventually returned to the only family who cared for him.

"Come on, buddy. Try me fer a drink."

Brown decided the best way to rid himself of this pest was to whip him. Besides, it meant a free drink. He put his right arm on the table, his hand open and ready for Marty's.

Marty grinned and sat down. He grasped the half-breed's hand with his. "One, two, three!"

Marty acted as if he was trying hard, but that his opponent was stronger. In a matter of seconds, his hand had been forced back and down against the table. "By gob," he groused, "ya beat me. Bartender, bring this man a drink."

The drink was delivered, and Marty raised his glass in salute. "You're a damned good arm wrestler, Mister. What's yur name, if I may?"

"I'm Luke Brown Horse. I'm half Cherokee Indian. Whadda ya say to that?"

"I say yur one strong fella. Drink up, pard." He raised his glass and the 'breed drained his in a single gulp. Marty carefully sipped his, spilling more on the table when he set it down than he swallowed. He grinned drunkenly at Brown. "Try me again, fer a drink?"

"No, I go now."

"All right then, a drink and a silver dollar." Marty flipped a shiny silver dollar on the table, and positioned his hand. This time the contest was more even, more intent. Marty finally allowed his hand to slowly be forced back until it touched the tabletop. "Ya win again, pard," he shouted. "Bartender. Another drink." He hoisted his old drink in salute. "Here's to you, Luke Brown. Yur one fine arm wrestler."

They swallowed the drinks, and Marty ordered another. Brown was visibly becoming drunker by the second. "One last time?" Marty queried.

"One more time. Then I go."

Again Marty allowed the man to force his arm back. The drink was quickly procured and as quickly swallowed.

Brown stood, swaying precariously. "I go now."

"I'll walk you out to yur hoss, pard."

As they reached the hitching post, Brown lowered his head to put a foot into the stirrup. As he did, Marty whipped out his gun and crashed it down on Luke's skull, knocking the 'breed senseless. He grabbed the unconscious outlaw and slung him over the saddle, facedown. He quickly tied the hands and feet of his prisoner and walked the horse and bound outlaw over to the hotel. He gathered his things and checked out. As he exited the hotel, he met Mr. Wilkins, standing by the horses, looking at Luke Brown Horse lying tied across his saddle.

"You planning on taking him all the way to Arkansas trussed up like that?"

"No, just until I get him away from here a ways. I'll have to let him up sometime."

"Well, I don't envy your problem. I wish you well, Marty Keller."

"Thank you, Mr. Wilkins. You've been a friend."

Marty led his bound captive away from the town, putting some quick miles between himself and any possible interference from any of Brown's friends. He stopped at sunrise and untied the now conscious captive. He slid the man off his horse and put the chains of captivity on his hands and feet. All he got from Brown were curses and promises of vengeance if he ever got the chains off.

In this manner they made their way from Preston back to Fulton, Arkansas, where they turned up the road toward Bentonville.

"You ain't never gonna git to Bentonville alive, Mister," Luke snarled for about the thousandth time.

"Luke, why do you take on so? You know it just makes your blood boil. You just ride easy and don't give me any trouble. Otherwise I'll tie you belly-down across your saddle for the rest of the trip."

Luke shut up, but his eyes never stopped seeking, watching for the opportunity to escape. He was going to make this impudent white man regret the day he ever crossed trails with Luke Brown Horse. That night, as they settled down in camp, Luke's fingers brushed against something hard as he laid his bedroll out. He brushed the dirt away from the object. It was a broken knife blade that had been discarded by some earlier traveler at the campsite. Cupping it in his hand, the wily half-breed made his plans.

Marty was completely unprepared for the attack when it came. The next morning, as he was assisting Luke on his horse, the half-breed swung the knife, slashing a deep gash in Marty's ribs. The shock and pain took Marty's breath away and he staggered back, trying to push the pain down with a bloody hand.

Brown slid off his horse and crab-walked as fast as his chained legs would allow toward Marty, the bloody blade in his hand. A malevolent grin was plastered on his face. Marty bumped into a tree and clawed for his pistol. As Brown reached him and swung the knife toward Marty's heart, Marty fired. The bullet hit Brown in the chest and drove him back. He was dead before he hit the ground.

Gasping in pain, Marty tied the dead outlaw to his saddle and continued the trip, enduring the pain in his sliced ribs, carefully changing the bandage every night with shaking fingers. His ride into Bentonville caused quite a stir with the slumped, blood-stained rider leading a horse carrying a dead outlaw. It was the thing of legends.

The local sheriff accepted the body of Luke Brown and took Marty's statement. He directed him to the town's only doctor, who stitched up the cut in Marty's side and assured him that he was not going to die from infection, probably because of all the blood that had washed the wound over the last four days.

Marty accepted the reward from the town mayor and the congratulations of the local citizens. Then the sheriff stunned him with his next words.

"Now that you've got yur money, Mr. Keller, I'd just as soon you head on outta town. There ain't no place here fer a bounty hunter."

CHAPTER 21
ANOTHER TRAIL,
ANOTHER OUTLAW

In three months, Marty was out of money. His funds would have lasted longer, had the demons in his head not drawn him to the saloons for the numbing release of whiskey. While drinking in a two-bar town outside of Monroe, Louisiana, he gambled with a cardsharp and got skinned of most of his money in one short night. Nursing a throbbing headache and a guilty conscience, he began looking for another quick payday.

He stopped in front of the town marshal's office and went inside. "Help y'all?" the marshal asked.

"May I see your WANTED posters?"

"Sure. What for?"

"Just looking, thank you."

The marshal eyed Marty curiously as he shuffled through the pile of posters. Most offered small sums for men whose crimes were nothing worse than chicken thievery.

He finished the pile and looked around the office.

"You lookin' fer somethin' more substantial?" the marshal asked.

"Is there?"

"You a bounty hunter? Or just some rube whose anxious to git his head blowed off?"

"Why do you ask?"

"If you know what yur doin,' I'd head over to Shreveport. They had a big bank holdup a few days ago. The sheriff was kilt, along with two of the bank clerks. The two robbers headed back to Texas, the posse chased 'em clear to the state line. Whoever goes after them is asking fer a handful."

"Why do you say that?"

"They was pure mean. Kilt the sheriff — he was a friend of mine — as he walked into the bank. Didn't give him a chance."

"The men responsible — were they brothers?"

"I ain't fer certain. Maybe the folks over to Shreveport can tell you."

"Well then, I suppose I'd better head on over there, hadn't I?" Marty saddled up and was on the road within the hour. He arrived in Shreveport to find the town still in a turmoil from the recent holdup.

He checked in with the chief deputy, an aging, balding man who was clearly in over his head. His round face was sweating, and his bloodshot eyes looked as if he had not slept in a week.

"It were plumb awful, Mr. Keller. The sheriff was a fine fellow. He didn't deserve what happened to him. They shot him down like a dog."

"Two of them, I hear?"

"Yeah. They rode due west on the Dallas Road. We had to stop at the border, but I sent word to the Ranger Headquarters in Austin. Maybe they'll git 'em fer us."

"I wouldn't count on it, Deputy. The Rangers are plenty busy just cleaning up Texas problems. Do you know, is the bank offering any reward for the capture of the robbers? Is the town?"

"Let me git back to you on that. I think somethin' can be worked out. Where can I reach ya?"

"I'll be over at the hotel. I'll stick around for a day or two. You let me know."

Marty lazed around the town the rest of the day. As he was finishing his supper, the deputy, accompanied by an equally portly man in a business suit, approached him.

"Mr. Keller, this here is Mr. Newark, the bank president."

"Hello, pleased to meet you."

"See here Keller, are you serious?" Newark asked. "You'll get these scoundrels if we offer a reward?"

"I'll give it my best try, Mr. Newark."

Newark passed a letter to Marty. "Here's a warrant signed by the town council and by me, as the bank representative. It offers fifteen hundred dollars reward for the capture of the two men who did this awful thing. Dead or alive, Mr. Keller, dead or alive."

"Fine by me, Mr. Newark. I'll try to bring 'em back alive if I can, I promise."

"Just get them, bounty hunter."

Marty winced at the crude address, but he nodded and took the paper. He would need it if the town tried to renege after he had accomplished their mission. "I'll be on my way at first light tomorrow. Thank you, gentlemen. Now if you don't mind, I'm not finished with my meal."

He turned his attention to his food and the two men, miffed at their abrupt dismissal, slunk away, muttering to one another.

"Serves them right for getting uppity with me," Marty mumbled to himself. He was as good as his word, though. The next morning, he chased the dawn shadows out of Shreveport toward Texas. He touched two fingers of his right hand to the brim of his hat as he rode past the fat deputy, who glared at him from the front door of the jail.

Marty rode into Texas on the Dallas Road. At the first town, a small village named Tyler, he stopped and talked with the local livery owner. The man was sitting on a chair outside his barn and had a good view of the street that ran the length of town.

Marty introduced himself and asked his questions. "Did you see two men, traveling fast, go through town a week ago Monday?"

The man scratched his chin. "Well now, let me see. A week ago Monday, you say? That was quite a while ago."

Marty took a ten-dollar greenback from his front shirt pocket and folded it together. "I'd pay well for the right answers."

The money disappeared in the man's hand faster than a cat's strike. "Yeah, I think I saw two men go through town faster than usual that day. Yep, I'm certain of it."

"And these two fellas. Did you see where they went?"

"Yep."

"Where?"

"Outta town on the south road."

"Did you by chance know these gentlemen in question?"

"Them two boys ain't gentlemen. They're

a long ways from it."

"How about names?"

"Well now, I ain't so sure I ain't satisfied what you paid me fer, stranger."

Marty sighed. He pulled out a five-dollar bill. He was almost out of cash. He would have to capture the bank robbers or go hungry for a while.

"Now, what're their names?"

Once again, the money disappeared in a flash. "There's two of 'em, you know."

Marty sighed. "All right, you highway robber. But I'm gonna need a place for my horse for the night, and a place for me in the hay pile. Agreed?"

"I reckon that's fair, Mister."

"The names, man. The names."

"It were the Hefflin boys. I knowed them since they moved here, after the war. Their pa was a no-good drunk. He's died now, near two year ago. They live on a hard-scrabble farm outta town a few miles to the south."

"Brothers?"

"Oh yeah. Ne'er-do-wells of the worst sort. Always fightin', drinkin', a'makin' money without workin'. It's plumb unlikely they're honest, clean-livin' fellas."

"They pale blond, lookalikes?"

"Naw, they've got the same sort of muddy-looking hair and dark complexion their pa had. Sam's near three inches taller than Joshua, and looks more like his ma. They're both Hefflins, though. Sneaky mean and too lazy to work fer a livin'. What'd they do?"

"Robbed a bank in Louisiana. Killed the sheriff during their getaway." Marty paused, thinking, then continued. "For my money, I'll expect a map to their place when I leave tomorrow."

The livery owner smiled faintly. "You ask a lot fer yur money, don't ya, sonny?"

"As little as necessary. But as much as necessary." Marty looked around. "Where's the best place to eat? Not too expensive, please. Suddenly I'm a lot shorter of cash money than I was a few minutes ago."

The livery owner cackled happily. "I know what ya mean, stranger. I know what ya mean." Then he got a crafty gleam in his eye. "There a reward fer the capture of the boys?"

"Maybe."

"Don't ya think I oughta git some, seein' as how I'm gonna put ya right on top of 'em?"

Marty sighed. "Tell you what. If they are the ones, and if your map does put me right on top of them, I'll give you a hundred dollars from the reward."

"There's two of 'em. Oughta be worth two hunnerd, iffen you ask me."

"For two hundred, I expect you to go with me to get them. Fair enough?"

"No thanks. I'll take the hunnerd. When do I get the money?"

"After I've got them. I'll swing back through town and pay you."

"And if you forget? To swing by, I mean?"

Marty began to get irritated with the greedy man. "Then come to Shreveport and put in a claim. Now, if you'll excuse me, I'm going to get something to eat."

Marty spent an uneasy night. He needed the succor of a few drinks of whiskey, but he also wanted to be sharp in the morning. He tossed and turned, and nightmares invaded his dreams, but he greeted the dawn with a clear head. The livery owner presented him with a map to the farm where the suspects lived.

The place was a dozen miles out of town, on the road to Henderson. Marty rode easily, until he crossed the creek depicted on the map. The house was visible in the distance. It looked run-down, as did the barn with a sagging roof that sat next to it. Only the corral holding two horses looked well maintained. Marty moved into the trees along the creek, and swung down from his pony. Taking his saddle rifle and a pair of binoculars he had purchased, he worked his way along the creek until he was closer to the house. Seeing no movement, he hurried back to his horse. Leading the animal, he carefully moved down the creek until he was covered from view of the house by the barn. Then he made a quiet dash to the rear of the dilapidated structure. He looked inside the barn through a door hanging on one rusty hinge. A couple of chickens flapped out of his way, but no one was inside. He tied his horse to the barn door and peered around the edge of the building.

From where he stood, he had a good view of the corral and the front door of the house. There was no way anyone could escape, except to run on foot across the fields. Marty could easily run them down on horseback. Marty hunkered down, awaiting some movement from inside the unpainted house. A torn curtain hanging over the one front window kept him from seeing what was happening inside. The two men in the house had to come out to him. Marty did not want them to barricade themselves inside the place if he could avoid it.

Finally, one man stepped outside and relieved himself off the front porch. He yawned and stretched mightily, his arms over his head. Marty saw that he wore a gun belt and pistol, even though he did not have a shirt on, only pants and boots.

"Josh," someone shouted from inside the house, "feed the horses while yur out thar."

"Okay," the bare-chested man answered. "You start breakfast while I do."

As the man stepped off the porch, Marty levered a round into his Winchester. He waited by the edge of the barn until the man came into view. Marty aimed his rifle at the man's chest and whispered, "Stay quiet and come here. Don't even think about going for your gun. Now, move!"

The young man, his mouth open in shock, warily did as he was told. "Who the hell are you, Mister?"

"Shut up and get back here."

As the man rounded the corner, Marty relieved him of his pistol. "Which one are you? Joshua?"

"I'm Josh. Who are you?"

"Never you mind. Just keep your mouth shut." Marty peered around the corner of the barn. The house was quiet. Apparently the other Hefflin brother had not seen the activity at the corral. Marty pushed the younger Hefflin against the barn door and took out his handcuffs. He cuffed Joshua to the iron latch of the barn door, hoping it was strong enough to keep the young man from freeing himself.

"Now, Josh, call for your brother to come here."

"Go to Hell, Mister."

"How would you like a quick rap to the noggin with the barrel of this rifle?"

"I ain't gonna say nothin', damn you."

"Hey, Josh, breakfast is ready," came a shout from the house.

Marty peeked around the corner again. A tall man stood in the door of the house, looking toward the barn. "Hey, Josh. Ya hear me?"

"Sam, look o . . ." That was all Josh got out before Marty swung the barrel of his Winchester against the young man's head, knocking him senseless.

Marty swung his attention back to the house. Sam had started inside, but stopped halfway in, his head turned toward the barn. He had heard his name called and then silence. He grabbed the shotgun leaning against the wall, just inside the doorway. Warily, he started toward the barn, alert to any sign of trouble.

Marty let his quarry get halfway to the barn before shouting. "Drop the gun, Sam. You're covered."

Sam swung the scattergun up and fired at

the corner of the barn. The first blast missed the building completely, and the recoil sent the second way high, where it splattered against the weathered wood, but did Marty no harm. He aimed and shot Sam in the right thigh, spinning the man around and dropping him immediately.

Sam lay on the ground, his hands wrapped around his leg, screaming in pain. Marty moved up and kicked the shotgun away, then dropped his kerchief to the wounded man.

"Tie it up tight, pard. You don't want to bleed to death before we get you to a doctor."

Marty watched as Sam bound up the bleeding wound, then slapped the cuffs on him. Sam lay on the ground, glaring at Marty, his face shiny with sweat from the pain.

"You ain't gonna leave me here, are ya?"

"Just until I find the money from the bank. The sooner you tell me where it is, the quicker we'll get on back to Tyler and you can see the doc."

"Take the money and go. My laig's broke. I can't stop ya."

"Sorry, Sam, it's not gonna be that way. Where's the money?"

Sam moaned and gave up. "It's under the

bed in the old man's room. A board there comes up if you pry it with the poker from the fireplace."

Marty soon had twenty-one hundred dollars and some stuffed in his saddlebags. He got the two Hefflin boys on their horses, chained their legs under the animals with the leg irons and started them back to Tyler. Sam moaned and groaned the entire two hours, severely trying Marty's patience.

Once there, he delivered Sam to the local doctor. After a quick examination, the old sawbones bound up the leg, which was not broken after all. Then he turned his attention to stitching up the cut on Josh's forehead. In an hour, Marty was out of the office with his two prisoners, and ready to ride. He stopped by the livery on the way out of town and gave the owner five new twenty-dollar greenbacks from the bank loot.

By early the next afternoon, he was riding into Shreveport with his two sullen captives. The excitement was immediate. Many of the town's citizens stood on the sidewalks gaping and shouting at the two unhappy men as they were pulled off their horses and delivered to the grinning deputy. Marty received many offers for drinks and free meals from the men surrounding him. Suddenly he was a very popular man.

He celebrated by getting completely soused with his new chums and sleeping until nearly noon the next day. After collecting the money he had been promised, he rejoined his new drinking buddies and spent another riotous night with them. This time, he bought most of the drinks. Hungover and sick to his stomach, he awoke the next morning and decided he needed to move on. Gathering his belongings, he headed to the livery barn, his head pounding and his stomach rolling, determined to ride on. He had just completed saddling his horse when a burly sergeant and two privates from the local Union Army garrison found him.

"Mr. Keller?"

"Yep, that's me."

"Major Logan wants to see you right away. Come with us, please."

"Who's Major Logan?"

"He's the commander of the Federal occupation forces in the Shreveport region. Follow me, please."

"What if I don't want to see Major Logan?"

"Then me and me boys will have to change yur mind." The old sergeant grinned, lightly tapping a gnarled fist into his other palm. "I'd like that, but you wouldn't."

"I get your point, Sergeant. Let's go see Major Logan."

CHAPTER 22
BRING HIM
BACK DEAD

Marty followed the sergeant into an office marked COMMANDER, NORTHWEST LOUISIANA DISTRICT. The officer, a red-haired major with Burnside-style whiskers covering his chin from his ears forward, nodded as the gruff NCO made the introduction.

"Major Logan, this is him. Keller."

"Come in, Mr. Keller. Thanks for coming so promptly."

"My pleasure, Major. Your sergeant led me to believe that you wanted me here immediately."

Logan nodded, and dismissed the sergeant with a slight wave of his hand. "Thank you, Sergeant Berkowski. You're excused."

The sergeant saluted, did a smart about-face, and marched out of the office.

"May I offer you some refreshments, Mr. Keller?"

"Thanks. You have any coffee?"

"Certainly." The officer shouted toward the outer office. "Corporal Hawes! Two cups of coffee, please."

The orderly quickly entered the office with two cups of steaming coffee. Marty sipped his and nodded his appreciation. "What did you want to see me for, Major?"

"I need your experience in tracking down outlaws, Mr. Keller."

"Where did you get the impression I track outlaws?" Marty asked.

"I'm a friend of the banker in Shreveport, Jerome Newark. I was talking with him last night about my problem and your name came up."

"I don't think I'm ready to go out again, Major. I just got a nice payday from the Shreveport folks."

"Oh, I believe I can change your mind, Mr. Keller. My problem is a deserter. One of my men, a galvanized Yankee, as a matter of fact, by the name of Wil Colby. He was a Confederate soldier captured in Atlanta. He joined the Union Army out of Camp Douglas in '65 and served a year on the western frontier. Then, he reenlisted for my command. Last Monday he severely beat one of my officers, a young lieutenant named Pennington, then deserted."

Major Logan angrily rapped his fist against

his desk. "Pennington hit his head on the corner of his bunk when he fell. The man's blind, and by thunder, Colby's gonna come back and pay for it. I'm authorized to pay a five-hundred dollar reward for his capture and return to this post, or for proof of his death resisting arrest."

"Why doesn't the Yankee Army find him for you?"

"The Army is too busy maintaining order in the defeated Confederate States to worry much about a single deserter. They'll happily pick him up if they run into him somewhere, but they won't particularly look for him. Logan glared at Marty. "Lieutenant Pennington is from a wealthy New England family. His pa is a U.S. Congressman. Young Pennington graduated from West Point just last June. He had a bright future in store for him. Now he's blind, on his way back to Connecticut, and I know his pa is gonna raise hell with my boss as to what I've done to apprehend his attacker."

"I sympathize with you Major Logan, but I'm still not interested in going after your deserter. I've other considerations."

"You mean looking for the swine that killed your family?"

"Yes, precisely. How did you know?"

"From Newark. He mentioned that two

of the men you seek were brothers named Swain?"

"Yes?" Marty leaned forward in his chair, his headache forgotten.

"I'm from Iowa, Keller. I grew up near the Swain farm. I know the Swain family. I'm a close friend with Warren Swain, went to school with him, in fact. He's the twins' older brother and the only member of the family worth a hoot. He's a schoolteacher and thoroughly ashamed of his twin brothers."

Marty was all ears. "Where can I find him?"

"I'll take care of that, Mr. Keller. You go find my deserter. When you get back, I'll have written Warren and got him to tell me where the twins are. If anyone knows, he will."

"I aim to kill 'em both, Major. You going to tell your friend that?"

"No, but believe me, the two have been courtin' just such a demise for a long time. Warren will be sad, but I don't think he'll grieve too much or too long."

"If I go after your man, Major, I'll expect you to honor your word. I can always go to Iowa and look up this Warren Swain myself."

"You'd not have as much luck as I will,

believe me. Warren and I are quite good friends. I feel almost guilty even asking him for information about the twins, but I want Colby even worse."

"What can you tell me about him?"

"He's from the Ft. Worth, Texas, area. That's one reason I thought of you. You know that area. You're friends with the Texas Rangers; they might be of some help. All this makes you the perfect man to ferret out Colby from wherever he's gone to ground."

"Have you talked with any of his friends? Maybe he told them where he was heading?"

"They all clammed up with me," Logan complained. "Perhaps you'll have better luck."

"I might. I think, if you'll ask the good sergeant — what was his name, Kowalski?"

"Berkowski."

"Yes, Sergeant Berkowski. If you'll ask him to sit with me, I might be able to get some useful information from his bunkies."

"Consider it done. Anything else?"

"A warrant, authorizing me to hunt for your deserter."

"Agreed." Logan smiled and stood. "Shall we get on with it?"

"Lead the way, Major."

Marty sat in the room issued for his use

by Major Logan. Sergeant Berkowski escorted in the first private — a young, towhead, barely eighteen. "This here's Private McKean, Mr. Keller. Sleeps next to Private Colby. Sit down, McKean. Answer the man's questions, unnerstand?"

"Yeah, Sergeant B."

"Hello, Private. May I call you Mac?"

"Sure enough, Mr. Keller. Everyone else does."

"You a friend of Private Colby?"

"Sort of, I guess."

"Did he ever say anything about cutting out, deserting?"

"No. Not to me. I got the idea he really liked bein' in the army."

"Any idea why he would take off like he did? Why he would beat Lieutenant Pennington like he did?"

"Nope. Nary a one. Somethin' was gnawin' at him these last few weeks, for a fact. He jus' never told me what it were." The young private looked at the old sergeant, sitting silently beside Marty, smoking a well-used brier pipe. "Willie had a good pal, fer a fact. Corporal Hawes and Willie was chums. I think they was that is. I ain't anxious to speak out of turn or nothin'."

"You have done the right thing, Mac. Colby needs to come back here and face the music. He won't be happy runnin' from the law all his life." Marty nodded at Sergeant Berkowski. "That's all for this gentleman, Sergeant. Would you get Corporal Hawes for me next?"

"Come on, Private. I'll be right back with Corporal Hawes, Mr. Keller."

When the old sergeant entered with the young corporal, Marty knew he had hit pay dirt. The man's face gave him away completely. It was as if the corporal had committed a crime himself, he was so guilty-looking. He avoided any direct eye contact, staring morosely at his shoes.

Marty sat him down and tried to put him at ease before he started the questions. It did not take long before Marty heard some real answers.

"Did Colby talk to you about going on the run?"

Looking miserable, the young corporal nodded his head. "He was very unhappy. Lieutenant Pennington was pickin' on him real bad. No matter what he did, Pennington didn't like it. Willie was always having to go over to the lieutenant's quarters after retreat and polish boots or clean weapons, and such."

Marty looked at Sergeant Berkowski. "That right, Sergeant B?"

"Yessir. The lieutenant said he was gonna make a real soldier outta Colby. Said he'd been spoiled by the time he'd spent in the 5th Infantry. He came down pretty hard on him."

"More than on any of the others?"

"Yeah. But not enough that I felt I had to say anything about it."

"You know where Colby might be headed?" Marty asked of Hawes.

"He's from Texas, a small town near Ft. Worth called McKinney. Has a ma there on a farm with some younger brothers and sisters. His pa was kilt durin' the siege of Vicksburg. Willie was talkin' about how he oughta git out and go back to help his ma. He always said he hated to leave, he liked the army so much."

Marty nodded. "I know McKinney. Where was his farm, he ever say?"

"Two miles to the north of town, that's all I know."

"Tell me all he ever told you about his family and home."

Marty took his leave of the army post, the warrant for Colby in his pocket and saddlebags filled with supplies for the trail. Major Logan had promised to have information for Marty upon his return with the deserter.

For the first time, Marty was enthusiastic about taking up the hunt for a lawbreaker. He pushed his animals hard and reached the small farm community of McKinney in only four days. He had ridden within ten miles of his old ranch, but had not detoured from the direct route, nor did he even consider it. There was nothing for him there. His path was the vengeance trail, and he was on it to the end.

He stopped at the saloon, hardly more than two planks on sawhorses in the general store. The storekeeper's wife acted as bartender for him. He sipped a lukewarm beer and asked questions about the area. He soon was talking about the subject of his search.

"I used to know a farmer hereabouts. Named Mose Colby. Heard he got killed in the war. You know him?"

The woman, in her late forties and showing every year of it, brushed a tendril of graying hair back from her cheek and nodded. "Yeah, sure enough. Ole Mose vas a good fella. He haf a small place north of town, on Sherman Road. You tinkin' about stoppin' by?"

"I'm headed north, to Sherman, so it's right on the way. I might."

"You can't miss it. Dere's a big cot-

271

tonwood tree right vhere de road splits, north to Sherman or east to Mt. Pleasant. It's about two miles outta town or so. Right dere, you turn vest on de little trail. About half a mile, you come to de Colby place. Iffen you do stop, tell Mrs. Colby dat I got some nice fabric on de last shipment from Dallas. We ain't seen her in de store in a vhile." The plump German woman gave him a toothy smile.

"I surely will. Well, I guess I'd better go find me a place to camp out. It's getting dark, and I want to get some sleep before finishing my trip to Sherman."

Marty took his leave and did not stop until he was at the cottonwood tree. He had a dry camp there, pulling his bedroll over him, after chewing some jerky and sipping from the bottle of whiskey he carried in the bottom of his supplies. He slept until the first, faint smudges of pink swept across the eastern sky. He saddled his horse and strapped the supplies back on the packhorse.

Nonchalantly, he rode up into the front yard of the Colby farmhouse. "Hello the house," he called out.

A slender, work-worn woman opened the door and looked at him, a wary concern on her face.

"Howdy, stranger."

"Hello, Ma'am. I'm on my way to Sherman and stopped for the night in McKinney. Met the storekeeper's wife there, Mrs. Nimitz. I told her I think I met your husband, during the Vicksburg campaign. She suggested I stop by. She wanted you to know that she's got some nice new fabric in from Dallas. Says to stop by the store real soon. Said you might fix me a hot breakfast, since I've got a dollar to spend on one."

The woman's face relaxed. "Howdy. My name's Clara, Mr. . . . ?"

"Martin Keller, Ma'am. Call me Marty."

"You met Mose afore he was kilt? Climb on down. I'd be pleased to fix yur breakfast. Won't cost you no dollar, neither."

"Be happy to pay it, Ma'am. I got the funds."

"Flapjacks and sausage do fer ya? Some of these German families 'round hereabouts make some mighty fine sausage." The woman shouted over her shoulder, "Willie, we got a guest fer breakfast. Git on out here, now."

A man, looking younger than his twenty-three years, with light brown hair, a fair complexion, and delicate features, stepped into the kitchen. He had on boots, and his undershirt was tucked into his pants. Marty

273

noticed the butt of an Army revolver sticking out of his waistband.

"This here's my boy, Willie, Mr. Keller."

"Hello, Willie."

"Howdy."

"Mr. Keller met your pa at Vicksburg. Mose got killed there, did you know? The first day of July, the letter said." She sort of turned inward for an instant. "We got a nice letter from his colonel. Mose was a first sergeant, you know."

"Sixteenth Texas, right?"

"That's right. You in the unit, too?"

"No, Ma'am. I was detached from General Forrest's command. Trying to slip in and out with dispatches." Marty looked at Willie, sitting quietly, watching Marty and his mother speak. "You in the Confederate Army, too?"

Willie nodded, "Yep. Hood's Command. I was a courier for him until I got captured at Atlanta."

"Tough break. Those Yankee prisons weren't much fun, from what I've heard."

Willie simply nodded his head, saying nothing more.

Marty and Mrs. Colby spoke for a few more minutes, then she got started on breakfast. "You must be starvin', Mr. Keller. We'll talk more about Mose after you eat."

After a good breakfast, Marty put down his coffee cup. "Mighty fine meal, Mrs. Colby. I'm surprised you're not a bit fatter, Willie, if all your ma's meals are as good as this."

"I've been away. Just got back."

"Willie was away till recently, Mr. Keller. Now he's home to stay, aren't you, son?"

Marty shook his head, "No, Mrs. Colby, you're mistaken. Willie's still in the Union Army. He deserted last week, and I've come to take him back." Marty drew and pointed his pistol at the surprised Willie. "Put the gun on the table, boy. Do it, now!"

"Damn you," Willie hissed.

Mrs. Colby's face reflected the shock and concern she was experiencing. "Oh, Willie. You ran away?"

"I had good reason, Ma. I'll tell you sometime." With careful fingers Willie lifted his pistol from his waistband and placed it on the tabletop. He glared at Marty. "Now what?"

Marty passed over the handcuffs. "Put 'em on. Mrs. Colby, get Willie some fresh clothes and such. We're leaving immediately for Shreveport."

"You'll never git me there, Keller. I swear it."

"Don't, boy. I'll kill you as quick as I

would a rattler on my doorstep. Just ride easy with me and face the music. Who knows, you might get off."

"Not with Lieutenant Pennington around, I won't."

"He's not there anymore."

"No? What happened?"

Marty watched the distraught Mrs. Colby hurry to do as he had commanded. He waited until she was out of earshot. "You blinded him, boy. He's on his way back to Connecticut."

"Good. He don't deserve no better."

CHAPTER 23
TEXAS TWISTER

Marty led the shackled Willie away from the farm, his mother crying bitter tears in the front yard as they rode down the dirt road. Willie was arguing the entire time. "You can't take me back there, Mister. I'll be strung up fer hurtin' Lieutenant Pennington. It ain't right. Ya hear me? It ain't right. You jus' can't take me back there."

"I've got three replies for you, Willie. One, you'll not get strung up, that is, unless the lieutenant dies. Stockade time, sure. But you'll not get hung or shot for a fight, even with an officer. Two, you're the one who ran away from your unit, instead of staying and facing the music, and three, I don't give a good gosh damn. You understand me, Willie? I don't care. I'm getting paid to bring you in, and that's just what I'm going to do. So shut up, and let's try and make our trip a little bit pleasant. Okay?"

"It ain't right. It ain't right, I say."

Marty sighed. He could see they were in for a long and aggravating trip. "Okay, it's not fair. Now, just shut up. Okay?"

Marty eyed the menacing thunderheads building up in the southwest sky. "Looks like a real gully washer headed our way. Let's hurry along. Maybe we can reach McKinney before it hits."

They just did, barely having time to tie their horse at the hitching rail in front of the Nimitz store before hard, pelting raindrops fell by the bucketful. Marty and Willie sat on the front porch, protected by the overhang. As the storm started to slacken, Marty stirred from his rocker. "You want to get anything from the store before we go on?"

"I wouldn't mind some canned fruit for after our suppers, if you don't mind."

"A good idea. I think I'll get a fresh slab of bacon. I can use what's leftover from my old slab to give the beans some flavor."

They went inside the store and made their selections. As they moved to the counter to pay, Mrs. Nimitz came in from the rear storage room.

"Vhy, it's Villie Colby and Mr. Keller. Hello, Villie. How have ya been? I ain't seen ya in a good long spell. Ya still in the Yankee Army?" Her eyes widened as she spotted

278

the cuffs on Willie's wrists. "Vhat's goin' on here?" Her gaze turned accusingly on Marty.

"He's under arrest, Mrs. Nimitz. Willie deserted from the Army and I was sent to bring him back."

"Vhy, vhy you lied to me den, Mr. Keller. You told me —"

Marty held up his hands in surrender. "You're absolutely right, Mrs. Nimitz. I owe you an apology, and I hereby offer it. I'm going to take Willie back to Shreveport and turn him in. But I'm going to treat him fair and considerate. He won't end up with a bullet in the back as soon as we're outta sight, like some might do."

"Never de less, I ain't so certain I vant yur business, bounty hunter."

"That is your choice, Mrs. Nimitz. But what I'm getting, I'm going to share with Willie on the trail. If you deprive me, you'll just be depriving him."

"And how about poor Mrs. Colby? You leave her brokenhearted and grievin'?"

"I imagine so, Mrs. Nimitz. You'll have to give her support until Willie can come back. In fact, if you will accept it, I'd like to leave you fifty dollars on account for her. As she makes her purchases over the next few months, slip her a little credit and make it up with my money. Will you do that for Willie and me?"

Mrs. Nimitz weakened. "Vell, dat's better dan she coulda hoped fer. Sure, I do it." She looked hard at Willie. "Villie, boy, you git this mess straightened out, and din come on back home. Yur ma need ya."

"Thanks, Mrs. Nimitz. I'll surely try."

Marty tied the new purchases on the packhorse and helped Willie into his saddle. "Well, here we go. Let's try and make Dallas before sunset."

They rode out of McKinney, over the small ridge that rose up a mile south of town. The sky was a peculiar shade of gray mixed with green, with dark, heavy thunderclouds rolling and boiling toward them. The wind picked up as they crossed over the ridge, and Marty grabbed his hat just before it was swept off his head.

"My God," Willie shouted. "Look!"

Marty jerked his gaze in the direction Willie was pointing.

"Good Lord in Heaven," he gasped.

Coming directly at them across the flat prairie was the biggest twister Marty had ever imagined. Although it was several miles away, it looked like it was a quarter-mile across or more. Dust and debris splayed out from the edge of the writhing, contorted funnel.

Marty quickly calculated the direction the funnel was taking. "Willie, it's gonna hit McKinney. Ride boy, ride hard. We've got to warn them." He jerked the reins of his horse around and slapped spurs to its flanks. Galloping like the Devil himself was after them, the two men thundered back down the slope toward the village, sitting serenely in the slanting rays of the sun, which had broken through the massive clouds sweeping past overhead.

Marty galloped into town and headed directly for the store. He shouted at the top of his lungs. "Twister coming, twister coming! Get in your root cellars! Hurry, hurry!"

He could hear Willie on the other side of the road shouting just as loud. Mrs. Nimitz stuck her head out of the door.

"Mrs. Nimitz, a twister's coming. A big one. Get under cover. Hurry! Hurry!"

She pointed toward the back of the building and shouted loudly. The wind was beginning to increase in fury. Marty glanced behind him. The top of the funnel cloud was just visible. The bottom would be coming over the hill in a minute or two.

"Mrs. Blake — she live in de white house vith green shutters, just down de road. Her

281

man gone on cattle drive and she has four little ones. Hurry."

Marty gigged his horse in the direction Mrs. Nimitz had indicated. As he rounded the corner of the store, he saw the house about a block away. As he galloped toward it, he continued to shout his warning. People stuck their heads out of the door and looked at him and then toward the southwest, where the roar was increasing with every passing second. The twister was clearly visible now. The dark funnel was writhing and flexing as it scooted across the ground. The roar sounded like an approaching train pulling into a station, snorting and steaming in fury.

Marty reached the house and swung down off his horse. Before he could even think of tying it to the hitching post, the animal bolted away. Marty was not too worried about his mount. It would instinctively run to safety, if it had time. He ran into the house, bursting through the front door. A woman looked up in terror at the abrupt entry, her children all gathered around her.

"What do you want?" she screamed in terror.

"Hurry, Ma'am. A twister's coming. A big one. Where's your root cellar?"

"Out back." She moaned and grabbed her

two smallest children in her arms. Marty grabbed the two older ones and ran for the back door of the house. A dog barked and snapped at his heels as he ran through the house, the terrified woman right behind him.

Marty stopped as he ran through the back door, then spotted the hump of earth that covered the root cellar. He ran to the slanted door and yanked it open. The roar of the twister was almost unbearable now. It was close. Marty looked over his shoulder as he jerked the door open. The front edge of the funnel was not more than a quarter mile from the first houses in McKinney. The path was taking the hellbender right through the town. "Sweet Jesus," he muttered. "It's gonna flatten the town."

Marty pushed the woman and her two toddlers inside and followed. He dropped the two crying older children on the dirt floor and turned to barricade the door. A crossbar had been fashioned to keep anyone outside from opening the door if those inside wanted it so. He dropped the heavy wooden bar in the iron straps and turned to the woman, who was crouched in a far corner of the room. Several shelves held canned goods or smoked and dried meats. Marty had to shout to be heard over the roaring wind outside.

"You have a lamp or candle?"

The woman nodded, pointing toward a shelf. Marty saw a half-burned candle sitting in a glass holder. Drippings had covered the holder until it resembled a convoluted wax mound. Marty moved to light the candle. As he struck a sulfur match, the roar increased to a mighty crescendo and the door vibrated and thumped against its hinges. Dust swirled around the cellar, extinguishing his match. The shriek of the wind drowned out the screaming cries of the scared children.

As Marty was finally getting the candle lit, the sound abated and the drumming of heavy rain could be heard again. He raised the door to the root cellar. It was as dark as night, with rain pelting down like it was never going to end. Marty looked at the house. Where it had once stood, only the crumbled ruins of the fireplace chimney could be seen against the dark sky. He ducked his head back inside.

He felt something touch his arm. It was the woman, her face tear-streaked, and her hair in ragged wisps around her head. "Is it over?"

"Yep, I think so. The twister has gone on by, thank God. Now if this rain would just let up a little. We need to get back to the town. There's folks there that need help."

"I wanna thank you, Mister. You probably saved me and the kids' lives. What's your name?"

"I'm Marty Keller, Ma'am."

"I'm Mary Anne Blake, Mr. Keller."

"My pleasure, Ma'am."

"I'll pray that God rewards you for your bravery, Mr. Keller. Every night, the rest of my life."

"Don't you fret, Ma'am. God has already passed me by. Me and Him are on the outs."

"I don't believe that, Mr. Keller. You did God's work today."

Marty merely grunted and moved over to reassure the children. They were still shaking scared. He spent some time talking gently with the older boys, urging them to be good helpers to their mamma. By the time the rain tapered off to a steady drizzle from the pounding downpour, he had the three oldest children laughing at an outrageous story about a horse and an elephant having a race. It was one he'd often told little Matt when he put him to bed at night. The tyke had loved hearing it, over and over again.

"Wish I could tell it to him just once more," Marty whispered to himself as he stood and brushed the dirt off the seat of his pants.

He escorted Mary Anne outside, where she promptly burst into tears when she saw the shambles that once was her home.

"Don't cry, Mrs. Blake. You and the children are safe. You can rebuild your house. Now, we need to get some stuff to the root cellar. That will have to be your home until your husband returns. Any idea when that will be?"

"At least six weeks yet, I guess," she sniffled.

"Then find what you can to make your new home comfortable. I've got to go back to town. There're liable to be folks in need of help there."

"You're right. Go on, I'll manage here. When you get tired, come on back. I'll cook you a meal and have a place for you to sleep."

"Thank you, Ma'am."

Marty looked around. The sky was lightening up a little. It was more like early evening now, as opposed to full dark. He spotted his horse, eating grass in a field on the far side of the ruins of Mrs. Blake's house. He whistled sharply and the animal slowly made its way to him. He rewarded the obedience by giving the nervous animal a sugar cube he had grabbed the last time he had eaten in an indoor restaurant. The little treat had been saved for just such an occurrence, and he wanted to reinforce the animal's subservience.

Marty rode into what had been McKinney. Now, it was a collection of stone foundations, splintered wood, and lonely chimneys standing in solitude against the dripping sky. The numbed citizens wandered around, looking at what had once been their homes.

Marty saw Mrs. Nimitz digging at the ruins of a building just across the street from her store. Surprisingly, her store was mostly still intact. One wall had caved in and half of the roof was gone, but the store was still standing. The front glass was in shattered slivers and rain was quickly soaking everything inside.

She saw Marty and waved him over. "Can you help me, Mr. Keller? Dere is someone callin' out from under dese boards."

Marty hurried over to join Mrs. Nimitz digging at the scrambled pile of boards that had once been a store.

"Dat's Mr. Packard. I knowed he vould not leave his store. He's too stubborn fer his own good. Hang on, Mr. Packard. Ve vill git you outta dere."

They kept a steady work pace, and soon were rewarded with a leg sticking up through a twisted pile of splintered wood. Marty pulled a section of wall off the pile and saw the man laying facedown, his clothing ripped and torn. As Marty eased him free, he saw that the man's arm was badly broken. He carried him over to the stoop of the Nimitz store, which at least got him out of the rain.

"Mrs. Nimitz, you need to bind up his arm. Is your husband around here?"

"No, he go to the Rummels' farm, tank goodness, to buy pigs fer to make sausage. I pray dey all right over dere."

"Where is the farm?"

She pointed to the southeast. "Dat vay, five miles."

"They'll be okay, then. The twister was headed northeast."

Marty left Mrs. Nimitz nursing the injured man, and headed toward a group of people pulling broken boards from a pile further on down the street. He thought it was where the hotel had stood. He saw Willie working along with several other men as he walked up.

"I see you made it," Willie spoke to him.

"Yep. What's up here?"

"They think there were some guests who

stayed in their rooms. We're just gettin' started."

Marty whispered to Willie. "If I unshackle you, will you give me your word you won't run off? That way you can work like a man among your neighbors."

"Will I? You bet. Can I go check on my ma?"

"We'll send someone out there as soon as enough men and boys show up." Marty could see wagons filled with farmers and cowboys on horseback headed toward the town. People were gathering around to help in the town's time of emergency.

Willie stood while Marty took off the hated chains, then he rubbed his wrists. "That feels good. Them damned things hurt yur wrists after a while. Come on, bounty hunter. We got folks to save."

CHAPTER 24
AT ODDS
WITH THE JOB

The effort was Herculean in scope. Every destroyed building had to be searched for people who might be trapped under the piles of debris. The new arrivals from the surrounding countryside provided the frantic searchers more manpower at just the right time.

Marty sent a young teenager out to Mrs. Colby's farm on horseback to check on her welfare. He returned to report she was safe and well, and that except for some wind damage to the barn roof and a destroyed chicken coop, the farm was intact. She promised to be in town the next morning to help the survivors care for the injured.

Marty and Willie worked relentlessly until it was nearly dark. By then, the men had found all the trapped citizens and freed them from the wreckage that once had been their homes or stores.

Marty wearily walked back to Mrs. Nimitz's store with Willie and several other exhausted men. They were all tired, dirty, and hungry. "Well, Mrs. Nimitz, what was the bill for the whirlwind?"

"Eight kilt, sixteen injured, and Mrs. Kostner vill not survive de night, I tink."

"I suppose it could have been worse. You did good work, Willie. You can be certain I'll tell Major Logan of how you worked to save the people trapped in the rubble."

"It won't matter, the major liked Lieutenant Pennington. He'll string me up no matter what you say."

"It's not so, Willie. My input can make a big difference. I see the women have some food prepared over there. Let's get something to eat and talk about it."

Marty led the way to where several women, including Mrs. Blake, had prepared a hot meal of roast beef, potatoes, and ears of boiled corn on the cob. They filled their plates and sat on a fallen tree, apart from the rest of the townsfolk, so they could talk while they ate.

Marty saw several men and women whispering and looking their way. He knew the word was being spread about Willie's problem with the army. Marty hoped he would not have any trouble getting away the next morning with his prisoner. Tired as they were, the hot food tasted delicious, and they both shoveled it in until they had their fill.

As they slowed, Mrs. Blake brought them both a cup of hot coffee. "I made a place for you to sleep tonight, Mr. Keller. You can bring Willie along, as well. My oldest should have a good fire going by now, so I'm headed home to get them fed. It's right outside the root cellar, in case any more twisters come along during the night. We'll wait for you before we go inside the cellar."

"Thanks, Mrs. Blake. We'll be along directly."

She hurried away, anxious to get back to her place before the daylight was completely gone. Marty looked to the west. The sky was awash in bright colors of red, gold, blue, and black. "Look at that sundown," he remarked to Willie. "It's like Mother Nature is trying to say, 'I'm sorry for all the trouble.' "

Willie looked long at the spectacle, but didn't reply. Marty took a sip of his coffee and turned his attention to Willie. "Now why don't you tell me about your trouble back in Shreveport?"

Willie clasped his hands together and put them between his knees, his face bowed. He did not reply for a long time. "It ain't nothin' you'd understand," he finally answered.

"Try me. I want to help you, boy. Tell me about it, so I can."

Willie's demeanor was like that of a young child explaining to his mother how he had broken her prized lamp. He talked quietly, obviously embarrassed. His speech stuttered in agitation as the story unfolded. He never lifted his head to look at Marty.

"When Lieutenant Pennington first arrived, I liked him a lot. He was nice to me, talked to me, you know? Asked about me. Gave me passes and didn't put me on any extra duty when I messed up. He'd tell Sergeant Berkowski to send me over to his quarters to clean up. At first he'd sit there and talk with me, then he asked me to shine his boots for him. He always wore 'em while I polished 'em. Later on, he started askin' me to rub his back. He'd take off his shirt and undershirt and lay facedown on his cot. I'd rub his back for a long time. I knowed he liked me to sort of, well, sort of rub against him while I was doin' it, so I would. Not hard you know, but just sort of push myself agin his legs and arms, sort of. Like I said, I liked him, and he was talkin' about gettin' me promoted to corporal. I wanted that promotion real bad. Every now and then he'd have me take off my shirts and he'd rub my back."

Willie looked up suddenly, the anguished expression on his face apparent even in the fading light. "He was always askin' me if it felt good, did I like it, on and on."

Willie stopped as a teenaged boy walked toward them and spoke excitedly. "I found him, Mister. I found both yur packhorse and the army horse. They was eating grass a mile or so over yonder." He pointed to the west, and then wiped his hand on his shirt. You gonna give me the two dollars ya promised?"

Marty pulled two silver dollars out of his pocket. "Right as rain, I am. Thanks, son. Where'd you tie 'em up?"

"Over to the corral where the livery was. I hobbled 'em both. They won't go nowhere tonight, fer certain." He took the coins and hurried away, as if afraid Marty would change his mind and take the money back.

"Well, there's our ride outta here tomorrow. We may as well get a good night's rest before we start."

"I don't wanna go, Mr. Keller. I told ya, they're gonna hang me out to dry."

Marty continued on as if he had not heard the protest. "I think we oughta leave before your ma gets here. That way you won't have to go through seeing her say her good-byes again."

Willie just looked at Marty as if he had a snake coiled around his neck. "You ain't listenin' to me, Mr. Keller. I can't go back."

"Come on, Willie. I'll help you. Go on, finish your story, so I can help."

Willie shook his head dejectedly. "One night, after I rubbed his back and shined his boots, he told me about how two men could make one another feel good. Said it would be our secret. That he would take care of me, get me promoted if I would do, well, do some things I never dreamed of doin'. He was a sodomite, Mr. Keller. He wanted to do some terrible things to me. I said no, and left right then and there. After that, he was mean and nasty.

"He'd curse me and make me clean up the stables or his room and then give me extra guard duty. He said he'd make my life hell iffen I didn't give in to him. The last time, he made me rub his back and then he grabbed me." Marty heard the embarrassment in Willie's voice. "Down there, you know where. I told him to leave me alone or I'd tell the major about what he asked me to do. He just smirked and said he'd already told the major I was a troublemaker and the major would never believe me. I got so mad I punched him right in the face."

Willie wrung his hands together nervously. "The lieutenant fell back against his bunk and didn't move. There was blood all over his head. I panicked and ran. Until you showed up, I thought that maybe I'd gotten away clean."

Marty listened in sympathy. "You've got a good case, Willie. I'll tell Major Logan what you told me. We'll make him believe you. First, we have to get back. You can't run away from this. The lieutenant's too important a person. They're gonna keep looking for you, no matter what."

"I can't go back, I can't."

"Come on," Marty said, rising and holding out his hand to pull Willie up. "Let's get a good night's rest. We deserve it. Tomorrow we'll make plans for your defense."

A sullen Willie followed Marty back to Mrs. Blake's root cellar. As they approached the fire, Marty whispered to Willie. "Will you give me your word not to run off tonight? If so, I'll not put the cuffs on you."

"Yeah, I promise. You ain't heard a word I said, have you?" Willie's tone was now harsh and accusing.

"I have, Willie. I promise you that I will help you. You deserve it, in recognition of all the fine work you did today."

Marty awoke the next morning to the smell of flapjacks being cooked over an open fire. Mrs. Blake made him and Willie a breakfast fit for a king, then thanked Marty again for saving her and her children. "Come visit us anytime, Mr. Keller. You'll always be welcome at the Blake house."

Marty and Willie walked back to the ruins of McKinney. They picked up the two horses at the destroyed livery, then headed to the corral behind the Nimitz store, where Marty's horse was hobbled. A white-haired man was busy feeding the animal a bucket of oats. He introduced himself as Mr. Nimitz, and he thanked Marty and Willie for their efforts on behalf of the town.

The three of them walked around to the front of the store, where Mrs. Nimitz was directing a half-dozen men and women concerning their duties for the day. She stopped as her husband, Marty, and Willie came around the corner. Marty tightened the cinches on his saddle and the pack animal. Then he turned to Willie, standing silently beside his horse, his face grim and showing a good deal of tension.

"Willie, if you promise not to make a break for it, I'll not put the chains on you."

"I can't make that promise, Mr. Keller. I can't."

Sighing, Marty took out the cuffs and threw them to Willie. The young man made no attempt to catch them, so they ended up in the dirt at his feet. "Go on, son. Put 'em on. We gotta get going. Your ma will be here shortly."

Willie bent down. As he did, Marty glanced at the people watching from the front of the Nimitz's store, their faces expressionless. He did not think they would try to help Willie escape, even though their sympathies were clearly with the young soldier. He turned back to watch Willie put the cuffs on his wrists.

His eyes widened in surprise. Willie was glaring at him, a pistol in his hand. "Where'd you get that?"

"Found it in the debris yesterday. Been carryin' it in my boot."

"Don't do this, Willie. We can make it right in Shreveport, I know we can."

"I ain't goin' back, Keller. You can't make me."

"Willie, Willie, don't be stupid. Don't do this. I'll just come after you again."

"Then I guess I'll just have to make sure you don't."

"Don't, Willie!" Marty shouted, but he could see it was too late. Willie was going to shoot him, right where he stood. Marty stepped back. His boot caught a piece of splintered lumber and he staggered to the side. As he did, Willie jerked the trigger of his pistol. The bullet cut through Marty's left sleeve, slicing a nasty groove across his shoulder muscle, but doing no real harm.

Instinctively, the result of long hours of practice, Marty drew his pistol and fired. He meant to hit Willie in the arm, but his practiced hand automatically aimed the pistol at the center of mass of the target. The bullet went straight into Willie's chest, mortally wounding the young soldier before he could take a second shot. He groaned and dropped to his knees, then slowly rolled over onto his side, blood soaking through his shirt.

Marty quickly rushed to Willie's side. "Oh, son, what have you done? It didn't have to be this way. We could have handled the charges. Willie, Willie, look what you've made me do."

Willie smiled through pain-filled eyes, his face relaxing in the quiet dignity of approaching death. "I told you I wouldn't go back." He died, his face dropping into the dirt, and he slowly relaxed, rolling to his back.

Marty stepped back, his throat choked and constricted, his heart aching in his chest. His voice quivered as he turned to the storefront. The people there glared at him with rage, revulsion, accusation, and condemnation.

Marty angrily wiped his hand across his eyes, pushing away the tears that tried to leak out. "You all saw it. I didn't have any choice. Mrs. Nimitz, I need a written statement from you and a couple of the others. Just say what you saw, and certify that this was Willie Colby."

"And if ve do dis ting, vill you leave our town and not come back?"

"Gladly."

The seething townspeople quickly supplied Marty with the statements he needed to prove he had fulfilled his assignment. As he stuffed the affidavits in his saddlebag, he glanced down at his feet. The piece of wood he had slipped on was lying there. It looked like a elongated triangle, with a sharp point like a spear on one end. He picked it up and went over to Willie's body. He looked sadly down at the young man, who seemed to be more asleep than dead.

"Rest in peace, brave soldier." He raised the wedge over his head and slammed it into the body, right through the bullet hole in Willie's shirt, driving it into the dead body.

"Hear now, you butcher," someone

screamed. "What in God's name are you doing? You — you animal!"

Marty looked only at Mrs. Nimitz. "For his ma. Tell her a falling wall killed Willie, while he was trying to save a trapped person. Let her have that memory to sustain her."

"Ja, dat is good."

Marty pulled his money roll out of his pocket. He held out the remaining two hundred dollars left from what he had from Shreveport. "Here's two hundred to help the town get started again."

"We don't want yur blood money, bounty hunter," someone shouted.

"It's not from me. It's from Willie." No person stepped up to take the roll of bills, so he tossed it on the front porch of the store and mounted his horse.

Marty slowly rode away from the town. Looking back, he saw the shocked town's citizens still standing on the porch, watching him, despising him, blaming him for Willie's death, scorning him for the man that he was.

"You gave me no chance, Willie. I have my reasons, damn you. Damn them. Damn the whole world." Marty whipped the ends of his reins against the flank of his horse. The animal broke into a ground-eating lope. "Meg, darlin', I sure miss you right now."

CHAPTER 25
A HATED NAME
IS BORN

When Marty arrived in Dallas, he went directly to local Ranger Headquarters. He immediately described the death and destruction that the town of McKinney had suffered. The Ranger commander, Captain Self, thanked Marty for the report and jumped up from his desk. Within a few minutes, he had three Rangers and a preacher from a nearby church dispatched to the town with instructions to provide whatever assistance they could, and then to report back with a listing of necessities needed, so that he could organize a relief effort.

Marty briefly explained why he was in McKinney when the deadly twister hit. Self listened incredulously to the story. "I can't believe what I'm hearin'. You're a bounty hunter? My God, Martin, don't you know that every decent lawman in the West has nothing but contempt for bounty hunters?

Most are no better than back-shootin' killers, just doin' it with the law on their side."

"Well, that's not who I am, Captain. Bounty hunting's the only way I can make enough money to keep looking for Meg's and little Matt's killers. I used up what money I got for my place a long time ago."

Self sadly shook his head again. "I just can't believe it. Look, son, if you want my advice, get outta that business right pronto. Meanwhile, I wouldn't tell any of your friends here in Dallas what you're doin'. I just can't believe it." Self motioned Marty away.

"Go find Doc Elders and git your arm looked at. When he's done, send him over to see me. He may need to take some medical supplies out to McKinney, depending on what Charlie says they need when he returns.

"I think you can count on it, Captain. There were sixteen people hurt when I left, eight dead, and maybe some more we hadn't found yet."

"Does that count the boy you killed?"

"No, it doesn't. I was just talking about the ones killed by the twister."

"Go on, git. Tell the doctor to stop by as soon as he fixes your arm."

Marty took his leave, disappointed with

the dismissive way the Ranger commander had talked to him. "He was a bit nicer when he wanted me to ride on posse for him," Marty muttered to himself as he walked toward the doctor's office.

The sawbones was the same doctor who had delivered Matt, and he greeted Marty effusively, truly happy to see him again. "I sure was sorry about yur loss, Marty. I wish I could have been there for you, but you was gone by the time I came by."

"Thanks, Doc. I know you would have. It's all right."

"Well, let's get yur arm stitched up. It's gonna be sore for a spell, but shouldn't give you any problems after that. The bullet came a mite close, didn't it?"

"I think I stumbled just as he fired, or I'd be pushing up daisies."

The old doctor finished wrapping Marty's arm, and immediately started packing a large bundle of medical supplies to take with him out to McKinney.

"You want me to show you the way, Doc?"

"No, if you killed one of their friends, you'd best stay away. I suggest you get a good night's sleep and take it easy for a couple of days. Check in with me Friday, and I'll have a look as to how yur healin'."

Marty wandered out of the office. He

stabled his horses, including the one Willie had stolen from the army, and indulged himself with a pricey room at the Sam Houston Hotel. He took a long, hot bath, had a shave and haircut, ate a hearty lunch, and then slept most of the afternoon, luxuriating in the clean linens.

As he took his leisure at the hotel's elegant bar that night, several Ranger friends came in. The word had already spread among the Rangers about the gunfight in McKinney and the death of the runaway soldier at Marty's hands.

Marty tried to explain his side to one of his friends. "Why, Hell's bells, Charlie. They're talking like I gunned him down in cold blood. Look at my arm. He fired first. I surely didn't want to hurt him. I tried to tell him that I'd help him fight the charges, once we got back to Shreveport."

"It's what yur doin', ole buddy. Nobody likes bounty hunters. You'll always be ridin' the lonesome trail. We're almost that way as Rangers. The only friends we got're our saddle pards and the six-gun on our hips." He looked sagely at Marty. "You won't even have any saddle pards, unless you join up with another bounty hunter. I wouldn't advise that. He might shoot you in the back jus' so he won't have to share the reward with ya."

Marty glumly acknowledged the truth of Charlie's advice. He twirled the shot glass of whiskey in the moisture ring it had made on the tabletop. "I don't have much choice, Charlie. I've got to get money to look for my family's killers, and that's about the best way I know how to get it. If I was any good at cards, I'd gamble. Unfortunately, I'm not, so that's that."

Charlie glumly agreed, finished his drink, and got ready to take his leave. "I'm off to Gilmer tomorrow, me and Steve Block. A gang of outlaws damn near wiped out the town yesterday. Robbed the bank, three stores, and the only saloon in the town. Kilt two and wounded five folks, including a pregnant woman. A real case of bad men."

"Robbed the town's only saloon? What on earth are folks coming to?" Marty and Charlie both chuckled, but just a little. "How many outlaws?" Marty inquired.

"Ten or twelve, it seems. Don't seem likely it's your gang, does it?"

"Probably not. Say hello to Steve for me. I guess he's all well from that bullet he took in Camp Verde?"

"Yeah, says it pains him some when it's rainin', but that ain't too often I guess. Well, so long, Marty. Take it easy."

"Thanks, Charlie. Same to you."

Marty sat alone, not interested in joining any of the drinkers at the bar, nor in trying his hand at any of the games of chance going on across the room. He steadily drank, his mood bitter. Without realizing it, he was a lot further gone that he should have been. Suddenly, a young man in a gabardine suit and celluloid collar with a string tie appeared at his table and sat down, uninvited. He stuck out his hand and introduced himself.

"I'm Bob Woodard, Mr. Keller. I'm a reporter for the *Dallas Daily Star.* I heard you were in McKinney when it was devastated by the whirlwind. Could you tell me about it?" He pulled out a notebook and pencil, and then looked expectantly at Marty, his hand poised to start writing.

Marty looked at the young man. He tried to shake some of the booze out of his brain. "Sure, I guess." Marty began to describe his impressions of the storm and its devastation. The young reporter scribbled furiously, nodding and urging Marty on with probing questions. As they talked, Marty ordered yet another whiskey. "You want anything, Mr. Woodard?"

"A small beer, thank you. Now, Mr. Keller. What can you tell me about the shootout you had this morning with the army deserter?"

Marty sipped his drink, swallowing a sizable amount. "You heard about that, too?"

"Oh, yes. I understand you were bringing the man back to face charges of desertion and assault against an officer? How did you come to take on that job?"

Marty blearily looked at the man questioning him. He seemed eager to hear what Marty had to say. The whiskey in him got the better of his common sense. Before long, he was pouring out his heart, telling the eager reporter the entire story of his life, the joy of his life after the war, the agony of Meg's and little Matt's deaths at the hands of the vicious outlaws, his determined search with such disappointing results, the gradual slide into bounty hunting, just to stay on the killers' trail. The reporter just kept nodding, writing in his little book and urging Marty to tell more.

"How many men have you killed?" he asked.

Marty did not stop to consider what he was revealing. "So far, just about all of 'em. Hell, I'll kill every outlaw in the West, if I have to, to find the men that killed my family."

"Every one?"

"Yep, just about. But, I always offered to let 'em live. All they had to do was give it up and come in with me. I don't just go shoot 'em. Nope, but if they try and brace me, I'm gonna cut 'em down."

The reporter closed his notebook. "Well, that's about it, Mr. Keller. Thanks for your story. It'll be in the paper tomorrow afternoon. People are gonna know about Marty Keller after this, I guarantee it."

"Wait," Marty's liquor-soaked brain finally realized what the reporter was about to print. "You gonna put in that stuff about my family? I thought you wanted to hear about the twister?"

"I'm gonna write both. You'll be a well-known man before I'm done with this story." He hurried away, while Marty was left struggling to grasp just what he had said, and if he should do something to keep it off the front page.

"To hell with it," Marty mumbled. "I'm gonna get some sleep." He drunkenly made his way up to his room and sprawled across his bed, not bothering to take off his clothing or boots.

The next morning, the interview nagged at him, but he shrugged it off and went about his daily business. He drank himself into oblivion again that night. By the next day, when he came down to the hotel restaurant, he noticed a difference in the way people looked at him. He was certain he saw several people talking about him, even pointing at him when they thought he was not looking their way.

He made his way to Doc Elders' office, uneasy with the reactions from people he met on the sidewalk. He walked into the old doctor's office, and was greeted with the title he'd soon grow to hate almost as much as the men he was searching for.

"Well, well. It's the famous Man Killer. How you doing, Marty?"

"What the hell are you talking about, Doc? Everybody in town got the crazies?" He started to pull his shirt over his head.

"Heck, son. Yur the talk of the town. Haven't you been readin' the *Star*?"

"No, what's it say?"

"Says yur the meanest, baddest, bounty hunter ever was. Calls you Man Killer, the deadly hunter of every outlaw in the West. That you'd jus' as soon kill an outlaw as look at him."

"What?" Marty was all tangled in his shirt, his arms still stuck in the sleeves. "Why that snot-nosed reporter, I'll wring his neck."

Doc Elders waited until Marty got his arms out of his shirt. He quickly inspected the stitches in the wound on Marty's arm. "Looks good. Well, yur about as good as I can make ya, Man Killer."

"Don't call me that, Doc. What on earth possessed me to talk to that sumbitch. I oughta go wring his scrawny neck."

"Why did ya talk to him, anyways?"

"Oh, dammit, I was drunk. I never would have, otherwise."

"Listen to me, Marty Keller. Yur headed down the road to death. If yur gonna be a bounty hunter — and as far as I'm concerned, that's yur business — then you gotta understand one pure fact: People are gonna be looking for a chance to kill ya deader than a squashed pond frog. You don't have the luxury of bein' drunk. Never! No place, no time, except maybe in a room with an armed guard standin' outside a locked door. You hear me, son? You can't drink. Period!"

Marty listened to the old doctor, his face set. "I don't drink much, Doc. It just helps me to sleep."

"I don't care boy. No more booze. I don't want you lyin' next to Meg and Matt. Do you? Not at least until you've done what you're settin' out to do."

"You're right, Doc, as usual. I'll put a lid on it right quick." Marty hoped he was telling the truth. It might take more than just a simple vow.

Doc Elders rested his hand on Marty's shoulder in a fatherly fashion. "Listen to your doctor, my boy. You'll live longer. Now, get on outta here so I can do some real work."

Marty returned to his hotel room and assessed his situation. Rather than become the object of stares and rumors in Dallas, he decided to return to Shreveport and report to Major Logan. Maybe he already had the information Marty would need to close in on the Swain twins. He was on the road within the hour.

Unfortunately, Major Logan had not heard anything new during his absence. Logan was satisfied that justice had been done as far as Colby was concerned. "You did a good job, Keller. I'll submit a voucher for your reward right away. I expect an answer to my telegram any time now from Warren Swain. Take it easy, and I'll be in touch."

Marty tried to explain to the busy major the reason that Willie Colby had deserted. "He got forced into something way over his head, Major. The lieutenant was putting too much pressure on him to do something he found abhorrent. You can't blame him for running."

"No, he didn't have to run. He shoulda

come to his sergeant and me. We would have taken care of it. Now a good man's dead and a promising young officer's career is gone. In my opinion, Private Colby got what he deserved. You just saved the army the time and expense of doing it themselves."

"Well, it's gonna cost me. I don't think I'll ever get over the pain of having to shoot that boy."

"Come on, Keller. After all, that's what you do. You're a bounty hunter."

CHAPTER 26
RIDE THE
OWL-HOOT TRAIL

"Boy, oh boy, was that a hoot and a holler." Bob Swain threw his head back and laughed with his brother as they rode north with the other ten members of the Longwood gang fresh from the raid on the northeast Texas town of Gilmer. It was a motley, semimilitary group of men led by an ex-Confederate guerrilla named Long Tom Carter. He ran the gang as if they were his own private army. He was a harsh and unyielding boss, but he planned his raids well, doubly insured that his men understood his plan, and then personally supervised the thieving and plundering. He was no coward, and his men respected him for that.

His cousin, Lawrence Thompson, was the sheriff of Bixley, Kansas, the nearest town to the ranch that Long Tom had stolen and where he set up his headquarters at the end of war. The unfortunate previous owner was buried in an unmarked grave behind the corral, with a pile of manure for a tombstone. The ranch was in an isolated section of central Kansas, near Lake Cheyenne Bottoms. It allowed him a safe haven where he could hide from the law and return safely, to lick any wounds received on a raid. The town of Bixley was under his thumb, and was a place where his men could let off steam with impunity and spend their victim's money on booze, cards, and women. Long Tom owned the biggest saloon and hotel in town, both lucrative properties where the money his men spent came back to his pocket. His cousin kept the townsfolk subdued and docile. It was a good operation, all around.

Andy Swain answered his brother. "You said it, Bob. I thought that saloonkeeper's jaw was gonna break, the way it dropped when you told him to put all his money in the sack. What did he think? Just because he sells rotgut whiskey, he thinks he ain't never gonna be robbed?" Andy slapped his thigh with the ends of his reins and laughed again. "We sure was lucky, runnin' into Long Tom when we did."

It had been advantageous timing for the two simpleminded, but vicious and amoral twins. They had ridden hard to the rendezvous site, just like Alva Hulett had instructed them to do after the bank job in Carthage. They had found the place easily enough, set up camp and waited in vain for either Hulett and Sanchez to arrive, or Ace Richland. For a week they waited, carefully husbanding their food and supplies, without any of the others showing up. Finally, out of grub and thirsty for whiskey, they went into Wichita.

Once there, they immediately got riproaring drunk and thrown in the city jail for causing a ruckus in one of the saloons. In that, they were lucky. The lawman that had talked with Marty and knew about the twins, Sheriff Sedgwick, was out of town collecting a wanted man from the sheriff of Conway Springs, fifty miles away. The part-time deputy who locked up the Swain brothers had not heard of Marty nor his reason to hold the two drunks.

Bob woke up first, his head throbbing. He kicked Andy's rump, who was snoring like a buzz saw, in the next bunk. "Wake up, Andy. Yur causin' my head to ache, yur makin' so much racket."

Andy rolled over, his face as slack as Bob's. "Oh, my head. We musta really throwed a whing-dinger, hey, brother?"

Bob called out through the bars, "Hey, jailor."

The part-time deputy looked in from the outer office. "Mornin', boys. You finally decide to wake up?"

"Yeah, and my head's splittin'," Bob complained. "What did you do, hit me with a ax handle, you ole mule skinner?"

"Nope, you fell down and thumped your thick skull agin the brass foot railin' at the Lucky Horseshoe Saloon. I think it made everyone there happy, since it shut you up." The deputy motioned to the twins. "You boys can git out fer a ten-dollar fine for drunk and disorderly or you can stay and serve ten days. What'll it be?"

Andy spoke up. "We'll pay the fine. I got some money in my boot." He pulled off a boot and retrieved a small pile of bills and pulled off a couple. "Here's yur money. We can go now?"

"Sure can, right outta town. You ain't wanted in Wichita. Git my drift?"

"Okay, we're goin'. Just as soon as we git our gear, we'll git goin'."

"And take ole Pecos there with ya."

"Who?"

"The fella in cell two. He's served his ten days. He's gotta leave town jus' like you do. Take him with ya. He's the sorta fella you two would like."

Bob and Andy were reluctant to have an

uninvited riding companion. Pecos did not say much as they gathered their belongings and left the city jail. As they were saddling their horses at the livery, Bob whispered to Andy, "Lookie at that nice hoss of his. Let's let him ride along with us till we're outta town a way, then leave him in a gully somewhere. We kin sell his hoss in the next big town we come to."

As they trotted away from the town, the man called Pecos, a balding, husky cowboy with a crooked nose and a nasty scar along his right jaw, opened up a bit more. "You boys on the dodge?"

"Why you askin'?" Andy replied.

"Oh, it jus' seems to me like you fellas could use a good thing. Maybe I got jus' that, iffen yur interested."

"We might be, might not. What ya got to tell us?"

"You boys ever hear of Long Tom Carter?"

"Can't say that I have. You, Bob?"

"Yeah. A Missouri raider warn't he?"

"Well, since the war he's put together a really sweet deal fer fellas like us. He's got a gang of men who can handle themselves, and a good place to hide out. He makes a plan and swoops down like a hawk on his target. Then we make tracks back to his ranch, where we'll git paid. He even has a town where we can go and spend what we've earned."

"And nobody gives ya no trouble?"

"Nary a one. It's the sweetest deal fellas like us kin git."

"Then why were you stuck in the Wichita jail, servin' a ten-day sentence?"

"I went home to Texas, 'cause my ma died and I had to bury her. I made the mistake of gittin' drunk on my way back. Don't worry, I'll git back at 'em some day."

Andy asked the most important question. "You think this Long Tom fella would have a place fer us?"

"I think Long Tom might. Our last raid, we lost a couple of men. I doubt if Long Tom has replaced 'em yet. If I show up with you two, it might make up fer me bein' ten days late returnin' from leave."

Bob and Andy rode ahead a bit, softly considering Pecos's offer. "Whatta ya think, Bob?"

"Maybe we oughta check it out, afore we kill that fella. I wouldn't mind joinin' up with a boss that's got it all together like this fella."

"And if he don't want us?"

"Then we'll head fer Colorado Territory. There's gold there, I've heard."

So it was that Andy and Bob Swain joined the outlaw gang of Long Tom Carter. He quizzed them long and hard, interested in their time with Alva Hulett. "You boys did the bank in Carthage, huh? I heard about it. Why'd you burn it down as well?"

Bob explained Hulett's grievance with the town. Long Tom smiled, his grin more akin to the Devil's grimace. He was lean, with a heavy, dark beard streaked with gray. Dark brows had grown into a near solid slash across his forehead. His dark eyes were cruel, his thin lips were perpetually turned down in a slight frown, as if he were never satisfied with his circumstances. He dressed impressively; the dark suit he wore cost more than a man could honestly earn in half a year. His boots were hand-tooled, and polished to a bright sheen. He looked hard at Pecos, standing meekly, hat in hand, awaiting judgment for his transgressions.

"Pecos you was late returning from leave. I could have you shot for that. However, you brought me two prime recruits, so I'm gonna be lenient with ya. Yur fined fifty dollars from our next take and one month of house arrest. You and these two can handle the midnight to dawn guard duty for the month."

Bob and Andy were not very smart, but

they knew how to take orders and to do the job assigned them, a by-product of their stern upbringing on the family farm. In a few months, they had earned the freedom accorded any of the Carter gang and eventually accompanied Carter on the raid to the small Texas town of Gilmer. After they returned to the ranch, Carter divided the loot in the standard manner. Bob and Andy ended up with four hundred dollars apiece. They requested permission to go into Bixley and spend some of their ill-gotten gains.

"You've earned the right, boys. I'll give ya twenty-four hours to spent yur money. Just remember the rules for any of my men. You can't kill nobody in Bixley. At pain of yur own life, you unnerstand me? Drink, gamble, cavort with the gals, you can do just about anything ya want there, but no killin' of Bixley citizens."

"We gotcha, Boss," Andy groveled, anxious to please his new master.

The twins rode into the town with four other men from the ranch. They ate and had a shave, then headed for the dry goods store, where they spent some of their funds on new clothes and boots. They sent their ma some money and a letter, asking a fellow outlaw who was going to Ft. Larned to post it for them. Finally, they headed for the saloon, determined to drink away several months of abstinence.

They drank hard, well into the early evening. By the time the sun had set they were stinking drunk. Their innate evil and cruelty was amplified by their intoxicated state. Bob slapped Andy on the head, rousing him from his stupor.

"Come on, brother. Let's get ourselves a good steak dinner. You game?"

"Yeah, I'm hungrier than a mule with a empty feed bag."

They staggered out of the saloon, holding each other up. They turned bleary eyes up and down the street, looking for the nearest restaurant.

"Hey," Bob blurted out. "Lookie over there."

A young woman was hurrying along the sidewalk, past the darkened windows of the stores along the walkway. Her light summer dress was swirling along as she walked, giving the two brothers tantalizing glimpses of her ankles and lower calves. Her blond hair peeked out from under a blue bonnet, tied by a velvet cord under her chin.

"Man, she's prime, ain't she, brother?"

"Come on," Bob urged. "Let's go see if she's willing to give us a ride. You got any money left?"

"Sure, I got plenty. I won that last hand."

"Well, come on then. She's as fine a filly as I've seen since we got some from that gal down in Texas last fall."

"Them was fine horses, warn't they?"

"I warn't talking about no horses, dummy."

They angled across the street, cutting the young woman off. As she tried to squeeze past them, Bob grabbed her arm. "Well, howdy there, Missy. You in a hurry, or could me and Andy buy you a drink?"

"No, thank you. Please excuse me, I have to get home."

"Whoa, now. Hold on. Me and Andy just wanna have some fun, don't we, Andy?"

Andy Swain took hold of her other arm, his foul breath making her wince in disgust. "Sure, Missy. We'll be happy to pay ya fer yur troubles."

"Let me go, please, please!" She clawed at Bob's face, raking her fingernails across his cheek.

"Oh, you damned bitch. That hurt." He slapped her, knocking her bonnet from her head. Her long, blond hair swirled around her terrified face. Andy grabbed a fistful of hair, and pressed his lips down on hers. She squirmed and moaned in fear, struggling to break free.

Bob grabbed the bodice of her dress, tearing it free almost to her waist. The woman screamed, trying to cover her exposed bosom and twist free at the same time. She stomped on Andy's foot, causing him to scream in pain and release her. He hopped on one foot, then staggered off the sidewalk and fell on his back in the street. The girl kneed Bob where it hurt, and he fell back, his fist tearing away a piece of the dress.

The girl ran like the wind down the street, far faster than either Bob or Andy were capable of. She turned the corner and was lost to sight. Bob moaned and tried to straighten up. "Damn her, she kneed me good."

"Well, she damn near broke my toe, so don't you complain none. It were yur idea to talk to her, anyways."

"To hell with her. Let's go git another drink."

"Yeah."

George Benson, her enraged father and the owner of the town dry goods store, was in Sheriff Thompson's office the first thing the next morning. He angrily related the story of the incident to the sheriff, who sat impassively behind his office desk, casually cleaning his fingernails with a small penknife. Two hulking brutes of deputies sat stoically in opposite corners of the room, watching the scene like the bodyguards they were.

"They damned near raped her, Lawrence. My Betsy came home in tears, her dress torn, her face bruised by those animals. You gotta do something about it."

"Now, George, calm down. Did they actually force themselves on Betsy?"

"Damned right, they did. I told you, they grabbed her, slapped her, tore her dress."

"Does she know who it was?"

"You know it was some of the men from your cousin's ranch. They were in town yesterday, drinking and raisin' hell at the saloon until all hours this morning. Who else would it be?"

"Well now, who knows? What was your daughter doin' out at that hour, alone, traipsin' past the saloon, actin' all snooty and uppity like she does?"

"What do you mean? She was coming home from church choir practice. She forgot her Bible and ran back to get it, or she would have been with the Sherwood sisters."

"Well, I can't say who done it. Your daughter'll have to come in and give me a description afore I can do anything else."

"Lawrence, she's badly shaken. I don't

want her to get any more upset. Just bring those fellas from the ranch in. One of 'em will tell you who did it. They were all so drunk, they'll think it was a joke."

"That's what it was, George, a joke. We'll just let it go this time and forget about it. Next time any of Tom's boys come in to town, I'll have a word with them. They know they're supposed to leave their amorous concerns to the floozies in the saloon."

"Well, what about Betsy? She has a right to see the animals that assaulted her put in the hoosegow."

Sheriff Thompson's eyes got cold, very quickly. "I told ya, I'll take care of it. You go on to work now and let it go."

"Dammit, Lawrence. If you ain't gonna take care of us, we may as well get ourselves a new sheriff that will."

Thompson made a quick motion with his hand. Immediately, the two deputies were on either side of George Benson, hauling him to his feet.

"We don't like talk like that in Bixley, George. You call me Sheriff Thompson, and you git on outta here like I told ya." One of the deputies slammed a meaty fist into George Benson's stomach, driving the wind out of his lungs.

As soon as he could stand and draw a

breath, they pushed him out the door, slamming it behind him.

Benson semistaggered to his store, his soul enraged at the treatment he had just suffered. "By God, there'll come a day when I'll help run that whole bunch out of town, so help me."

Chapter 27
Closing the Ring

Marty impatiently awaited word from Major Logan. When he explained to Sergeant Berkowski what he had learned about Willie Colby and Lieutenant Pennington, the old NCO was aghast.

"I can assure you, Mr. Keller, if Private Colby had confided in me about what was happening, I'd have taken immediate action. That sort of thing happens, now and then, but I don't condone it, nor do I allow officers to take advantage of my enlisted troops, in any capacity. I'd have been in the major's office in a heartbeat."

"I sure wish Willie had come back with me instead of trying to shoot it out."

"I sympathize with you, Mr. Keller. Fortunately, Private Colby's untimely death may help this command in the long run, and for that, I'm grateful. It's not a very desirable assignment, acting as occupation troops, I mean. If your side had won instead of mine, you might be doing the same thing in Ohio or somewhere. The major's demonstrated that he won't abide with desertion, and that may keep some of the men here who otherwise might try it later."

Marty stayed close to his hotel room and waited out the days and nights. He never drank in the saloons, only in the privacy of his lonely room. He tried to cut back on his consumption, until he was taking only a small amount each night. He rode out into the countryside daily to practice his marksmanship and fast draw. He spent many hours and a lot of gunpowder, and he saw improvement with every passing day.

Major Logan started to accompany him, enjoying the respite from his duties and the challenge of shooting with a good marksman like Marty. He started bringing Sergeant Berkowski, as the grizzled sergeant was an outstanding shot himself. The old sergeant had served in Berdan's Sharpshooters at the beginning of the war. Berkowski taught Marty several useful strategies for long-range shooting and stalking of his targets.

Berkowski took a real liking to the .50-caliber Sharps buffalo rifle that Marty had from his hunting days with Buffalo Bill. He would often hit a ten-inch-diameter target at five hundreds yards with it. Before long, so could Marty.

"Yur just a natural at the long shot," he complimented Marty. To the ex-Ranger, it was a high praise, coming from the veteran sharpshooter.

Marty was eating breakfast a couple of days later, when Sergeant Berkowski came into the restaurant. "Mr. Keller, the major's compliments, sir. He wants to see you immediately."

"You haven't had another man go on the run, have you?" Marty groused good-naturedly.

"No, sir. The dispatches came in from New Orleans. I think he has a telegram you'll be interested in."

Marty sopped the last of his gravy with a remnant of his biscuit, swallowed a mouthful of coffee, wiped his mouth with his napkin, dropped a silver dollar on the table, and pushed back his chair. "In that case, lay on, Macduff."

"Who the hell is Macduff?" the old sergeant asked.

"From a story by Shakespeare, my good fellow."

"Who the hell is Shakespeare?"

"Never mind, Sergeant. Come on, let's go see Major Logan."

Logan looked up as Marty came into the room. "An answer from Warren, Marty. His ma has heard from his brothers three times in the last year. Letters mailed from Wichita, Salina, and Ft. Larned. She thinks they're working on a ranch somewhere in the area." He took a map of Kansas out of a drawer and spread it on his desktop. "Here, here, and here." Logan drew a circle around the three locations, lying in a triangle of about one hundred fifty miles to a side. "I'd bet you they're located within this circle some-where."

"Damn, Lo. That's over twelve thousand square miles. Take a lot of searching."

"At least it's closer than you've been up to now."

"Yep, there's that."

"Also got a message from your Captain Self."

"Oh?"

Logan passed it over to Marty. "Says that the raid on Gilmer was done by the Carter gang, and that one witness saw two men who looked exactly alike among the gang."

"I've heard of Carter. Ex-Confederate raider along the Kansas-Missouri border wasn't he?"

"That's him. Has a gang of cutthroats riding with him now. Likes to ride into a town and take it over. Cleans out the banks and stores, and then disappears for a while. Look at this." Logan took his pencil and started putting "X"s on the map. "We know he's raided the towns of Ozark, Arkansas; Gilmer, Texas; Olathe, Kansas; Sterling, Colorado Territory; and Grand Island, Nebraska. He's probably responsible for many more, but these I know of. And look at this, Marty."

Logan drew a line back toward the circle he had drawn earlier. "They all converge on this area. An animal doesn't like to soil his own nest, so he goes out a ways to do his business. Longwood doesn't rob around where he has his hideout. Makes things easier that way."

Marty and Logan went over the messages and the map again. "I think I'll start in Wichita," Marty announced. "From there, I'll start a leg search from Wichita to Salina. A gang like Carter's can't survive without somebody knowing about him. I'll just have to dig him out, I reckon." Marty looked at his friend. "I hope I haven't made it bad between you and Warren Swain."

Logan shook his head. "Warren knows what his brothers are. I told him I had no interest in them if they weren't active around here. I doubt if he will equate the capture of his brothers with my inquiry. If he does, I'll accept it, since the twins have to stand accountable for what they've done to your family and to others."

"Well, I reckon I'd better get ready for the trail — daylight's burning." Marty held out his hand. "Thanks for your help, Lo. I appreciate it, even if you did sort of back me into a corner."

"I sincerely hope you get them, Marty. Best of luck. Let me know how it comes out . . . or will I get to read it in the paper?"

"You mean you've seen the article about me?"

Logan laughed. "Sure have. It's been passed around the entire post by now. Berkowski's a real hero among the men, since he calls you his friend. Makes you seem about ten feet tall to the younger troops. They sort of take up for the underdog, since they're not too well liked around here either."

"Believe me, they wouldn't want to be as shunned as I've been at times."

"I suppose it goes with the territory, doesn't it?"

"So long, Lo. I'll send you a letter once I've looked things over out in Kansas."

"If you need me or Berkowski, just let us know. I think we'd both like a little excitement after all these months of garrison duty."

"Maybe I will, Lo. Maybe I will. All right if I go say my good-byes to Berkowski?"

"Certainly. He's probably at the stables, with the new recruits."

Marty bade his farewell to Berkowski and was on the trail before noon. As he rode, he mused over Logan's offer. It would be easier with someone watching his back. He decided to get a good look at the situation before busting ahead this time. He had moved too fast against Ace Richland, and all he got was a dead man for the effort.

"Not that he didn't deserve to die, ole hoss. I just wanted more information out of him before he did." His pony continued to jog on down the road, unresponsive to the musings of the man on his back.

Marty entered the office of Sheriff George Sedgwick in Wichita several days later. A stranger was seated in a chair beside the desk, talking to the sheriff. The two men looked up expectantly as Marty opened the door.

Sedgwick's eyes widened. He recognized Marty from their previous meetings, when Marty first hunted the Hulett gang of outlaws.

"Well look what the cat's drug in. Howdy, Ranger Keller. It's a pleasure to see Mr. Marty Keller, the famous bounty hunter. Man Killer? I sure hope you ain't here a'huntin' me." He laughed loudly.

Marty winced. "You saw the paper, too?"

Sedgwick laughed. "Shore did. One of the drovers from Texas had it in his saddlebags. Showed it to me when I mentioned about a Texas Ranger who was a'lookin' for some killers who slaughtered his family. You're gettin' plumb famous, boy."

"I sure wish I'd never said anything to that damned reporter."

Sedgwick laughed again. He turned his eyes to the young man sitting beside his desk. "Marty, this here is William Masterson. He's my new deputy. As soon as his brother, Bat, arrives from Kansas City, I'm retiring to my rockin' chair."

"Givin' up on the law?"

"It's a young man's game. I'm gettin' too old and slow. Will, meet Marty Keller, of Texas fame."

"Hello, Will."

"My pleasure, Mr. Keller." The young deputy had clear blue eyes and a heavy, dark moustache on his boyish face. His dark hair was long, almost to his collar. He was taller than the sheriff, but not as tall as Marty. He looked to be in his early or middle twenties, at best.

"Will, I imagine Marty has some palaverin' to do. Why don't you go on and make the afternoon rounds."

"Sure thing, Sheriff. See ya later, Mr. Keller."

Marty waited until the young deputy left the office. "My God, Sheriff. He looks like a babe in arms."

"He's gonna be a great lawman, mark my words. He says his brother, Bat, funny name ain't it? Bat Masterson. Says his brother is gonna be even a better deputy than him. Big things coming to Wichita, Keller. The railroad is buildin' this way. When it gits here, so will the trail herds. That means cowboys, money, drinkin', gamblin', and such. It'll be too much fer me to handle. So, I've arranged fer the Masterson brothers to become Wichita's law enforcement officers."

They exchanged small talk for a minute or two, then Marty got down to business. He pulled the map he and Major Logan had written on back in Shreveport. Marty explained the reasoning behind his theory regarding where the Carter gang might be located.

Sheriff Sedgwick looked at the map, tracing his finger over the area circled by Major Logan. "So you think the Carter gang might be hidin' out somewhere in this circle?"

"I think there's a very good chance that's so." Marty answered. "I plan to head up that way and see if my idea holds any water."

Sedgwick nodded, his face grave. "I have some information about that area you might find useful then. I've been gettin' disturbin' rumors that the law in a town right here" — he pressed his thumb down on the map — "has gone rotten."

"How's that?"

"I mean the rumor is that the law's bad there. Maybe in cahoots with outlaws and such. I ain't certain there's any truth to the story, but just the same, if you're headed to Bixley, Kansas, ride easy. Somethin's not right there."

"Thanks, Sheriff. I'm leaving for Bixley in the morning. Buy you a beer?"

CHAPTER 28
STAND ALONE AND
DIE

The route to Bixley was not marked by trail or road. Marty rode across the rolling prairie, heading north until he cut the stage line from Topeka to Santa Fe. "You just go north," Sheriff Sedgwick advised, "hit the Santa Fe Trail, and then follow it west until you see the turnoff to Bixley. It's up by a big lake, called Cheyenne Bottoms, I think. The town is built right on the eastern shore. I was up there just before the war, hunting renegade Arapahos raiding from Colorado Territory."

"How big a place is it?" Marty inquired.

"Wasn't much of a town then. Doubt if it's grown much since. Maybe a hunnerd people, a few more."

Marty rode steadily, determined to reach the suspect town as soon as possible. He felt as if he was finally approaching the fruition of a long and arduous search. He scanned the passing countryside, always alert for his need to know where he might find cover if needed. He also did not want to ride into any kind of ambush from his quarry.

He cut the Santa Fe Trail and turned to follow it west until he came to the turnoff to Bixley. The trail skirted the lake for several miles. As he crossed a small rise, he saw the little town lying before him. It was built in a long T-shaped layout, with the main north-south street crossing a single side street at the center of town. Off the long east-west main street, several side streets allowed the townspeople to live away from the main street, yet walk there with very little effort.

Marty paused, surveying the layout of the town. The livery was at the far south end of town, a church with a pointed steeple at the north end. The saloon was at the intersection of the two principal streets, across from what had to be the hotel. There were only three entrances to the town, as none of the cross streets intersected the north-south street. In the portion of town where the citizens lived, all the streets ran north and south, paralleling the main street.

Marty patted the neck of his horse as he sat there. "Be fairly easy to defend, old hoss. Block off any two of the intersecting streets and your enemy will be channeled up the other street, right into your guns."

He sat there a few more minutes, resting his horse and studying the town. Finally, he chucked his horse along and rode toward the livery. He climbed down, stretched the kinks out of his legs and loosened the girth of his saddle. As he untied the packs on his packhorse, the livery owner walked up. He was obviously the town blacksmith; his brawny arms were covered in soot from the furnace.

"Howdy, stranger. Name's Stephens. I own this livery and the smithy. Welcome to Bixley. Be stayin' long?"

"Can't rightly say at this time, Mr. Stephens, maybe just a bit. I've just about run out of cash. On my way to California. May have to work a spell and build up my poke again. Anybody hirin' at the moment?"

"Can't say as I know of anyone. My rates are on the wall there. Can you handle it? If not, I'll stake you to a night, oats fer the horses, and a bed in the straw pile fer you."

Marty glanced at the rate list tacked on the barn wall. "Fifty cents a night for my horses. How 'bout I give you five dollars? That take care of the three of us for a week?"

The smithy's eyes widened in surprise. "Shore will, Mr. . . . ?"

"Keller's the name. Call me Marty, if you like." He placed his saddle on a stall railing and piled the packs on the floor beneath. "I suppose I oughta mosey on over to the sheriff's office and check in. He'll likely be interested in a stranger showing up outta the blue like me."

The brawny blacksmith's eyes narrowed in concern. "That bastard will likely do more than that. If you're broke, he'll likely throw you in jail, fine you your saddle and packs, then run you outta town."

"I declare, Mr. Stephens, you don't seem to hold the law in much accord around here."

Stephens wiped his thick hands on a dirty rag pulled from a pocket. "You seem a bit strange yourself, Mr. Keller. You ride in here, supposedly on your way to California, out of money and looking to stay for 'just a bit.' Your clothes ain't dirty, your guns are cleaner than my wife's dinner plates, and your horse ain't been ridden hard in a month. You're supposedly broke, yet you pull a five-dollar bill outa your pocket faster than a cat can spit. A fella might think you'd like to look around without drawin' too much attention to yourself. That you might be the answer to a problem this town has with its law. Are you a Federal marshal,

341

Mr. Keller?"

"No, but I'm more than I seem, Mr. Stephens, that much is true."

"I don't care what you are, as long as you clean up Bixley and get rid of Thompson and his deputies."

Marty smiled. "Well, Mr. Stephens, I may do just that. As long as it gets me to some men who are riding with Long Tom Carter."

"You have to. If yur not gonna try, I may as well tell Sheriff Thompson and save myself any trouble later on."

"No, I don't think so, Mr. Stephens. I suspect you're tired of what's going on around here. You've been waiting for someone like me for a long time. The question I have is are there more who feel like you do?"

Stephens nodded. "I'm certain there are some. I just don't know if they're mad enough to risk gettin' killed to make a change. Some are just too afraid, I guess. I'm pretty certain George Benson feels the way I do. His daughter, Betsy, was assaulted by two of Carter's hooligans. That's who runs this town, Long Tom Carter, the foulest scum a man can be. He raids other towns, kills, robs, takes what he wants, then hides out here in Bixley. And we've allowed it, been too cowardly to stop him. I'm ashamed, Mr. Keller, and I'm ready to help you."

"Why don't we sort of ease into this, Mr. Stephens? Let's go see Mr. Benson as soon as it's dark. See what he has to say."

"Then you are here to take care of Carter and his outlaws?"

"Sort of, I suppose. I'm here to kill a couple of them, at least."

"It'll have to include Longwood, or there'll be hell to pay."

Marty nodded. He was getting in deep, but it might be his only chance to get the Swain twins. He busied himself rubbing his horse with a piece of burlap sack. He would go along with the hopes of Stephens, and see where they led, for now.

"Well, it's near suppertime. Would you care to eat with the missus and me? It may be plain fare, but there'll be plenty of it, and my Sarah can cook a right smart meal."

"I accept with pleasure, Mr. Stephens. Then, we'll visit your Mr. . . . ?"

"George Benson. Owns the dry goods store here in Bixley."

After the meal, they walked along the darkened street to Benson's store. It was just after eight, and Mr. Benson was bringing in the outside displays before locking up for the night. Only the saloon was active;

every other business in the town was closed.

Even as they walked past the tack shop, the owner put out the inside lights, plunging the store and sidewalk outside into darkness.

Benson answered the knock at his front door. "Hello there, Nicholas. How's business at the livery?"

"Hello, George. I'd like you to meet Marty Keller. He's gonna kill Long Tom and his gang."

"What?" Marty protested. "I never said that."

Stephens laughed. "Had you going there for a minute, didn't I? Seriously, George, Mr. Keller is here to help us get rid of Sheriff Thompson, Long Tom and all the others."

"By himself?"

Marty held up his hands. "Wait a minute, fellas. Let's start over. I may be able to do something, Mr. Benson. First, I'd like to get the lay of the land, see what can be done. Second, Mr. Benson, is to find out who else can we count on, if it comes to a showdown."

Benson shook his head. "I'm not certain. I think there are several folks who want a change in Bixley, but we're not gunfighters, Mr. Keller. I don't think you can count on anyone. Well, me, I guess. But I can barely shoot a rifle. I'm certainly no gun hand. To make matters worse, Sheriff Thompson has pretty much confiscated most of our weapons. We got a few shotguns for game birds and such. But not much in the way of fightin' weapons."

Marty thought for a minute. "Weapons can be obtained. Maybe I can also get some help from a few friends of mine. First, I need some time to look around." He turned to Stephens. "What can I do to spend some time here without bringing the sheriff down on me?"

Stephens turned to Benson. "George, why not take him on as a your new clerk? You can say he's your nephew, stopping off on his way to California. He's working to build up his stake before he heads on west."

"I suppose so. I imagine Sheriff Thompson will want to talk to him as soon as he knows he's here."

"Don't try and hide him. Make it all seem out in the open like. Thompson thinks he's got us so buffaloed that he don't have to worry about us, anyway."

The three men discussed several options without making any definite plans as to how to rid the town of its crooked sheriff or how to get Longwood and the Swain twins into town to face Marty. He slept in the hayloft of Stephens' livery, and was at the dry goods store when it opened the next morning. Reluctantly, he left his pistol rolled up in his bedroll at the livery.

Marty actually enjoyed interacting with the customers who came in. He was introduced as Benson's nephew, a man who needed money to continue his trip to California. By ten a.m., he had met several citizens, and even made a sale of fabric to the wife of the local butcher. He looked up from stocking a display counter as a tall man with a sheriff's star on his chest walked into the store. A huge man wearing a deputy's badge on his scuffed leather vest and a dark scowl on his face followed the sheriff. The burly deputy took a position where he could watch the door and Marty at the same time.

"Well, howdy there, friend. I hear you're gonna be workin' for ole George fer a spell. What's yur name?"

"I'm Martin Keller, Sheriff. Pleased to meet ya."

"Just so you know, Keller. I'm the law in Bixley. Stay outta trouble. Don't butt in or mess with the local citizens. Let me know if you plan on leavin'. Unnerstand?"

"Certainly, Sheriff."

"Good. Come on, Butch. We need to make the rounds." He spotted George Benson standing in the doorway of his office, off the main business area. "Hello, George. How's yur daughter?" Laughing, the sheriff walked out of the store, the hulking deputy right behind him.

Marty watched them walk down the sidewalk. He turned to George Benson. "I think I have an idea, George. Let's meet with Mr. Stephens tonight."

The three men sat at Stephens' dining room table that evening. Marty laid out his tentative plan. "You'll need me to go to Wichita to pick up goods, Mr. Benson. I'll send the telegrams from there."

"Will you wait for them in Wichita?" Benson was visibly uneasy, his eyes darting from the door to the windows, checking to see if anyone was spying on them.

"No, I want to get on back here. If this thing is going to work, there are some things that have to be done in advance."

Marty stopped the empty wagon in front of the sheriff's office the next morning. The deputy who had accompanied Thompson the previous day sat in a chair, leaning back against the wall of the building. He dropped the chair to all four legs and went inside the office.

Thompson stepped out of the office. "Howdy there, Keller. Goin' somewhere?"

"My uncle is sending me to Wichita to pick up some goods. You said to let you know if I left town."

"Be back shortly?"

"Yep. Seven, eight days at worst, I reckon."

The sheriff gave Marty an insincere smile and nodded. "Be seein' you then."

Marty tipped his hat and chucked the reins of the team. He slowly rode out of town and once out of sight, pushed hard to Wichita. Arriving there, he checked in with Sheriff Sedgwick. "You were right, Sheriff. The sheriff there is a cousin of Long Tom Longwood. He's got the town sewed up tight, with a couple of thugs as deputies."

"What's your plan?"

"Any chance I can get help from the state of Kansas or the Federals?"

"Maybe. But it will take a good while. You can ask the army fer help, but they're busy with the Injun problem, so they might not act fer a spell, either."

"So it appears my best bet is to handle the problem myself?"

"Can you? You're talkin' about being outnumbered by ten to one."

"I'm going to send a telegram to a friend over in Shreveport. He said he might be interested in helping."

A week later, Marty was sitting on the hotel veranda when Sergeant Berkowski drove up in the Conestoga wagon. A well-built soldier, dressed in patched pants and a faded shirt, was sitting beside him, a rifle cradled in his arms. Two other men — dressed, like Berkowski, in civilian clothing — were riding alongside the wagon on mules.

"Hello, Sergeant. Where's Major Logan?"

"He sends his regrets, Marty. He's been recalled to Baton Rouge for meetings with the area commander. He shore wanted to come, but couldn't. He did send Privates Conway, O'Brien, and McKean with me. McKean's brother was kilt by Longwood's raiders during an attack on Ft. Gibson during the war, so he's got a blood feud with the skunk. O'Brien is the best shot in the company, 'cept fer me. Conway is a smart lad, a good soldier. Maybe he can help you with yur plans, and he'll do in a pinch, I'm certain. Hell, all the lads will."

"Good enough. Climb on down. Did you bring the stuff I asked for in my telegram?"

"Yep, it's all in the wagon."

"I picked up two Winchester rifles and six

hundred rounds of ammunition, just in case. Well, I've gotta get back to Bixley before the sheriff gets suspicious. You three come along in four days. Understand?"

"You got it, Marty. We'll be there a week from tomorrow, four lost souls on the way to Santa Fe."

"Stop at the livery. The owner, Mr. Stephens, is one of ours. He'll be looking for you."

"Be seein' you then."

"Come in ready. There's gonna be gunfire shortly thereafter."

"Marty, my friend, I can't wait."

CHAPTER 29
BAITING THE TRAP

Marty made certain he rode into Bixley in the light of day. He stopped behind the Benson store and immediately began to unload the supplies he had purchased in Wichita. At the bottom of a barrel of crackers he had hidden the ammunition. Marty was manhandling the barrel off the wagon when Sheriff Thompson suddenly appeared. He engaged Marty in small talk about the trip, while he carefully inspected the goods Marty had in the wagon.

Marty acted politely disinterested as he worked at unloading the boxes and barrels. The rifles were wrapped in bolts of cloth, bright calico prints and plaids, something he hoped the sheriff would be unlikely to investigate. His short, blunt response to the sheriff's questions soon drove Thompson away, convinced that the new clerk at Benson's store was just a half step above a dimwit.

Marty carried the goods inside Benson's store and stacked them in the storeroom. As he finished, Mr. Benson came back into the room, wiping his hands nervously.

"Did you git the stuff you needed?"

"Yessir. Also got the army to lend me four soldiers. They'll be here in four days. Once they're here, we can put our plan into motion."

"Only four. Damn, Marty. Carter has fifteen, twenty men at his place, plus the two with Sheriff Thompson. We'll need more than four."

"Perhaps. But, we'll deal with Sheriff Thompson before we start anything with Long Tom's bunch — and in fact, a few good men can take the starch out of a much larger group if they do it right. I'll tell you how once we start our planning. Were you able to get any recruits for our cause?"

Benson nodded glumly. "I suppose. Nicholas convinced the preacher to help. Reverend King says he'll help in anyway he can, but he won't take a life, so I don't know what good he'll be. I talked to Joey McDonough and he'll join us. He's not yet twenty, but last year one of Carter's men got into an argument with him and pistol-whipped the snot outta him. Sheriff Thompson put him in jail for ten days and let the other man go free. Joey's been nursin' a grudge ever since. I don't know how much help he'll be in a gun battle, but that's all we've found so far. I've been a little uneasy about pushin' the folks too hard. Some of 'em still think it's good to have the money Long Tom Carter spends in the town, and some are too scared to try anything."

"We'll make do with what we've got, Mr. Benson. Can you come over to Mr. Stephens' house this evening, say right after supper? Deliver a bolt of cloth to Mrs. Stephens, or something as an excuse for the visit."

"Sure, I'll be there."

"Ask the preacher to stop by, too. Bring Joey with you. Have him carry whatever you bring to Mrs. Stephens. I'll talk to everybody then, see what I think."

At the meeting that evening, Marty took stock of his citizen recruits. Young Joey, still filling out a body that was at best average, was eager but untested. The preacher, nearing sixty, slight of frame and with a full, gray beard, was worthless except as a messenger or loader of empty weapons. Still, they were ready to serve, agreeing that Sheriff Thompson had to go, and the town needed to rid itself of the influence of Long Tom Carter.

"Preacher King," Marty probed, "you understand that I mean to kill some of these vermin, don't you?"

"God forgive you, Mr. Keller, I do. I'll not take human life, as I believe that's God's prerogative, but I'll help you act as God's right hand in this matter. We have to purge these evil men from our midst. I'll load your rifles for you, treat you if you are hurt, and hide you from them if you fail, but I'll not shoot at anyone."

"How about you, Joey? You ever shoot at a man before or been shot at?"

"No sir, Mr. Keller. But I'm ready. I got good reasons to stand with you, and I won't let you down."

Marty simply nodded; he'd heard men boast before. Once the bullets started flying, it was a new game. Some men stuck and some ran at the first whisper of hot lead past their ear. He pulled out a pencil and a sheet of paper. He began to draw a map of the town, aided by the men. Marty needed to know exactly where every entrance and exit into the town was, and what was located in all directions for a four-hundred-yard radius.

By the end of the evening, he had a pretty accurate map to refer to while he planned the coming action. Marty gathered the others around the table, all looking at the map.

"It's not too bad. Main Street runs north-south, and Lake Street runs east-west. No other way to get to the saloon or jail unless you come down the alleys, or through the buildings on either side of the saloon, or the stores on either side of the dress shop across the street. When we start this, we'll send the shopkeepers and customers home and barricade the stores so Long Tom's men can't move through them easily. A couple of men on the roof of your place, Mr. Benson, can pin down anyone in the saloon and stop any charge down Lake Street to the jail."

Marty pointed at the church. "Here's where we hit them first and hopefully hurt them badly. I'll have a man with me who can shoot accurately at long range like I can. We were both snipers during the war. We'll both open fire from the bell tower. Our objective will be to engage Long Tom's men at long range, getting as many as we can early. Then, he'll be forced east around to the gully outside of town and work his way to where he can come down Lake Street. If we're ready for him there, and if we hurt him badly enough, they should go on to the south side of town and attack up Main Street past the livery."

Marty tapped his pencil on the rough

map. "What I want is for him to head to his saloon. If we can trap him in there, we'll beat him. At least that's how I want it to go. Someone will have to make certain he doesn't come down from the north along the lake's edge to the west of town. A single man in the church bell tower could stop them easily. That will be you, Joey. Once we have them moving around town toward the south, Sergeant Berkowski and I will come to either the center of town and join you, Mr. Benson, or go on to the livery and join you, Mr. Stephens. Each of you will have at least one soldier with you. Reverend King, I think you should be with Mr. Benson to start. You can load for him and my soldiers."

Satisfied that his new recruits understood what he was thinking, Marty suggested they depart, one at a time, to their own homes. He went to his bed in the hayloft of the livery. For a long time he lay awake, reviewing his plan and wishing he had some whiskey to dull the nervous energy building up in his gut. His day of retribution was fast approaching.

The next morning, Marty walked over to the church. Reverend King was sweeping out the sanctuary when he showed up. "Morning, Reverend."

"God's blessing on you, Mr. Keller. What

can I do for you?"

"I'd like to see the view from your bell tower."

"Don't let Sheriff Thompson or his deputies see you."

"I checked. They're eating breakfast over at the restaurant. They just started. We've got an hour before they'll be out, if they hold to form."

Marty followed the preacher to an anteroom where the stairs to the bell tower were located. He quickly climbed the steps to the belfry, and cautiously peered over the parapet at the surrounding countryside. He had a clear view to the north, from which Carter and his men would most likely ride into the town. As the ground fell away to the east, the gully that Stephens had described became visible. It was heavily wooded and made good cover, but was well over three hundred yards from the tower. "No way they can hit anyone here, unless it's pure, blind luck," he muttered to himself.

To the south, the gully opened up into clear countryside again. Waist-high wheat grew in a broad field there, all the way to the edge of town and the southern end of Main Street. Marty could even see movement on Lake Street, the second artery into the town. "We'll have him in our sights for a long time," he muttered. "We oughta be able to hurt him bad, long before he gets in close."

He climbed back down the stairs to the sanctuary. "The wood up in the tower is way too thin to stop a rifle bullet, Reverend. We'll have to reinforce it. I'll have one of my soldiers do that when they arrive. You mention it at services tomorrow. Ask for donations to cover the repairs. That will allay any suspicions when we start."

"I don't care for the house of God being used for such ungodly acts. Mr. Keller." The preacher glared at Marty, and swept the dirt viciously with his straw broom.

"Just think of the results, Reverend. God will be happy about that." Marty walked away, not interested in arguing religion with the man. He had more pressing things to worry about.

He returned to Benson's store and climbed on the roof. The city jail and office building were next door to the south. It was a story higher, so he went back and got a small ladder. After climbing onto the jail's roof, he had a clear shot down Lake Street to the edge of the woods that marked the gully outside the town. Additionally, the building's façade, of heavy wood, made for very effective cover. The saloon, which was Longwood's, thus a logical place for his men to hole up in, was directly across the street from the jail. While Marty's men on the roof could do great harm to anyone trying to ride into town on Lake Street, the overhang around the saloon, which was built in the shape of a boxy "L," would protect anybody on the ground floor from fire. He would have two men at ground level firing into the interior of the building. One man could cover the windows of the sporting girls' rooms on the second floor, he decided.

Jotting his observations and plans into a little notebook, he then climbed back down into Benson's store. The busy owner looked at him, but said nothing. Marty helped Benson package some goods for a customer, then walked down to the livery stable.

Mr. Stephens showed Marty every nook and cranny of the place, as Marty expected the stable to be where he would have the final showdown with Longwood. "I'll need two wagons filled with full grain sacks to block off the north end of Main Street, Mr. Stephens."

"The feed store is at that end of the street. We can get the wagons from Fritz Diehl's freight business, right next door."

"Will he help us?"

"I ain't too certain. He's a dour ole Dutchie — don't say much, or socialize much, neither. I'd say wait until it's time to fish or cut bait."

"What about the doc or the apothecary store owner?"

"Old Doc Adams is too much of a boozer to trust. He'll fix us up, but he spends a lot of time swillin' booze at the saloon. The apothecary owner is in St. Louis, visitin' his kin. His store is shut up till he returns."

"How about the empty store east of the saloon on Lake? Either it or the doc's place have a door to the saloon?"

"No, there's the two back doors of the saloon and the front door at the corner of Lake and Main. That's it, 'cept for the windows to the front."

"How about in back?"

"They got wrought-iron bars over 'em to keep people from breakin' in."

"Good. I want you to make me a block for each of the back doors. That will keep anyone inside from getting out that way once we put them up. I'm hoping to funnel the few remaining outlaws into the saloon from the rear as we wear them down out here. Then we'll block the doors, and stand them off until they surrender or try and come out the front, right into our massed fire."

"How do you want the blocks made?"

Marty drew his design in the dust. "About half the height and width of a door, made out of one-inch rod. Then two long legs off at an angle. We'll jam the bar against the door and drive the long legs into the dirt. It should be a formidable barrier to getting out."

"I see where you're goin'. I kin do it easy. Be done in a few hours."

"Wait until the day before we strike. My men will be here in three days, if you need any help."

"The widow Jenkins' house is right behind the saloon. I'll make 'em and put 'em there fer safe keepin'. That way we don't have to carry 'em too far — they'll be pretty heavy."

"Good. By the way, I'll need all the horseshoe nails you have."

"Oh?"

"Yep. I'm gonna make hand bombs and land mines."

"How?"

"I'll explain as soon as my men arrive with the wagon. They'll have a couple hundred pounds of power along with them. We'll use the mines to stop a rush down Lake Street, and the hand bombs in case they get too close for us to shoot."

"Well, I got a couple of barrels of nails. You oughta have plenty."

Over the next two days Marty walked around the town as much as he could, delivering items for Mr. Benson, learning the exact location of every house, alley, and empty lot — whatever might have an impact on his plans.

Four days after Marty returned from Wichita, Sergeant Berkowski and his three men rode into the town. They stopped at the livery as instructed, quickly hid their smuggled arms and explosives in the hay, and drifted over to the saloon or restaurant. Sheriff Thompson soon found out they were in town, and cornered Berkowski at the restaurant, where he quizzed him about his intentions.

"We'll let my lead hoss get his feet shod and shake off that bruise, then be on our way. Say, there any chance of findin' any work whilst we're here? We could use some more spendin' money."

Thompson ruefully shook his head. "Nope, I doubt it. We're a poor place — hardly enough to keep the townsfolk busy. I suggest you boys head on out as soon as yur hoss is able. Meanwhile, obey the laws and don't bother the folks. We aim to keep it nice and peaceful hereabouts."

"You got it, Sheriff."

Marty had the men walk the town the next day, familiarizing themselves with anticipated positions critical in their coming fight. From Benson's store, they all studied the view across the street toward the saloon, their prime target. O'Brien and Conway climbed up onto the jailhouse roof and looked down Lake Street and at the second floor of the saloon, just across the fifty feet of Main Street.

The next morning, Marty put the three soldiers to work making the hand bombs and land mines. They used empty, one-quart whiskey bottles or one-gallon whiskey crocks, filled half and half with powder and nails. He had the men make a dozen of the deadly bombs.

Benson spoke up. "I just cut up twenty-five dollars worth of sulfur matches. You sure you'll need that many?"

Marty nodded. "Yeah. We add them to the powder. When a bullet hits the mixture, a match head will light, igniting the powder and *boom!* we have our explosion. We did it like this during the war. It'll work."

Marty inspected the first land mine, and nodded his approval. He turned to Sergeant Berkowski. "You bring another buffalo gun, like I asked, Stan?"

"Brought two. One fer me and one fer O'Brien. We stopped outside of Wichita and got real familiar with 'em. Both of us is hittin' the targets at three hunnerd yards every time and at four hunnerd most of the time. Conway and McKean are both hitting targets with their Spencers at two hundred."

"Good." Marty beamed at the old sergeant. "Send McKean and Conway over to the church as soon as they're done here. Have them line the inside of the bell tower with the heavy boards I had delivered yesterday. Be sure they cut the firing slits as I described them to you."

"Understood, Marty. They will."

"Excellent. Now, let's take a walk." Marty led the old sergeant to the area just out of town on Lake Street. "If we put the mines here and here" — he pointed to the spot — "could O'Brien hit 'em from the top of the jail?"

"You say they'll be made from one-gallon whiskey crocks, and that they'll go boom iffen he hits 'em with a rifle slug?"

Marty nodded. "Yep. They'll be filled with powder and horseshoe nails. I plan to put two here and two more there." He pointed back closer to town. "I want the outlaws to ride on to the south, not enter here on Lake."

"Iffen he can't, I'll drop-kick his sorry ass all the way to Shreveport, Marty."

"If he can't, we may be too dead to worry about it, Sergeant."

"Understood, Marty. It'll get done. What next?"

"Tomorrow. We take out the sheriff and send out our challenge. Then we hunker down, wait for Carter to react. I hope he'll come all out, ready to shoot up the place. If he does, we'll have a nasty surprise waiting for him. And I'll get to meet the Swain brothers with a gun in my hand."

CHAPTER 30
THE TRAP IS SET

After a leisurely breakfast, Marty headed for the livery stable. Sergeant Berkowski, his three soldiers, George Benson, Reverend King, Joey, and Mr. Stephens were already there. Some sat and smoked, while the Reverend and Benson paced back and forth, nervously.

"Good morning, everyone," Marty said. "Well, today's the day. Everyone ready?"

The assembled men nodded or grunted their agreement. Marty looked at each one in turn. "It's gonna be a hard day before it's over. Anyone not ready for come what may oughta take off now." He waited for a second, then nodded his head as everyone stayed put. Marty turned to Private O'Brien. "You finish reinforcing the belfry like I showed you?"

"Yessir. Wood reinforcement all around. Three firing slots, cut low on the north, east, and south sides."

"Why'd you cut 'em low like that, Marty?" Berkowski asked.

"Something I discovered in the war, Stan. When we shot at you Yanks from a high window, if we cut a firing slit low, the return fire tore up the area around the opening of the window, but few ever hit down where we were. It must be human nature to shoot at the larger opening, even though your mind tells you the fire is coming from below it."

Marty turned to Joey. "Joey, you'll start out in the belfry with Sergeant B and me. When we leave, you'll be on your own. If they rush you to where you can't get a shot at them because they're right below you, toss a couple of the hand bombs at them. I cut the fuse at three seconds, so you'll have plenty of time to throw it after it's lit. You have two candles in your pocket?"

"Yep, I shore do."

"Keep 'em lit once we leave, so you won't have to keep striking matches. Mr. Benson, you bring the fishing pole and the strips of colored cloth?"

"Yes. Red, white, and blue — twelve of each."

"Joey, you'll be our eyes once Sergeant B and I leave. You hang out a strip of blue for every man you see going through the houses toward town north of Lake Street, a strip of red for every man coming toward the saloon from south of Lake Street, and white for every man you see working his way toward the livery at the south end of town. I'll give you my binoculars when I leave. Got it?"

"Yessir. I'll keep a good eye out."

"You must make certain nobody comes down the back road next to the lake. That puts them behind us. If someone does get past you, tie three strips together, like a kite tail. Understand?"

"Got it."

Marty looked at O'Brien. You'll be on top of the jail. You certain you can hit the mines when they ride past them?"

"You can count on it, sir."

"Good. I will."

"Conway, you, McKean, the Reverend, and Mr. Benson will hole up in his store. You'll have to take on any riders coming up Lake Street that get by the land mines and O'Brien's fire. Once the outlaws go into the saloon, which is what we want them to do, just keep them pinned in until the rest of us join you. Mr. Stephens, you'll start off alone in your barn. As the outlaws move around the town, someone will join you. Don't let them get past you before we get there."

Marty passed out the heavy Sharps buffalo rifles, one to Sergeant Berkowski and one to Private O'Brien. He gave each of the others two Spencer carbines and one hundred rounds of ammunition. He gave Reverend King a case of bullets for the Spencers and several boxes of .44s for the Winchester rifles he and Berkowski carried.

"You'll be responsible for refilling the rifles of the men with Mr. Benson, Reverend."

The preacher nodded, his face white and his Adam's apple bobbing up and down in his skinny throat.

"Now," Marty smiled. "It's time we started. McKean, you and Conway take the wagons down to the feed store and load them with sacks of grain. Then park them at the north end of Main, where I showed you. You'll fight from the backs of the wagons after you've moved them out to block the street. Once the outlaws break off and head for the woods east of town, take up your positions at the center of town."

The two troopers nodded, unable to conceal their excitement at the upcoming battle.

A heavy-set man with a balding head stepped into the livery. He paused at the sight of eight heavily armed men gathered together. In a guttural voice, he spoke to Stephens. "Herr Stephens, de vagons you haf ordered. Dey are ready. Vat is goin' on?"

Quickly, the livery owner outlined their plans. "I hope you won't oppose us, Fritz."

The old wagon master shook his head. "No. Dey need to be put avay. Dey are not good fer Bixley. Vat can I do to help?"

"Grab a rifle and stand with me, Fritz," Mr. Stephens declared. "We'll be in my barn, if the outlaws try and come into town from the south."

"Good. I am vit you, by tunder."

Marty sent the two soldiers off with the wagons. Then he turned to the others. Mr. Benson, you all stay out of sight while I take care of Sheriff Thompson. If I fail there, you'll not be involved. Sergeant B, you ready to take on our crooked sheriff and his men?"

"Ready, sir."

"Call me Marty. I'm not in the army anymore."

"Can't — not when I'm thinkin' about fightin'. You're Cap'n Keller, and that's that."

"Well then, let's get it done."

Marty led the way out of the livery, followed by Benson and the others. He waited until they had entered Benson's store, then pointed at the alley beside the doctor's office.

"Watch my back from here, Sergeant. I'll stand on the corner and call Thompson out."

"You got it, sir." The old soldier ducked into the alley, blending into the shadows until only the tip of his buffalo gun was visible.

Marty glanced around as he walked to the corner of Lake and Main Streets, just across from the door to the sheriff's office. He could see McKean and Conway rapidly piling sacks of grain into the two wagons. Marty stepped off the sidewalk onto the dusty street. He had the sun on his back. He wiped his lips with the back of his hand, then shouted loudly.

"Sheriff Thompson, you sorry son of a bitch! Step out here and look at me."

The door to the office opened, and Thompson peeked around the corner of the doorjamb. When he saw Marty standing alone in the street, he grinned and stepped out, followed by one of his hulking deputies. "You lookin' fer trouble, store clerk?"

"Thompson, you're done for in Bixley. Drop your guns and raise your hands. I'm arresting you in the name of law and order."

Thompson glanced around. Several store

owners had heard the commotion, and watched from the doorways of their establishments. He could not allow the challenge to go unanswered. "You just put the last nail in yur coffin, store clerk." He nodded to his deputy, who had moved off a few steps to get a better angle on Marty, then pulled his pistol, as did the deputy.

Marty was as smooth as the long hours of practice had made him. His first shot hit the sheriff square in the middle of his chest, knocking him back into the open doorway of the office. His second hit the deputy's right wrist, breaking it and causing his shot to fly harmlessly into the ground at Marty's feet. The burly deputy screamed in pain and fell to his knees, cradling his broken wrist in his other hand. Marty ran toward the two downed men, his pistol ready for the second deputy to come out of the office.

As he started up the steps to the sidewalk, Sergeant Berkowski's big rifle boomed, and Marty felt the whistle of a massive bullet fly past his head. He ducked and looked at Berkowski. The soldier had his rifle aimed down the street, toward the church. Marty spun that way. The second deputy was sprawled on the sidewalk beside the dry goods store, so obviously dead he did not warrant a second look.

"Sorry, Cap'n. He came outta the store and had a bead on ya. I couldn't wait." Berkowski hurried toward Marty, loading his rifle as he did.

"Looks like you saved my bacon, Sergeant. Thanks."

"No problem. How's our two fish?"

"Go get the doctor. They're gonna need some patching, I think."

The men in Benson's store came out, rifles in hand. Marty pointed toward the saloon. "Private O'Brien, take some men and arrest the bartenders and gamblers in the saloon. They'll all be on Thompson's side. Quickly, before any get away."

O'Brien and Benson ran toward the saloon door, where the bartender stood frozen in amazement, watching the activity. Soon, he and three gamblers were in the jail's cells, along with the body of the slain deputy. Sheriff Thompson was gravely wounded, and lay sedated on one of the deputy's cots in an inner office. The wounded deputy was getting his broken wrist fixed by the rummy doctor, whose hands shook as badly as the injured man's.

After the groaning deputy had his wrist wrapped and immobilized in a sling, Marty marched him to the livery, motioning for Stephens and Diehl to stay out of the moaning deputy's sight. Marty did not want to risk the man getting an accurate count of how many men opposed the Longwood gang.

"Ride out to Long Tom's place," Marty ordered the deputy. "Tell him he's banned from Bixley forever. If he ever shows his face in town again, he'll be shot down like the mangy cur that he is. He's to also send in the Swain twins, unarmed, to stand trial for murder. If he doesn't, I'll hang his cousin in their place, then raid his ranch later for both of them. Get going now."

"My arm's hurt, Keller. I don't know if I can make it."

Marty helped shove the injured deputy on the horse. "You're lucky I don't shoot you again, just for the pleasure of watching you bleed. And I will, if you're not outta sight in one minute."

The man galloped away, holding his injured wrist to shield it from more painful jolts than necessary. Marty returned to the front of the jail. Benson was there waiting for him.

"We're sending everyone home from the town. We're locking up all the stores and boarding up the windows."

"Good. Be sure and get those whores outta the second floor of the saloon while you're at it."

"What'll I do with 'em?"

"Lock them in one of the empty stores, I don't care." He looked at Benson. "You certain about the time we have?"

"Sure. There's no way on earth they can get here before noon." Benson hurried off to clear the second floor of the saloon.

Marty saw Joey McDonough ducking out of a store across the street. "Joey, come here, please."

The young man hurried over. "Yessir, Mr. Keller?"

"Take some sandwiches and my binoculars. Get on up in the belfry. I want you to keep watch, in case anyone tries to sneak into town. Be sure and take the fishing pole with you. I want to see how the streamers look from back here. Put it out for a minute and then pull it in. Shout when you're ready for us to see it."

"Yessir. I shorely will." Joey hurried off, thrilled at the importance of his mission.

Marty and the others placed the land mines at the edge of town beyond Lake Street. Four of them were staggered along a hundred-yard line on either side of the road. Marty went up on the roof of the jail and made certain O'Brien had a clear shot at each one. He called out for everyone to stand where they could see the whiskey jugs, then told O'Brien, "Let's see you hit the farthest one on the left."

O'Brien flashed a confident grin, aimed his Sharps and fired off a round. At the mine, a tremendous explosion shook the ground and a mighty cloud of smoke and dust boiled upwards. As the sound reverberated off the building, Marty heard a shout from the onlookers.

"That's what Long Tom's riding into when he tries to come down Lake Street," Marty shouted down to the excited spectators. He patted O'Brien's arm. "Good shooting, Private. When the first rider passes the jug, you cut loose. If any keep on coming, light off the others as they pass. Got it?"

"Yessir, Captain." He grinned at Marty.

Marty glared at Berkowski. "You tell your men to 'sir' me?"

"You bet, Cap'n. Soldiers like discipline. They want you to be a cap'n. I'm glad you are."

They both turned as Joey shouted from the belfry. They watched as the pole with the streamer on it snaked out from the back side of the opening. "We can see the streamers fine, Sergeant. Make certain everyone knows what they mean."

"That I will, Cap'n." Berkowski hurried off to check everything again.

Marty headed for the two wagons parked on both sides of the northern end of Main Street. A rope had been tied to each wagon tongue, then looped around a pillar of the store roof across the street. In turn, the rope was tied to a draft horse, standing patiently in the sun, awaiting the next command from its masters.

Upon command, the two horses would pull the wagons into the center of the street, where they would impede any entrance by riders. Marty saw the feed sacks piled along the wooden sides. The two men crouched inside would be protected from any bullets that penetrated the thin walls of the wagon box.

Marty looked up. Joey was leaning out of the belfry, scanning the horizon with the binoculars.

"See anything?" Marty shouted up.

"Nope, nary a thing, yet."

"Don't worry, they'll be here. You can count on it."

"And we'll be ready for 'em," the young man shouted down. "They can count on that, and they ain't even countin'."

Marty walked back toward George Benson's store. It was almost time to get ready for the dance. "Meg, darlin', here I go. Two more notches to carve on your casket. Pray to God I get it done."

CHAPTER 31
RETRIBUTION

Long Tom Carter was not in the best of moods when the injured deputy from Bixley rode into his ranch yard. His head had been pounding for two days now, and even whiskey was nothing more than a momentary cure. When he heard that his cousin had been ambushed and cruelly shot down, his rage was monumental.

"How many of them sumbitches was there?"

"I ain't certain," the deputy groaned. His wrist was throbbing badly, and he felt light headed and feverish. His wound was bleeding again, and he worried about bleeding out while the enraged Thompson quizzed him. "I think there was two, maybe three. Maybe more, I dunno."

"What the hell do you know, you worthless piece of horse shit. You was supposed to protect Lawrence, not let him get shot and captured."

"They caught us by surprise, Long Tom. They shot me afore I had a chance to draw."

Long Tom's face grew livid with anger. "So they're gonna hang my cousin, are they? So I'm banned from Bixley, am I? So they think they're gonna come on my ranch and take two of my men, do they? Well, by God, it's time we showed the people of Bixley just what happens to towns what don't get in line. You men saddle up. Big Joe, how many men we got here?"

"We're at full strength, Major. We got twenty-two, plus you and me."

"Good. Everybody goes. Men, we're gonna git our fill of whiskey, women, and money from Bixley. Get yur guns and saddle up. We ride in ten minutes."

The motley crew of outlaws whooped a ragged cheer as they ran to do his bidding. Nothing was more fun than pillaging a town from top to bottom. Every man grabbed his weapons, extra ammo, and a sack to carry stolen booty in. No one wanted to be the last man ready to ride.

As Long Tom stepped out of his front door, a rifle in his hand and twin pistols in holsters on his hips, the wounded deputy spoke up from the edge of the porch. "Whata 'bout me, Long Tom? Ya want me to wait here alone? I need some doctorin'."

"Vince Varrier, you worthless sack of dog droppins, yur a'ridin' into Bixley with me. Yur gonna be the first man of the pack, and if ya even try and slack off, I'm gonna fill yur worthless hide with lead. Now, git on yur hoss and shut yur mouth, afore I kill ya right here and now."

Long Tom mounted his horse and shouted to his men. "A fifty-dollar gold piece to the man who brings me the head of the sumbitch that shot my cousin."

To the cheers of his mongrel followers, he led his band of cutthroats out of the ranch yard toward Bixley, riding hard. The Swain twins were in the forefront, howling like the mad dogs they were.

Marty climbed the ladder to the belfry, followed by Berkowski. He looked to the north after squirming through the trapdoor in the floor. The wood hammered to the waist-high parapet still smelled fresh and green. "Two-by-six undried wood. That oughta stop most rifle bullets, wouldn't you think, Sergeant B?"

"Ain't nothin' gonna get through save maybe a buffalo gun. Sure hope they don't bring none to the party."

Marty nodded and inspected the half-dozen whiskey bottles filled with powder and nails that Joey had placed in the far corner. Everything was in readiness for their standoff. All they could do now was wait and hope Thompson took the bait, riding into town without a proper reconnaissance.

Marty inspected the firing slots, cut about six inches above the top of the boards lining the floor. "Don't pull the cutouts away until they begin to return our fire. We'll shoot first from over the parapet. That'll get them used to seeing their target higher."

Berkowski merely nodded and shifted the plug that he was furiously chewing from one side of his face to the other. He looked down at the two wagons poised to move, the two soldiers, McKean and Conway, holding the reins of the horse on his side of the street. "You boys look alive. We'll start shootin' at four hunnerd yards. You pull the wagons together at the first shot and take yur places. You'll be the main line of defense once they git to two hunnerd. See the rag on the stake out there? Don't start firin' until they reach it, but when they do, pour it on 'em."

The two soldiers nodded, looking anxiously to the north. Joey was peering through the binoculars. Marty saw him stiffen.

"Riders, Mr. Keller. A bunch, coming this

way fast."

Marty grabbed the field glasses and looked to the north. He could count at least twenty men riding through the dust kicked up from the horses' hoofs.

"Here they come, Sergeant. Duck down; I don't want them to see us until we're ready to fire."

Marty knelt at the corner of the enclosure, his head partially obscured by the upright that supported the roof. He watched the riders come on, the men in back strung out as their slower mounts struggled to keep up with the faster horses in front. At the top of a small rise, about half a mile out of town, the riders slowed and stopped, the dust slowly dissipating in the noon breeze.

Long Tom looked through his well-used collapsing telescope at the town below. He scanned the street and briefly swung up to look at the belfry, but saw nothing. The town looked deserted. He prodded the deputy, "What say, Vince. Where are they?"

"Maybe at the sheriff's office, Long Tom. God, my wrist's a'killin' me."

"Yur lucky I ain't broke the other, ya damned coward. Now, git yur hoss a'goin'. We're gonna ride in hard, surround the jail, and do some serious work with the guns. Men, the saloon is our rally point, if you get separated. Ride in and collect there. Git goin', Vince. Remember, I'm right behind ya."

The mass of riders slowly stirred into motion, fanning out slightly as they approached the north end of Bixley. "Get ready, Sergeant B. They're almost to our first rag. Now!"

Marty and the old sergeant rose to one knee and sighted in on one of the many galloping men. Their mighty guns boomed within half a second of one another. Two men pitched out of their saddles. One, the unfortunate Vince, was drilled through the chest by Marty's shot.

Long Tom realized he was under fire only when Vince pitched backward off his horse, directly in front of Long Tom. He threw up his hand, motioning his men to spread out in a fighting line. "They're in the church steeple!" someone shouted.

A second round of heavy lead whizzed into the group, driving another man from the saddle. The second bullet hit a horse in the head, and its fall flipped its rider over the top like a discarded wad of paper. He ran to the horse of a dead comrade and galloped after the rest, shouting obscenities at the men who killed his favorite mount.

The outlaws spurred their horses even

harder, as two more fell to the deadly fire from the church steeple. Suddenly, Long Tom spotted the two wagons criss-crossed in the street. He held up his hand just as more fire came from the wagons themselves. Two more men fell to the ground, sprawling in the dust of the trail in the limp position of death.

Long Tom shouted and motioned with his arm. "Head fer the woods to the east. They got us blocked here. Move, move!"

Another man jerked stiff and slid from his horse. Several of the riders beside him rode over his flopping body without an instant's hesitation. As they rode away from the carnage, yet one more man fell out of his saddle, his scream of agony lost in the thundering hoofbeats.

They galloped hard until they were in the trees of the gully and away from the deadly fire that whizzed past from the church steeple. Several men crawled to the edge of the trees and banged away at the steeple, their shots harmlessly whizzing past and over Marty and the others, or smacking into the wood without penetrating the reinforced walls.

Long Tom cussed like a sailor, then settled down long enough to think about his situation. "Big Joe, listen up," he shouted over the rifle fire his men were pouring at the church. "I'm gonna take five men and work my way to the saloon through the south end of town. You wait five minutes and come in hard down the street yonder." He pointed at Lake Street, three hundred yards to the front. "Bob, you and Andy take two men and come in from the south end of Main. We'll meet at the saloon and go from there. Bob, you git goin'. Big Joe, you wait five minutes and charge. We'll all come in together and meet at the saloon, unnerstand?"

The men nodded and ran to their horses. Big Joe let his men continue to fire at the steeple. That would keep the men in there pinned down while Carter moved against them from another direction.

Marty stopped firing his rifle. He hurriedly counted the downed bodies on the ground. "Eight, nine. Looks like we got nine of 'em, Stan. Come on, they're all in the trees now. Joey, it's up to you here. If you shoot at the men in the trees, use the firing slit. Don't let anyone get around you to the back road."

"Don't worry, Mr. Keller. I won't." Joey lit his two candles and set them beside the four hand bombs, ready for use.

Marty nodded and ducked through the

trapdoor and down the ladder, followed by Berkowski. As they ran out of the church, he called to the two soldiers in the wagons, "Head for your next position. The outlaws are on the move." He ran down the street to the jail. Looking up, he saw O'Brien on the roof and shouted. "You're next, O'Brien. Be on your toes."

O'Brien threw him a half salute and moved to his position behind the façade of the jailhouse. He had a good view of the four whiskey crocks positioned along the far extreme of Lake Street.

Marty glanced back at the belfry. He saw smoke issue from one of the slits, and knew Joey was firing his Spencer at the men still hidden in the trees. As he looked, a pole snaked out with four white streamers tied to it. "Four men headed south," he alerted Berkowski. He leaned his buffalo rifle next to the door of Benson's store and grabbed his Winchester. Checking to insure a load was chambered, he thought about running down to help Stephens and Diehl in the livery, when Berkowski grabbed his arm. "Look, Cap'n."

Another pole was out, six red strips hanging from it. Marty shouted, "Six men working through the town toward the saloon. You see that, Conway? Get your men ready, they'll be there soon. Don't let them get out."

He had taken only one step when he saw the men ride out of the trees at the far end of Lake Street and gallop toward him. He stopped, his rifle poised, wondering if his mines would stop them. He counted — there were six of them. They rode hunched low over their horses, guns in their hands.

O'Brien watched as the men approached his corridor of death. He waited until all six were in the zone, then fired his Sharps. A mighty explosion rent the air, causing men and horses to go flying. Methodically, the young sharpshooter walked his rounds down the four crocks, the last and closest one going off almost directly under Big Joe, splattering him and his horse all over the landscape. Not a man emerged from the mushrooming cloud of smoke and dust.

"Good shootin', O'Brien," Marty shouted as he headed for the livery. "Come on, Stan. We're needed down at the livery." Both men heard the sound of gunfire in that direction. They ran toward the stable, rifles at the ready.

Just as they reached the door entering the stable from Main Street, it opened, startling them both into almost firing instinctively. Stephens ran out, right into Marty's arms.

"What's wrong?" Marty shouted.

"My gun jammed. Fritz is down. Hit in the head. I think it's just a nick, but I was alone. Four, no, three men headed this way around the stables."

"You get one?" Berkowski asked.

"Yeah. Two went right and two left. But I knocked one on the left out of his saddle with the first shot."

"Where was Diehl?" Marty asked.

"He was in front, in the hayloft. I was at the back door."

Marty pushed Stephens away from the door. "Get over to the widow Jenkins' place and get the door blocks you made. As soon as six men enter the saloon, put 'em up. Here, take my Navy revolver." Marty handed Stephens his .36 Navy backup pistol and a handful of ammunition. "Don't let anyone leave, once they go inside. Stan and I will handle these three. Carter's men are headed for the saloon, so be careful and hurry."

Stephens ran off. Marty opened the door a crack and peeked inside. "Stan, you take the back door. I'll go up the ladder and take Diehl's place."

"Okay, Cap'n," Berkowski answered as he ran toward the back door. As Marty climbed the ladder to the hayloft, he could already

389

hear Berkowski's rifle coughing out rounds at the outlaw trying to work his way around the corral. Marty ran to the open door of the hayloft, located directly over the double doors of the barn. Diehl was lying on his side next to the opening, fresh blood dripping from a wound to his head. His body lay still, but he was still breathing, so Marty ignored him momentarily and stuck his head out of the opening, looking for targets. A bullet drove him back, but he quickly returned the fire in the general direction from which it came. He pushed aside a coiled rope that was looped through a pulley at the end of the extended center pole of the barn. It was used to hoist heavy items from the ground to the hayloft level.

As he picked up the looped end of the rope, a horse and rider dashed beneath him, heading hard for the street. Almost by reflex, Marty dropped one end of the rope, which was tied in a slipknot-style noose, over the rider's head. He grabbed the other end and jumped to the ground from the open hayloft door. His arms jerked when the rope grabbed the rider and pulled him off his saddle. As the unhorsed rider swung back, the rope slipped up until it caught on his chin. The noose tightened until the man swayed back and forth, slowly choking to death.

Marty held on as he hit the ground, then quickly wrapped his end of the rope around the wooden latch of the barn door. The man was as strung up as if he had been the guest of honor at a proper necktie party. With his arms and legs flailing the air, he struggled to loosen the rope around his neck. Every move, however, drew the noose tighter.

Marty stared in wonder at the man. He was big and blond, and his open mouth revealed a pronounced gap between his two front teeth. "A Swain brother," Marty hissed.

The man reached for the bone handle of a knife stuck in his right boot. Marty pulled his pistol and shot the man in his right elbow, breaking his arm and leaving it dangling uselessly at his side. For good measure, he shot and broke the other arm. With no help from his hands, the man struggled even more frantically. He tried climbing air, his legs pumping like a man running up stairs. "No use trying to climb to Heaven, Swain," Marty muttered. "You're on a long drop to Hell."

Marty ran over and hid behind a pile of manure collected from the barn. He looked on as the hanging man's struggles weakened and finally stopped. Hoofbeats announced the coming of another man, who galloped around the corner, nearly running into the hanged outlaw, slowly rotating at the end of the rope. Seeing the gruesome scene before him, the blond rider slid his horse to a stop and ran to the dangling body. It had to be the other Swain. Grabbing the limp legs, he tried to push his sibling back up, taking the weight off the dead man's neck and screaming for someone to help him.

Marty stepped out from his hiding place. "Swain," he shouted. "It's time for you to die, just like your brother."

The man turned and shouted wildly at Marty. "Who are you? Help me, Bob's dyin'."

"He's dead, Swain, and so are you, you just don't know it yet."

"Who are you?" Swain screamed, his grip on reality shattered by the events unfolding too fast for him to comprehend.

"The man whose family you slaughtered back in Texas a year ago. My wife, my son, my hired hand, you killed them all. You and the rest of Hulett's gang. I killed Ace Richland and your brother, and now I'm gonna kill you. You gonna die empty-handed, or are you gonna draw?"

Swain let go of his brother's legs and

clawed at his pistol, but Marty was faster. He put four bullets into Swain's gut, just above his belt buckle, each within a hand's span of the other.

Swain fell on his back, trying to hold his life's blood in with both hands while it poured out, staining his fingers claret red. He moaned in agony, pushing his heels against the dirt. With his smoking pistol in his hand, Marty walked over to him.

Marty mercilessly looked down at the dying killer, his eyes bleak and hard. "Tell your brother what I told you when you see him in Hell — say in one minute."

Marty shook himself and shifted his attention back to the larger battle, still underway. There was no sound from inside the barn. He ran in shouting for Sergeant Berkowski. "Stan, Stan. You all right? Where are you?"

"Over here, Cap'n. I got the one by the corral. A clean shot to his head. How 'bout you?"

"I got two. Come on, we'll be needed at Benson's."

The two men ran down the street toward the center of town. As they approached the doctor's office, shooting erupted from both the saloon and Benson's store. The final phase of the gun battle was on. Marty and

Berkowski skidded to a stop and ducked into the doorway of the doctor's office. From there, they were protected from any bullets shot down the street at them.

From the roof of the jail, O'Brien was shooting at someone on the second floor of the saloon. O'Brien saw Marty and held up his hand, two fingers up. Grinning, he mimicked chopping them both off, then made a slashing motion at his throat. "O'Brien got two," Marty announced. He pointed at his eyes, then at the saloon, signaling O'Brien to keep watch on the upper floors. O'Brien nodded his understanding.

"Two down," Marty said, "leaves four in the main saloon." Marty reloaded his pistol and spun the cylinder to check for jamming. He slid it back into its holster and looked around the corner of the doorway at the half-empty rain barrel standing, in case of fire, in the alley behind them. "Stan empty that barrel and bring it here."

Sergeant Berkowski hurried to comply. He quickly returned with the empty barrel. Marty whispered, "I'd guess one man at each window and two at the door. Agree?"

Berkowski nodded. Marty continued. "I'll ease down until I have a shot at the man at the window next to the doc's office. When I do, you throw the barrel through the window and we'll dive in. Then I'll take the two at the door, you take the man at the far window."

It was almost a perfect plan. As Marty and Berkowski snuck toward the window, the men in Benson's store saw what was happening and intensified their fire at the other two openings of the saloon. The outlaws inside tried to reply, but the fire was too intense. They ducked back, their attention focused on the store diagonally across the street.

Marty peered through the saloon window. He waited until the man firing from the window shifted his head a few inches, then shot him square in the face. As he did, Berkowski threw the barrel through the glass, shattering it into a million slivers. Marty dove into the saloon, his pistol out. A man at the front door turned, his eyes widened in surprise. Marty's shot hit him in the throat, and he fell immediately, his would-be screams nothing more than a loud gurgle. Berkowski's shot hit his man in the side, knocking him through the window onto the sidewalk outside the saloon. Marty scrambled to his feet. Where was the other man?

Long Tom had run to the back, hoping to

sneak out of the saloon during the fighting. He hit the back door running full steam and nearly broke his shoulder. The door was blocked solid. To top off his bad luck, someone outside began shooting through the door panel. Cursing, he headed back to the main room of the saloon. It was time to surrender.

As he entered, a barrel flew through a window, followed by two rolling figures, both firing at his men by the front door. Carter's hand streaked to his holstered pistol. He drew down on the nearest man, who was standing with his back turned. His finger squeezed the trigger and the gun bucked in his hand.

"Marty, look out," Stan shouted at the same instant.

Marty turned, his gun blazing. One bullet hit Carter in the side, and two of Stan's followed into the outlaw's chest. He was dead before Marty hit the ground.

Marty felt the hammer blow of a bullet ripping into his side. He was spun in a circle and fell back, his head smacking hard on the windowsill. Marty saw stars, then all went black.

CHAPTER 32
RIDE ON,
BOUNTY HUNTER

Marty opened his eyes. A fuzzy outline sharpened into the face of a young woman. She sat next to him, a damp rag in her hand. As he squinted to focus, she wiped his brow. "Papa, I think he's finally coming to his senses."

Marty turned his head toward the man standing on the other side of the bed. It was George Benson. "Hello, Mr. Benson. Is it all over?"

"Yep. How you feelin'?"

Marty took stock. "My side is sore and my head aches like I've been on a two-day toot. Other than that, I'm just fine." Marty grinned at Benson. "Since I'm layin' in a nice bed instead of a hole in the ground, I take it we won."

Benson nodded, his face beaming. "Did we ever. Every last man of Long Tom's gang is dead or wounded and in jail. We got every last mother's son of them."

Marty tried to recall the battle. He had some wide gaps in his memory. "We have any casualties?"

"Fritz Diehl got a slice along his scalp. Your Private Conway was hit in the shoulder. Didn't break any bones, though, and old Doc Adams got him fixed up. Private McKean has a nasty gash on his hand from flyin' glass, but he's fine as well. You were hurt the worst of anyone. Did you know that you've been unconscious for three days?"

"No, you're joshin' me."

"It's true. You got a nasty bullet wound in your side, and you musta hit your head on somethin' mighty hard. Ole Doc said he had grave hopes fer you at first."

"You don't say."

"Yep. Your Sergeant Berkowski wouldn't hear none of it. He had us pour about a gallon of coffee down Doc Adams and march him back in here. Berkowski said iffen Doc didn't fix you up so you was better than new, he was gonna fill Doc's hide with so many bullets we'd have to use a hoist to put him in a coffin. Berkowski watched ole Doc like a hawk ever' time he worked on you, his eyes as mean as a hungry wolf's. Doc was so scared of him I think he done went and performed a miracle on ya. Anyway, yur gonna be fine. Ya just have to take it easy for a spell. Let yur side heal and yur head get well."

"Where is Stan?"

"Him, Stephens, the other soldiers, and Joey took the wounded outlaws down to Wichita in a couple of wagons two days ago. They're gonna deliver 'em to the law there. The town voted to make Joey a temporary deputy." Benson smiled down at Marty. "We hope you'll become the full-time sheriff."

Marty was surprised by the sudden offer, but said nothing for a moment. Then he asked more questions. "What about Sheriff Thompson?"

"He died sometime during all the fighting. You got Long Tom, jus' before you went down."

"The rest of his men?"

"Kilt all but seven, and them ya wounded. Two each lost an arm, four got shot up legs or ribs, and one was hit in the gut. Why he ain't dead, nobody can figger."

"So it's over. Good. I got both of the Swain brothers, thank God."

"Did you ever. I think just about everybody in town went down to see 'em. One lying gut-shot dead right under his hanged brother. It was a pure ole sight to see."

Marty was suddenly very sleepy. He yawned, and Benson immediately excused himself. "You need yur rest, the doctor said. We kin talk later. If you need anything, just call fer Betsy here. She's taken up as your private nurse."

Later that day, Marty had a visit from the Reverend King. "How you doing, Reverend?"

"I'm fine, Marty. I came to help you ask God for forgiveness."

"What for?"

"For murdering the Swain brothers. You executed them, you killed them like rabid dogs. You have to ask God's forgiveness."

"Reverend, I'll not do that until God asks me to forgive Him for allowing my wife and baby son to be slaughtered by vermin like the Swain brothers."

"You can't demand that God reveal his plan, my boy."

"I can. Until then, God and I don't walk together. Go on, Preacher. Spend your time with someone who can use your help. It's too late for me. I'm tired. I'm going to grab some sleep now."

"I still will pray for your immortal soul, Marty Keller."

"Do what you want, Preacher. Just let me sleep." Marty turned away on his side and shut his eyes, not moving until the disappointed preacher left, muttering something to himself.

Marty rested and slept a lot until Stephens and the others returned a week later. Everyone crowded into his room at once to describe the excitement the news of Long Tom's killing generated.

"It were all in the paper, Cap'n," Stan informed him. "I brung you one to read. The sheriff in Wichita says there's a big reward fer Long Tom. He'll hold it fer ya to pick up when yur better."

Marty waved his hand to brush the news aside. "You and the men all okay?"

"Sure, Cap'n. Conway will be ready to ride in a couple of days, then we'll head on back to Ft. Lewiston in Shreveport." He paused. "Oh, by the way, the sheriff — Masterson is his name — says to stop by when you're in Wichita. He says you'll have about seventeen thousand in reward money coming."

"I'm going to send some of it to you and the boys, Stan. I couldn't have collected it without you. You can count on it."

"I won't tell 'em until it gets there, Marty. That'll make it a nice surprise."

"I'll sure miss you, Stan. You were a good man to have at my side. I wish you didn't have to go."

"Well, we ain't goin' until after the big

shindig Saturday night."

"Oh?"

"Yep. The town is throwin' us a thank-you party. Seems like everybody in Bixley was jus' a'waitin' fer someone like you to come around. Long Tom ain't too popular hereabouts, especially since he's dead and planted in boot hill." Berkowski grinned at John. "Jus' wait until you can git around. You'll not believe how many folks was jus' itchin' to have a go at Long Tom."

Berkowski's remark on the money. By the time the big town social rolled around, Marty had met twenty men who proclaimed their intention of running the outlaws off. The right time had just not presented itself to them.

Every citizen in Bixley attended the town social. An abundance of good, home-cooked food was spread across several tables. The young women of the town laughed and danced the night away with the three young soldiers, and the older women tried to catch Berkowski's eye. Partway through the festivities, George Benson stood and gave a speech. He made the destruction of the outlaw gang seem to be one of divine intervention, and Marty Keller the deliverer of the largess from above. After his grand oration, he called up Stan and the soldiers,

402

and presented them each with a new, one-hundred-dollar gold piece.

Beaming in satisfaction, he called up Marty to thundering applause. He presented him with a cherrywood box. Inside were two pistols, nickel-plated and shiny, with ivory handles and the initials "M" and "K" inlayed in filigreed silver on each handle. The weapons were beautiful and menacing.

Marty thanked everyone in a short and sincere speech. He was embarrassed by the fuss. He came back to his table and showed the gift to Stan and the others.

"They're Smith and Wesson .44s with seven-inch barrels, Marty," Stephens announced proudly. "I had the gunsmith put yur initials in the handles. Ain't they nice?"

"They certainly are, Mr. Stephens. I deeply appreciate them."

Marty bade a sad farewell to Sergeant Stan Berkowski and the three young soldiers the next day. He stood on the front porch of Benson's house and watched until his four friends disappeared over the hill to the south of Bixley. Sighing with regret, he returned to the rocker in the living room. Benson accompanied him, anxious to talk about something.

"Marty, the town has authorized me to

offer you the job of sheriff. We want ya to stay in Bixley, put down roots here. Everyone knows about yur loss. We think we can help you to git past it." George smiled at him. "I think Betsy's ready to help you there, if she can." He winked, his cherubic face beaming.

Marty sat silent for a minute, then leaned toward Benson, his face serious. "Thank you, George. I certainly appreciate the offer. I think it would be a bad idea. Once the news of this gets out, every riffraff, no-good in the state is liable to come around, hoping to make his reputation by bestin' me. My presence in Bixley would be more aggravation than good for the town."

Marty rocked back and forth for a few minutes. "I've got a cancer, George. It's called revenge, and it's eating at my gut with every passing day. It's a rage I can't run away from. My vengeance has to be complete for it to go away and allow me to find some peace again."

Marty offered his hand. "I'll leave tomorrow morning, early. I'm not gonna say anything to the folks hereabouts. Please don't you, either. After I'm gone, thank them for me and ask them to just as promptly forget me. Bixley doesn't need me, or, to be frank, really want me. It wouldn't take long for that to become evident."

George shook his hand. "I think you're wrong, son. But I'll go along. I owe you that much."

"Good night, George. Thank you and good-bye."

"God go with you, Marty. Good-bye."

The next morning, Marty left envelopes for George, Joey, Stephens, and Diehl on his dresser. In each he had put the last of the money he had brought into Bixley. It would be their shares of the reward he would receive in Wichita. He left a short, thankful note to Betsy for her devoted nursing, then walked to the stables, his possessions slung over his shoulder.

He had just finished saddling his horse and pack animal when Stephens walked in. "I figgered you'd be on yur way one of these days. I'll miss you, Marty."

"I'll miss you, Nicholas. It's best this way. I need to get on with my hunt, Bixley needs to get on with its life."

Marty shook hands and rode out of town. At the top of the hill where he had paused on the way in, he paused again. He turned his horse toward the little town. People were beginning to stir, the town was awakening. Already they were beginning to forget him.

He reined his horse back to the trail and nudged him with his spurs. He had some men to kill.

ABOUT THE AUTHOR

Thom Nicholson was born in Springfield, Missouri, and grew up in northwest Arkansas and southwest Missouri. After college he worked in a uranium mine in New Mexico before entering the U.S. Army. He served as a Special Forces officer in Vietnam, South America, and Africa. In Vietnam he was an A-team executive officer, then a Raider Company commander. In 1996, with more than thirty years of commissioned service, he retired at the rank of colonel. A graduate of the National Defense University and the U.S. Army Command and General Staff School, he is a registered engineer and holds an MBA. After retirement, he started writing novels. Thom Nicholson and his wife, Sandra, have five children.

The employees of Thorndike Press hope you have enjoyed this Large Print book. All our Thorndike and Wheeler Large Print titles are designed for easy reading, and all our books are made to last. Other Thorndike Press Large Print books are available at your library, through selected bookstores, or directly from us.

For information about titles, please call:
   (800) 223-1244

or visit our Web site at:
   www.gale.com/thorndike
   www.gale.com/wheeler

To share your comments, please write:
   Publisher
   Thorndike Press
   295 Kennedy Memorial Drive
   Waterville, ME 04901